TEAS OF JOY

LOVE ON BELMONT
BOOK THREE

LORI WOLF-HEFFNER

Editing by Susan Fish and Phoebe Wolfe

Cover design by Fresh Design

Cover photograph from Shutterstock

Print ISBN: 978-1-989465-34-9

Ebook ISBN: 978-1-989465-35-6

Head in the Ground Publishing

Waterloo, Ontario, Canada

headintheground.com

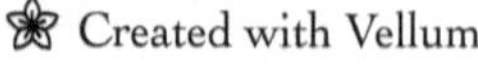 Created with Vellum

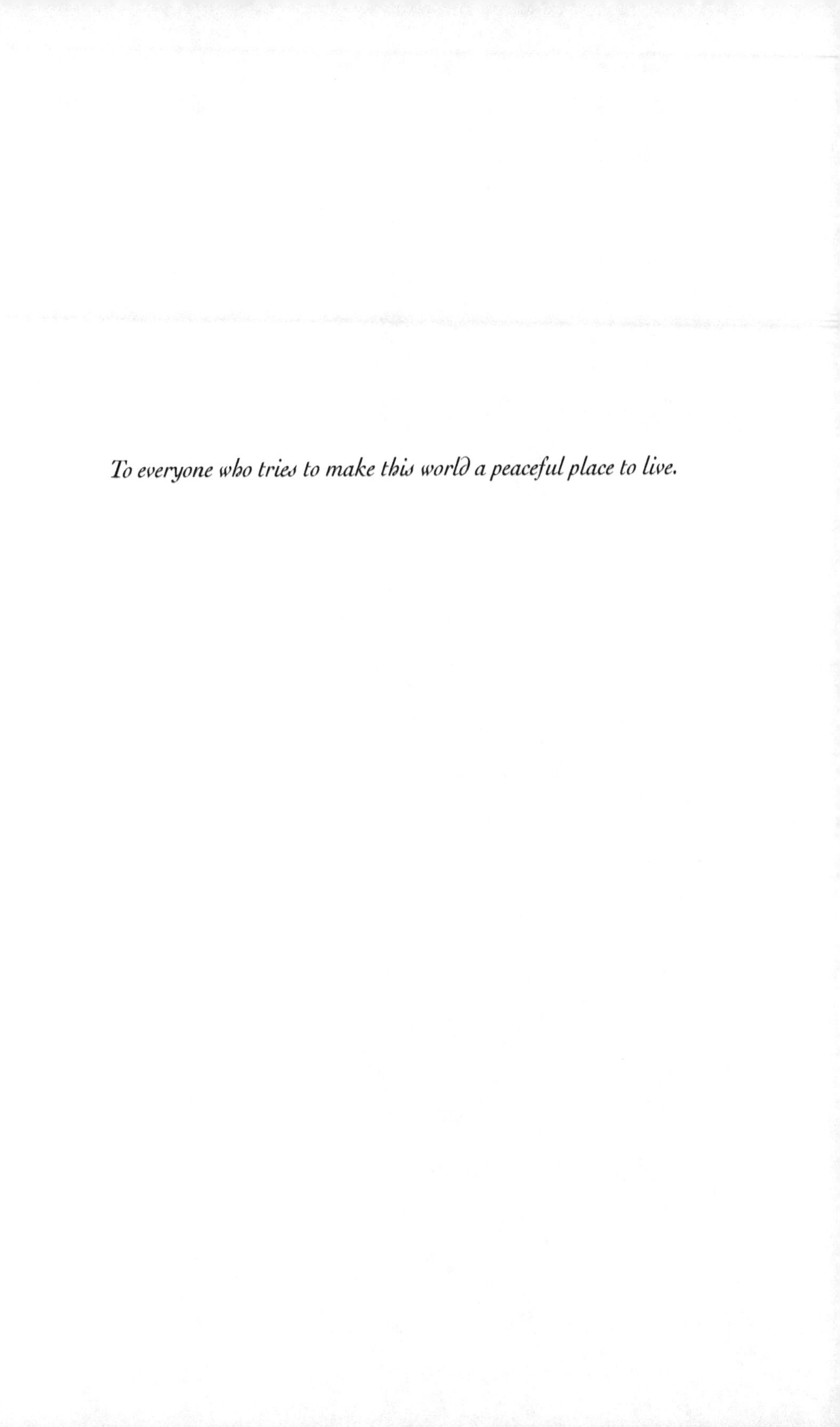

To everyone who tries to make this world a peaceful place to live.

CHAPTER 1

Claire Robinson tried her hardest to focus on her speech as Jan poked and prodded at her white hair. "I should've started this earlier. What if I bore people?"

Claire's daughters stared at her.

"Bore people?" Pauline, at forty-eight the older of Claire's two daughters, raised an eyebrow. "You've sold tea to tens of thousands of people over the years, Mom. You have lots of stories to tell."

Dawn, four years younger, nodded. "What would make you think that?"

Claire shrugged. "I'm used to addressing people one at a time, not a room full of dozens. Each person has a different story, a different history. You know what I'm talking about, Dawn. You only talk to a few people at a time when you sell homes."

Dawn nodded.

"Addressing eighty people is easy." Pauline peered over Claire's shoulder and touched up her own short hair a little.

"Sure, *if* entertaining thousands each game was your career for thirty years," Dawn said in defence of their mother.

Jan removed a hairpin from her mouth, hid it in Claire's hair, and then said with a hint of mischief, "I'm certain Pauline would be happy to mime your anniversary speech for you, Claire."

Pauline parked her hands on her hips. "Hey! Being a professional mascot is a lot more than miming."

Jan lit up with the kind smile she was known for. "I'm just teasing. You have a gift for entertaining people, Pauline."

"Entertaining silently," Dawn added with a wink. "Which would've been nice when we were kids."

Pauline playfully punched Dawn in the arm. The sisters got along well now but in their childhood, their differences had clashed. By her mid-teens, Claire's oldest daughter had used the house as a makeshift gymnastic club, while Dawn tried quietly to work on her art somewhere away from all the shaking caused by her sister jumping over furniture. If there was one thing Pauline had never been, it was a soft lander.

Claire was still thinking about the speech she had to give that evening at her fiftieth anniversary party. "Maybe that's what I should talk about—how unexpectedly life can change. I wouldn't have dated your father if he hadn't walked into my tea shop."

Dawn nodded. "And I wouldn't have met Dean if I hadn't gone on that artists' retreat that summer."

Pauline smiled softly. "Just like I wouldn't have met Todd had you not fallen off that chair, Mom. Not that I would've wished that on you!"

Claire quickly glanced at Jan in the mirror at her next thought: She wouldn't have opened her tea shop if another accident hadn't happened. But that was something she never thought about unless it forced itself into her consciousness—and then she would she push it back into its box.

Pauline began pacing along the carpeted hallway of her parents' apartment, but Claire could see in the mirror that she still walked with a slight limp. The continual stunts she'd performed in her previous career as a professional sports mascot had caused so much wear on her body that she'd needed a hip replacement a month before. The surgeon had said she would return to walking in no time, given her fitness level, age, and how well she'd gone through the surgery itself.

Jan picked up the next few hairpins, stuck them between her lips, and held up a small rose with a few pieces of lavender. "This will look so striking against your hair," she mumbled to Claire. She artistically placed the flowers—an inspiration from Claire's go-to tea blend, Earl Claire—in her hair.

Claire's best friend was a born flower child with a touch of sophistication. Like Claire, Jan had also been a business owner, running her own hair salon for decades in Belmont Village, the quaint shopping strip that was also home to Claire's Tea Shop. Even though she'd sold her salon ten years ago, Jan could never picture herself fully retired, and still worked part time.

As the hairstyling continued, Dawn gave her mother's purse an extra polish, while Pauline began bouncing like a boxer warming up for the next fight.

"I thought you weren't supposed to jog," Dawn said.

"Technically, I'm not jogging. Our parents are celebrating fifty years. The real question is, how can you sit still?"

Claire suggested Pauline might want to drink a lavender tisane to calm herself but Pauline shook her head. "Once I burn off the energy, I'll be fine."

"And possibly sweating profusely. You're reaching that age," Claire said, meaning perimenopause.

Pauline winced and immediately stopped. "Ow." She

massaged her hip. "I don't know if I'll ever get used to this. Not being allowed to jog in the morning makes it hard to deal with any kind of stress, even the good kind."

Claire suggested getting an ice pack from the freezer. "I don't understand why you won't use a cane. It makes walking much easier and will ease the pain for you on a long day like this."

"I'll be fine once my muscles relax."

Obviously Claire had never intended to fall off that chair at the tea shop in the summer of last year. But it was one of those painful twists of fate with a silver lining: the required minor knee surgery, bed rest, and rehabilitation time just when she was about to train a new employee had meant she'd needed help with the store. Because Pauline had been working for the Toronto Peregrines men's hockey team just an hour away, Claire had called on her for help.

Pauline had come back, initially just for a week. But the physical strain from her career, plus falling in love with Todd, the new employee, had led Pauline to stay and take over the tea shop. Claire and her husband, Richard, had wondered if Pauline would ever settle down.

By contrast, Dawn had fallen in love with Dean Glover over twenty years ago, and the two of them, with their three kids ages twelve to eighteen, lived out West where Dawn ran her own real estate brokerage and Dean worked in movie animation. In fact, he'd just gotten a promotion.

Dawn's phone dinged.

"It's Dad, wondering if you'll be on time," she said.

Claire had a coy smile on her face. Richard Robinson, the man of Claire's dreams. Dashing when they'd met in their twenties, and still dashing in his seventies. "Tell your father perfection is worth the wait. And that he'd better not be playing a Rolling Stones song."

The feud that had started it all: Were The Rolling Stones or The Monkees the better group? The Robinson jury was still out on that.

"And tell him we'll be on time," Claire added. "If he wants me walking across the dance floor to a Stones song, I'll respect his choice. You don't survive fifty years without making concessions. Just so long as it's not 'Can't Get No Satisfaction.'"

Jan snorted and the hairpins fell from her mouth. Pauline doubled over in laughter, a hand still tight on her hip, and Dawn laughed almost silently, the delight in her eyes showing how much joy she carried in her.

After everyone had calmed down again, Pauline nudged her sister. "So? What do you think Dad's gift is for Mom? A romantic getaway somewhere?"

"The way Dad thinks? Yeah." Dawn's eyes got starry. "He *is* a romantic."

Jan shook her head. "That's true but your mother's lucky if she can get your father to go away for an extended weekend."

"I don't know," Claire said. "We managed a full week away for our twenty-fifth anniversary, and a week to celebrate my retirement. Surely our fiftieth is worth him sacrificing another week from the brokerage."

Dawn joked, "I'll bet he's going to announce his retirement."

"Hmm…" Jan said thoughtfully. "You never know. It *would* be like him. And he has really built up this party—ordering a limo for us, having a song for you to walk into the party…he likes his grand gestures."

Claire shook her head. "As wonderful as that sounds, Richard loves his work, and I can't blame him. After covering for you at the shop for a few weeks, Pauline, I have to say, I miss my work a little, too. I don't miss the sixty-hour weeks, but I miss seeing and talking to so many people."

Jan parked her hands on her hips. "And what about me, Brenda, and Cecilia?"

Their women's group that had sprouted up over the past six months. After Claire had handed the store over to Pauline—officially on New Year's Day this year—she and Jan had begun taking day trips and enjoying evening romps around town. Cecilia, a new widow, and Brenda, freshly retired from Richard's brokerage, had eventually joined them.

"There." Jan pushed in the final hair pin. "Done."

Claire stood up from her chair and took one last look at her hair. "Perfect, like you always do, Jan."

"Oh! Wait, Mom, your lipstick." Dawn dug through her mother's purse.

Claire smiled. "Later, my sugar. I wouldn't want to get lipstick all over your father's face." Claire and Richard had always had a passionate life. That hadn't changed as they aged either. Lipstick would go on after she kissed him. She enjoyed the thought of kissing him—and she enjoyed Pauline and Dawn's eye rolls.

Dawn handed Claire her cane, and she slipped into her dress shoes.

"Photos?" Jan held up her phone and everyone moved together.

Claire stood between her two daughters: six-foot tall Pauline and five-foot-four Dawn. In their personal styles, the girls had not changed. Pauline had dressed up the bare minimum in a sleeveless purple blouse and black dress pants. She always said she found dress clothes too restrictive and requiring a certain way of acting to fit in that she found difficult. Dawn, on the other hand, loved visual aesthetics and therefore getting dressed up: she wore a fitted red dress that stopped a few inches above the knee.

After a few rounds of photos—including several of Claire

and Jan—the women headed downstairs where the limousine was waiting.

As she slipped into the limo, Claire realized what she'd talk about: how embracing change, but always with a nod to tradition, had helped her reach this day and its celebration of fifty years of marriage to the most amazing man in the world.

RICHARD ADJUSTED HIS BOWTIE. "Are you sure it's not fifty degrees in here?" he asked Sedrick, Jan's husband and his best friend.

"I've asked the staff to check the thermostat three times already, Rich. It's you."

"Or I'm not used to wearing a tux anymore."

"Just a little stage fright," Todd said as a professional photographer took their photos.

"Easy for you to say. You had an international ballet career."

It was almost time for Claire to arrive. Friends and family were seated at tables adorned with white tablecloths, and the chairs had fancy white covers pulled over them, too. A beautiful floral centrepiece from the flower shop in Belmont Village provided a refined accent against all the white, and party favours from the Belmont Village Chocolate Shop sat at each place: a pairing of a sample of Earl Claire with one of Richard's favourite truffles—lemon cream. Sedrick and Jan's daughter, Tracy, co-owned the chocolatier with her partner, Ben, who now stood by the podium as emcee, ready to begin the evening.

Todd leaned in. "Pauline just texted. They're here." He signalled to Ben who then asked anyone milling about to please take their seat.

Richard fiddled with his tie. "Does it look right?"

Sedrick attempted to make adjustments, but Richard

declined his assistance. "I'm going to go with the man who has decades of costume experience. Your job is to keep me standing: when I see her all dressed up, I melt."

Sedrick stepped out of the way so Todd could make any final adjustments to Richard's appearance. When Richard was set, Sedrick gave him a brotherly clap on the back to calm his nerves.

Or at least try to.

Richard took a moment to appreciate the men standing with him. Only one was missing from the lineup: Dean, his son-in-law of twenty-one years. But Dawn had said Dean couldn't leave his job after his new promotion, and the kids were up to their eyeballs in schoolwork. Richard would've loved to see his grandkids, but he understood how important work was, too, and that included schoolwork.

Tracy stood at the door, keeping an eye out for Claire. Richard's heart beat in his throat. One year of courtship, fifty years of marriage, two daughters, one-and-a-half sons-in-law. That was what Richard had started to jokingly say after Todd and Pauline had become a couple last year. Claire was now retired, enjoying time with friends, and Richard was still running a business he loved: his real estate brokerage.

It was a good life.

Yes, they were up there in age: Claire was seventy-six, Richard seventy-nine. But what had carried them through all these years was their mutual respect for each other's dreams. Richard couldn't wait to give Claire his gift later tonight and hopefully fulfill one of hers.

Todd whispered, "Here she is."

A moment later, "Can't Get Her off of My Mind" by the Monkees began to play over the sound system. Most in the room laughed—they knew of the musical feud between the two —and stood. Just as Richard had hoped, Claire was positively beaming as she entered the small ballroom that was filled with over eighty friends, family, and business colleagues. She wore a beautiful, pink, knee-length, short-sleeved dress. She held her cane in one hand and a small bouquet reminiscent of her wedding bouquet in the other. Roses and lavender adorned a spot off to the side in her hair, obviously inspired by her favourite tea.

Sedrick passed Richard a tissue, and only then did he realize he needed it: Did Claire look more beautiful today or on their wedding day? He'd shed a few tears out of happiness back then, too.

When Claire finally made it across the dance floor, Richard wrapped her in his arms. "Hello, my Darjeeling."

Claire smiled from ear to ear. "The perfect song, my Keemun."

Yes, tea was their love language.

Within seconds, Richard lost himself in a passionate kiss with his true love. Only when he returned to reality did he hear everyone cheering.

Claire, her face aglow, gestured to Dawn for her purse. "Now I can put on my lipstick."

But Richard took her hand and pulled it behind his back. "Oh, not yet." He moved in for a second kiss. Because it was, of course, important to ensure that the woman you'd been in love with most of your life understood just how much you loved her.

His life with Claire was perfect.

Richard didn't want a single thing to change.

CHAPTER 2

"So," Todd said at the podium, Pauline's arm around his waist. "When Claire asked if I'd be able to learn that there was a tea for every emotion, problem, and celebration, I assumed she had those hundreds of jars somehow grouped into emotions, problems, and celebrations, and then further summarized into something like a cheat sheet."

Claire chuckled along with the crowd. She'd felt a little badly for Todd back then: he'd had to learn so much.

Todd reached under the podium and pulled out a two-inch thick black binder, and the crowd broke out into full laughter.

"I didn't know what I was in for." When the laughter died down, Todd continued. "I would've understood if my first day of work had been my last: How could the shop run with a one-day old employee at the counter and the owner in hospital?" Todd paused as he gazed at his partner, and Pauline smiled back. "That's how I met the Robinson family, and I got to hear story after story about how Claire and Richard changed people's lives." He smiled at Claire, and then nodded over to Richard. "They certainly changed mine for the better."

Todd raised his glass for a toast, and everyone followed suit.

Claire's heart filled with warmth. A full hour of speeches about how her and Richard's lives had affected family, friends, and even strangers in their community. Fifty years of dedication to family and work. That was a long time.

Todd introduced the last "speakers" on the program: Tracy's son, Austin, and a girl from his ballet studio, dancing a duet from the ballet *Romeo and Juliet*.

Austin wore a long-sleeved, billowy white top over white tights and ballet shoes. His dance partner wore a flowing, single-layered dress made of white chiffon and Lycra, with beautiful lace decorations on the front. Anytime the young girl danced on her toes, Claire held her breath in case she'd fall. But the girl danced like a princess.

Claire held Richard's hand as the two teens danced the most beautiful duet Claire had ever seen. She tried to make quick eye contact with Jan, but Jan was enraptured by her grandson's performance.

Jan and Sedrick's other grandchildren lived only an hour or so from Kitchener. Claire wished she could have been so much more involved in the lives of her grandchildren, but they lived three time zones away. Dawn and Dean had managed to visit at least once a year with the children, and sometimes twice, so Claire, busy with running the tea shop, had never travelled to see them.

In fact, Claire had only flown once in her life—on her and Richard's twenty-fifth anniversary trip to New York City. That was it.

When the young couple finished their duet, Austin waved at Claire and Richard, and his classmate took another curtsy.

Now it was Claire and Richard's turn to speak. Claire's heart thumped in her chest as they approached the podium. After some playful banter about who got to speak first, Claire pulled the microphone in her direction. Best to just get this over with.

"If chance hadn't thrown this wonderful man in my path, none of us would be here today." She explained how they'd come to their terms of endearment: "Darjeeling" because it was close to "darling," and "Keemun" because she'd decided that Chinese Keemun tea, with its clean, floral taste, reminded her of Richard.

Claire continued with heartwarming stories about the girls—the first time Dawn's art landed in the school board's student art exhibit at the downtown art gallery, the time when Pauline landed her first professional gig as a mascot for the local hockey team, and much more.

But as Claire gazed over the crowd while she spoke, her mind automatically took note of those who had travelled to the most interesting corners of the earth, those who had gone on fascinating family vacations, those who had retired—including some before they'd turned sixty-five.

"But if it hadn't been for that chance encounter just over fifty years ago," she said, finishing her speech and looking over at Richard, "all these adventures in my life wouldn't have happened."

Richard gave her a quick kiss as everyone clapped, and then he began his speech.

"Speaking of chance, the reason I'd walked into that tea shop was because I'd gotten to know her while she was trying to broker a deal with the building owner. The stealth she negotiated with, and pride she carried, the dreams she talked about—like creating a café for families—stayed in my mind long after she'd signed the contracts. Had I not been assigned that building, I don't know if I'd have ever walked in there."

Chance indeed, Claire thought. But also embracing change. Claire had sworn when she'd opened the tea shop that she'd never marry again. And here she was, happily married and retired! Claire loved all the day trips and evenings out with her girlfriends. They'd travelled west to nearby Stratford to see some plays, northwest to the shores of Lake Huron in the summer to spend time on the beach, and, of course, frequently to Toronto for many events and exhibitions. Not to mention all the restaurants they'd already tried near Kitchener. Locally sourced food, exotic food, something called "fusion food" that was usually tasty, or even a top hamburger locale. She wanted to keep discovering because look at what had happened just by taking the leap that fateful summer in 1967 when she and Richard had enjoyed their first kiss.

"And we've had some travels, haven't we?" Richard asked. Claire nodded.

She thought of the time they'd gone to Muskoka for a cozy weekend in February. They'd wanted to take in the beautiful Ontario winter with a real fireplace. Although they'd hoped to go outdoors at night to try to catch the Northern Lights, the thought of being food for wild animals had kept them inside. Claire smiled at the memory. Staying inside had been the right decision. She and Richard had had a lot of fun.

In bed.

Then there was their weeklong trip to Niagara a year ago to celebrate Claire's retirement. The day after they returned, Richard came home from work and couldn't stop talking about all the tasks that hadn't gotten completed in his absence. Claire made a mental note back then to not ask again about work the day after returning from a trip.

But the limo, the grand evening of celebration, that special song, those kisses… She remembered what Dawn had said about Richard possibly retiring. Maybe there was something to it. Richard wasn't one to make a private announcement in public, but was it possible he would tell Claire tonight that he was going to sell the brokerage? His speech covered so many fun memories, but they'd squeezed those in around their jobs. Now that they were both nearing eighty, wasn't it time to stop work and enjoy whatever time they had left on this earth together? Going with Richard on day trips, going out in the evenings as they'd done when they were younger, instead of sitting in front of the TV because Richard was exhausted from work…

That did sound nice.

But no. Something as big as selling the brokerage? He'd have talked that over with her.

But as Richard squeezed her hand and stared at her for a moment, love and adoration in his coppery-brown eyes, Claire realized that the idea of Richard retiring was very appealing to her.

He faced the microphone again. "All I know is that I wouldn't change a thing." He gave Claire another kiss to a roomful of cheers.

Back at their seats, Claire couldn't stop thinking about his last statement: he wouldn't change a thing. He was referring to everything up until now, right? He didn't mean he'd never change a thing for the rest of their lives, right?

Right?

IT WAS NEARLY two in the morning by the time they got home. They were so tired, they sank into the couch, laughing at their exhaustion.

Richard straightened the little bit of hair he had left. Not that it mattered. Messy hair, either a full head or not, always turned Claire on. He kissed her on her ear and then down her neck. She shivered and reached for Richard's top button, then shook her head and laughed some more. "I'm far too tired."

Richard also conceded defeat. "We should've had sex this afternoon. Enough energy for gifts, though?" he asked.

Claire's eyelids wanted to close but she sat up and lifted herself to her feet with a groan.

They both went to retrieve their anniversary presents: Claire in the den, and Richard apparently in the front closet, on the top shelf Claire couldn't reach. Being the shortest in the family was usually so unfair.

Back on the couch, they exchanged gift bags.

"Of course you've done yours up with bows and dried flowers," Richard said. "This looks beautiful."

"Bergamot," Claire said. "Jan's idea. All that's missing to make it an Earl Claire is a vanilla pod, but I thought that might smell too strong."

Richard insisted she open her gift first and handed her a simple lightweight gift bag that said, "Happy Anniversary!" with gold tissue stuffed in the top. Cute: gold for their golden anniversary.

When she opened the gift, she laughed and kissed him: the bag contained a pamphlet for tea gardens on Vancouver Island.

"Since you've never seen real tea gardens before," he said. "But why are you laughing?"

Claire pointed at her gift without saying a word. When Richard opened it, he also began to laugh. Claire's gift was the same pamphlet plus a brochure for a luxurious hotel.

Claire shook her head in disbelief. "I don't know if it's a good thing that we thought of the same gift or if it says we've been together too long."

Richard held her hand and looked deeply into her eyes. "We can never have been together too long." He let go and studied the hotel brochure. "This hotel is in Vancouver, though."

"I've booked us for a few days in the spring. It's so we won't be encroaching when we visit Dawn and her family on our way to Vancouver Island. I thought it was about time we made the effort to go see them."

Richard shifted and scratched his neck. "That sounds like you're planning for a whole week. I can't take that much time off work, especially in the spring. It's the start of high season."

Richard had finally reduced his hours a few years ago to thirty-five from sixty or seventy. Claire had—mistakenly, it appeared—believed he was now more willing to take a week off here and there.

That meant that retirement was definitely not on the horizon.

She began pulling out the pins from her hair as disappointment crept in. "It's just that we're both in excellent health, all things considered. We should take advantage of that now. Your business isn't going to collapse with you gone for a week. That's what your staff and sales team are for, isn't it? And why wouldn't you want to visit your grandchildren for once?"

Richard sat back. "We could visit them for a day, I suppose, or they could come and meet us on the island. It's just that, even though Terry's doing a wonderful job as Brenda's replacement, he's not fully up to speed on everything. And if I lose a sales rep, we risk losing sales unless I jump in until we've found a replacement."

Claire played with the pins in her hand. After fifty years of marriage, she should've known better. But Claire hadn't gotten this far on pure realism either: A woman starting her own business in 1966 had been unrealistic. Bringing both girls as babies into work had been unrealistic. Forbidding smoking long before the legal ban on indoor smoking had been unrealistic. But what had grown out of those unrealistic dreams was a community cornerstone that welcomed anyone who needed a kind place to stop by.

Asking your husband for a week off in the spring seemed rather realistic. *Maybe that's the problem*, Claire thought facetiously.

Richard placed his hand over hers. He spoke in a gentle voice. "I'm sorry, but the timing's just not right."

Claire thought back to everyone she'd noticed as she'd delivered her speech. Did they wait for the right timing to follow their dreams? Take their family vacations? Retire?

Or did they do what she had always done: take life by the horns and yank it in the direction she needed?

But Claire didn't want a debate to be the nightcap on their fiftieth wedding anniversary.

"I understand. A weekend it is then." She gave her best smile, followed it with a kiss, and headed for the bathroom before bed.

But the nagging feeling that Richard didn't believe their fifty years of marriage were worth more than an extended weekend trip wouldn't leave her.

CHAPTER 3

Richard grimaced as Pauline followed behind Todd, carrying a heavy box into his and Claire's apartment the day after the anniversary party. Although Pauline was exceptionally strong, Richard couldn't envision any surgeon allowing his daughter to carry something heavy so soon after an operation. But she hadn't let him take it from her.

"Finally! This is the last of the decoration boxes from our storage locker," Pauline said. Richard and Claire had moved into an apartment last year just a few doors down from the young couple.

Richard caught a fleeting look of worry on Todd's face.

They set the boxes on the table where Claire set out tea for everyone.

"Dawn's Delight," she announced.

Dawn blushed. Her mother had named the tea in her honour. "Hopefully I can take some home with me?"

"Of course, my sugar."

Dawn and Pauline had both expressed gratitude that their parents called them sweet nicknames rather than tea-based ones. Being called "my oolong" in front of their friends would've embarrassed them, especially when they were teens.

Pauline and Todd carefully shifted the boxes around the table so everyone had one to open. "Before we get started," Pauline said, "I have something for Mom—I'm sorry, Dad, but it might give Mom a leg up on your musical debate."

Pauline pulled something out of her shoulder bag and hid it behind her back. She enjoyed putting on a show, no matter how small. Richard loved that about Pauline: you could always count on her to keep everyone's morale high.

"I think the truly successful bands put out a Christmas album." She drew a CD from behind her back. "And the Monkees just released one!"

Claire clapped for joy.

Richard laughed. "I don't know if a Christmas album is a requirement for a fully successful band, given that the Stones have sold more records. But I will concede a point here."

Claire was all smiles as she inspected the CD—she and Richard still used a CD player—and then handed it to Pauline. "Why don't we put it on?"

Pauline parked a hand on the back of an armchair and stopped. Richard knew what she'd wanted to do—throw her legs sideways into the air and jump over the chair. Furniture for Pauline had always been a speed bump, never a barrier. But with her new hip, stunts like that were no longer allowed. She had been encouraged to take up activities like walking, which Pauline couldn't fathom doing for exercise: it was too slow. But she could return to weightlifting as long as she followed her physiotherapist's instructions, so it wasn't all bad news.

Pauline walked around the armchair, slid the CD into the player, and turned on the music. "So, Mom? What do you think?"

"A nice festive touch to our evening."

Having returned to the table, Pauline straddled a chair—her favourite way of sitting down when she was among family and close friends—and then Richard saw it: a tiny wince on her face that indicated she had indeed done something she wasn't supposed to.

Normally, the Robinsons didn't begin decorating for Christmas until after Remembrance Day, November eleventh, which was tomorrow. But because Dawn was in town, they had made an exception this year. Besides, the task before them was daunting: Pauline wanted to use Christmas decorations from years past at the store that reflected Richard and Claire's fifty years. She believed the story of their almost eternal love would help with sales. When Claire and Richard sold the family home last year, they hadn't sorted through the Christmas decorations: they were already in boxes—some for years because Claire hadn't had the heart to throw them out—and Claire and Richard still had *so much* to pack.

Pauline opened the box in front of her and peered in. Her eyes lit up as she pulled up the gaudiest, largest red bows Todd had ever seen.

"We had these going up the banister at our old house," Pauline said. "We definitely need to hang these somewhere."

Dawn burst into laughter, and Claire raised an eyebrow. "You mean in a dark corner?"

Pauline playfully moped as she set the bows aside.

Dawn opened the flaps to her box. "I'm so glad I could help this year. It's nice to have this peace and quiet for a few days." Dawn pulled out red bell-shaped plastic ornaments. "I remember these! I loved them!" Then sadness came over her face. "I remember breaking one."

Claire added, "You cried until Grandma Sutton gave you a box of Smarties from her purse."

Dawn broke into a smile at the memory. "I'd completely forgotten."

Richard smiled, too. Claire's mother had been known for giving kids far too many sweets. Although his own grandparents had showered him with love, times had been tough in Richard's family when he was a child. Christmas, for example, consisted of only one gift, while tree decorations were made from whatever Richard could find lying around outside, plus his grandmother's leftover yarn and a little glue.

A feeling of fatherly warmth swept over Richard as he watched his wife and two daughters rediscover Christmases past. Last Christmas had been hard because he and Claire had just moved out of the family home to the much smaller apartment. To see everyone together like this, laughing, chatting, loving one another's company... Richard couldn't think of a better way to spend a Saturday evening.

Todd smiled politely at the stories. Richard wondered if all this talk about childhood was making him a little sad: he'd had his own share of family difficulties as a child.

Or was Todd saying nothing because he still felt like an outsider? Richard remembered last year, when Claire had invited Todd over to their home for an afternoon tea, how moved Todd had been when she'd served tea from the tea gardens on Vancouver Island. Claire didn't carry them herself because of their price—considered a rare tea, they were expensive—but with Todd coming from the city of Vancouver, it was her special way of showing she appreciated him and how he'd handled himself in the unique situation he'd been thrown into. Richard recalled how Todd seemed as though he couldn't fathom that someone would make such an effort for him.

Garlands, hundreds of ornaments, crafts made by the girls when they'd been in school... Claire and Richard's apartment was beginning to look a lot like a Christmas decoration store.

Then Claire gasped as she opened a box.

"Everything all right?" Richard asked.

Claire nodded as she gingerly pulled out a blue-and-white teapot. "I thought I'd lost this years ago." She held it toward Pauline. "Where did you find it?"

Their eldest shrugged. "I'm not sure. That box was from the tea shop. We stored it there from the move last year because it said 'Christmas shop.'"

Claire raised it for everyone to see. "My father bought it from a Dutch man immediately after the war. He said the man was clearly selling anything he could to soldiers just to make a little money. Dad gave it to my mom as a gift, knowing how much she loved teapots."

"Goes to show how lucky most of us are today," Richard said. "Very few of us are directly affected by war anymore."

Claire nodded. "It was my favourite teapot as a child: I loved its simplicity, just white and blue. But eventually Mom had to put it away." She placed it on the table in front of her. "Every time it came out, Dad's mood darkened. I understand now it triggered his PTSD, but when you're three or four, you don't get it. You just knew he became angry really fast."

Richard reached out his hands. "May I?" Claire passed it to him. "Such a beautiful design." The white teapot featured a Dutch countryside—complete with windmill—painted around it in blue.

Claire motioned for Richard to turn it over so she could read the bottom. "A Royal Delft, definitely hand-painted. These letters—AJ—stand for the year. I don't know why they didn't just use numbers."

Pauline pulled out her phone. "I'll look it up."

"This could even have been a family treasure," Claire continued. "Mom always took care of the teapot. She said that tea is the cornerstone of a family in many cultures across the world, so it must be doing something right."

"1914," Pauline announced.

Everyone stared in awe for a few moments at this heirloom that was over a hundred years old.

"Well, this has been a nice trip down memory lane." Claire carried the teapot to a shelf. "I'm glad you found it, Pauline."

"I can't take much credit for it—it was simply in that box."

Claire rubbed Pauline's shoulder thoughtfully before sitting down again.

"So?" Pauline asked. "Are Dawn and I allowed to know what anniversary gifts you exchanged? Will they also last a hundred years?"

Uh-oh. Richard had noticed Claire hadn't been truly happy with his version of their trip last night, even though she'd tried to end their anniversary on a happy note. Were their daughters going to agree with their mom? Or with their dad?

"We're going to travel to Vancouver Island in the spring to see the tea gardens," Richard said, hoping no further details would be requested.

Dawn smiled. "Then you could visit us for a few days! I know a few lovely B&Bs."

Richard took a deep breath. "We're not exactly sure how long we can be away for."

"What do you mean?" Dawn asked.

Claire tried to appear polite, but Richard could hear the subtle edge in her voice. "I'd like to go for a week, but your father said that, since it's high season, he can't be gone for that long."

Richard fiddled with the hook of an ornament lying in front of him. "I thought flying to see something you haven't seen before would make that extended weekend special."

Claire placed a hand on his. "You're right. I also understand how important work is to you. I miss it myself a little. But it bothers me that you don't think our fiftieth anniversary is important enough to take a week off."

Richard understood Claire's point of view, but one lost deal could cost the brokerage easily twelve thousand dollars for an average-priced house, plus potential referrals, depending on the situation. Because of Richard's reputation and skill, he'd saved more deals than he could count. The brokerage had lost two deals while he'd been in Niagara with Claire last year. On top of that, sales this year were down compared to last year.

Dawn sat forward in her chair. "I'm just surprised you wouldn't want to spend more time enjoying life at your age."

Richard let out a heavy sigh. "I'm not dead yet."

Dawn shot him a look of exasperation. "That's not what I mean. I mean: Why work yourself to death?"

"I'll retire before then."

"But Dad," Pauline said, rubbing her hip, "life can change on a dime. Why wouldn't you want to spend extra time with Mom and your family?"

What part of "no" did his family not understand? "My business needs me. It hasn't been long since Brenda left so right now is an especially challenging time. It's the first time in a long time that I've had a transition of this nature."

"It's rare for someone to stay with a company as long as Brenda did," Dawn said. "Which is why you should have processes in place to quickly train someone so they can manage in your absence. It'll make your staff more self-sufficient so you can step away more."

"I don't agree. Hands-on, with the owner there is best. Otherwise, how will you know someone's working?" He'd been at this for decades. Why were his management choices suddenly being questioned? Because he couldn't step away when everyone wanted him to?

"You can't just fire people these days by watching them," Dawn said. "You need documentation. I can show you some of the software we use at my brokerage."

"Thank you, but we're fine. We have the important software —website manager, accounting, customer relationship and deal manager. Too much software complicates matters."

Claire leaned into him, her eyes pleading. "But Richard, if you allow Dawn to help you a bit, then you'd be free to—"

"I said no."

A tense silence filled the room. Richard's response had come out harsher than he'd intended. "I'm sorry. It's just that my business means the world to me, and any time I leave for any extended period, things happen that we all end up paying for later."

Claire shrugged, acquiescing to his decision, and Dawn and Pauline exchanged glances, also allowing Richard's decision to stand. Todd, in his usual way, smiled awkwardly and then continued unpacking his box.

Everyone else took their cue from him. Pauline moved over to the couch to begin sorting through the decorations, disposing of ones everyone had already decided could be tossed.

"You could visit us before Christmas," Dawn suggested. "Do half your weeklong trip that way. You know, separate the two plans. You could give your gifts in person to the kids."

Claire clasped her hands in front of her heart. "That's a brilliant idea! Your dad and I can tour the city when you and Dean and the kids are busy, but we could join you for suppers."

"Claire, my Darjeeling…"

Claire's shoulders drooped.

"I'm sorry," Richard said. "I'm still hiring an agent, and Terry's too new." Richard needed to lift his wife's spirits somehow. "What if Jan joined you?"

"That sounds like a great idea," Pauline said, though Richard didn't miss her accusing glance in his direction.

"Well, she is working three days a week right now…" Claire said.

"Just ask her, Mom. Maybe she can move her appointments around."

Claire stroked her teacup. "Jan and I have known each other for more than sixty years but we've never travelled before. My dad wouldn't let me out of his sight until I was married."

Richard's wife rarely talked about her first husband, so Richard had learned to piece together what he knew about the man from statements like that. Richard didn't even know the man's name, only that he'd died in a car accident two years into what had been a painful marriage for Claire. His death had left Claire free and clear to date Richard. But Claire's words struck Richard with a wave of sadness: it sounded as though Claire had felt some pressure into marrying that man in order to get away from her overbearing father.

"Jan and I could also visit your father, Todd, if he's available, so if there was anything you wanted us to take for you, we could."

Todd nodded. "I'm sure he'd be happy to see you."

Pauline's eyes lit up. "Can I send you my gifts for Dawn's kids, too?"

Claire smiled. "Of course! The more I can leave there, the more space in my suitcase for bringing back things I can buy while shopping in Vancouver."

Richard had thrown out the idea of Jan accompanying Claire, assuming she would say no, but now his wife would be thousands of kilometres away from him where he couldn't help her if she needed it. The thought unnerved him.

CHAPTER 4

*N*ow that Claire and Richard were alone in their apartment, she could not contain her resentment.

"How can you *not* find a way to travel with me and visit our family? It's *your* business!"

Richard leaned forward on the counter. "You never left your business for a week except to give birth. Even if you had the stomach flu, you were gone at most two days! And now I'm supposed to leave my business because you suddenly feel like travelling?"

Claire stood on the other side of the counter, supported by her cane. "First, you have staff. Second, this is why you should have sold your business by now: so we could spend more time together in our later years."

"'Our later years'? Claire, please. The only reason you're retired is because everything lined up: Pauline was forced to retire from her career, and your accident forced you to see how exhausted you were with running the shop. I love what I do as much as you did—"

"I still do. I just see the writing on the wall."

Richard rubbed his hands over his face. "Which is supposed to mean what?"

"That we're still both healthy and should take the time now to fully enjoy ourselves!"

He took a deep breath to calm himself and Claire realized she should do the same thing. Getting angry with the love of her life wouldn't solve anything.

Richard continued. "It's just that I'd rather see you for a few hours a day for the next ten years than have an intense two years ending in one of us dying."

Claire drew her eyebrows together and lowered her voice. "Is something wrong with your health that you didn't want to tell me this weekend?"

"No, no, I'm fine. Nothing like that."

Claire let out the breath she'd been holding. "Then I don't understand. I'd rather take advantage of what we have *right now* and have the best time of my life with you, instead of seeing you only in the evenings when you're tired. We spend more time in front of the television than we do talking to each other. We could be travelling, trying different restaurants, going on long walks when the weather's perfect…"

Richard stuck his hands in his pockets. "You know I don't like flying. This trip to Vancouver Island will be hard enough as it is."

Claire continued, trying hard to keep her voice calm. "Then let's use that trip—or a shorter one before it—to see how we can help you. Medicine has changed a lot since we last flew somewhere. I'm sure our doctor could give you something. It's just that I've really enjoyed all these new experiences this year, but one person has been sorely missing from most of them: *you.*"

They stared at each other for a few moments, and Claire wondered if Richard might change his mind.

Then he shrugged. "But apart from us selling the house last

year and you retiring, almost nothing's really changed. Why would you want to rock the boat?"

Claire threw her hands into the air. "Almost nothing's changed? Where have you been? We not only sold the family home, but our daughter had to give up the career of her dreams and is struggling with the effects of her surgery. We both saw that today. And retirement is *huge*! I sorely miss the business I built over fifty-two years, but on the other hand, Jan and I are having a blast with Cecilia and Brenda. What do you mean nothing's changed?"

Another shrug. "You heard all the speeches on Friday. They all said the same thing: We were dedicated to our family, the community, and our businesses. We still are. Nothing has changed, Claire, and nothing needs to."

At those words, Claire was filled with fear and her voice became quiet, almost a whisper. "I need to change. I have changed. I am changing. Richard..." She walked toward the den. "You don't want to travel? Fine. I will. I already spend almost every day barely seeing you. What difference does it make if I'm here or on the other side of the country?"

She disappeared into the den, where she kept a special collection of teas, and closed the door behind her.

RICHARD COULD ONLY STARE in Claire's wake. He had no idea his decision to keep working would upset her this much: he'd always worked, and so had she until just this year. He had assumed Claire was enjoying her free time. He didn't expect her retirement to turn into a demand that he change his work schedule.

And why had he suggested she fly to Vancouver with Jan? Yes, he wanted Claire to enjoy her life, but if she was far away from him, he couldn't get to her if she needed help. At least with Vancouver, she'd be by family, but what if her next trip was halfway around the world?

Maybe he could turn his anniversary gift into a week if he really tried.

He shook his head at the thought: general wisdom—and his experience—said that it took a good year to onboard a new employee, and Terry would have only been working for him for six or seven months by the spring. Plus, another agent had quit two weeks ago and needed to be replaced.

Richard stared down the hallway. Would Claire really travel across the world without him? She loved him as much as he loved her. They'd only ever been apart for maybe a few days at a time, when one or the other had a work-related conference in Toronto, for example. But otherwise, they'd done almost every-thing together: it'd been that kind of love affair for fifty years. Richard and Claire weren't only lovers and parents—they were best friends.

No. She'd never fly that far without him.

But that didn't help how she was feeling right now. If there was one thing Richard had learned in his many years, it was to deal with one problem at a time. Claire and Richard always respected each other's need for quiet after a fight. It was one of the many "secrets" that had helped them last this long. The next step was to keep talking this out, so after he gave her a bit of time on her own, he had to get Claire talking to him again.

A smile came across Richard's lips as he looked across the kitchen at the tea kettle. Soon enough she'd have to come out to get water.

When people asked Richard for marriage secrets, another one was this: "Get the water ready."

Most people required further explanation, but Richard filled the kettle and turned it on to boil.

～

CLAIRE SLUMPED into her desk chair. Their fiftieth anniversary was supposed to be such a special celebration. Learning that Richard had no intention of relaxing his work hours had soured the joy.

Why was he so insistent on working? Why? Aside from mild pain in her knee leftover from the operation, and Richard's slightly elevated blood pressure, they were both in good health. Why on earth couldn't he see that?

She needed a cup of tea.

The nice thing about their old house had been that her office had had everything: a kettle, small water cooler, and her Goddess of Teas, a collection of seventy-eight tins of tea.

The den in this apartment was too small for all that, but she needed a tea to calm down.

"Act your age and just go and apologize," she said to herself. "You know what it's like to struggle with work, and you know that he supported you all these years."

Back in the kitchen, she found the kettle almost at a boil.

"I assume Earl Claire?" Richard asked from where he was getting out Claire's mug and container of loose-leaf tea. "I'd honestly feel out of sorts if I didn't smell lavender after an argument."

The remainder of Claire's anger melted immediately. This was why they'd been married for fifty years.

She stroked his arm. "I'm sorry for my outburst. I'm angry, but that was uncalled for."

Richard put the tea and mug on the counter in front of Claire. "Please understand that my work fulfills me as much as yours did, and I'm very much aware of the responsibility I have for my twenty-four employees. If I'm not there, things fall apart fast."

Claire wasn't cold-hearted. Far from it. In fact, she had a hard time growing her business because she'd had difficulties surpassing that threshold where growth stopped incurring losses and became profitable. It didn't help that she needed to pay wages, whereas almost everyone at the brokerage worked on commission.

However, she only had one life to live, and she was going to live it. "I refuse to spend these years living like an 'old person.' We've both been so dedicated to our businesses, families, and community... Richard, we've forgotten ourselves."

Richard passed her a measuring spoon and strainer. Some might have interpreted that to mean he expected her to finish making her tea out of anger. But fifty years let you understand your spouse on a deeper level: he was saying he knew Claire preferred to decide for herself how to make her tea.

He knows me so well. So why doesn't he understand these desires I have?

Claire and Richard said nothing while her tea steeped. She then placed the strainer into the sink and lifted the cup to her nose. She breathed in deeply, and the aroma of Earl Claire flowed through her.

Richard held her hand and looked at her with a caring but inquiring expression.

"I say little about my first husband." She stared at her tea. "But I did not enjoy being a silent partner."

Richard dropped his hand. "Claire, when did I ever say that was my expectation?"

"You didn't. You never have. And that's why I love you so much." Richard relaxed. "But refusing to acquiesce to someone else's fears—because I can only assume he feared strong women —is why I am the way I am. And I'm growing, Richard, in ways I don't understand yet. I'm excited to travel to Vancouver this month, excited to take Jan along, but angry that you can't find the time to join me. Who knows? Maybe it would've turned into a fun short trip with Sedrick, too? But so long as you bury yourself in your work, you'll never know. You can have the same-old, same-old, but I'm going to live what's left of my life. Starting with flying to Vancouver."

She walked back to the den.

Didn't he understand that if he didn't start making changes, too, he and Claire would start moving along diverging paths?

The answer was obvious to Claire. Why wasn't it to him?

CHAPTER 5

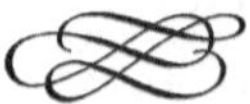

"Todd didn't have to stay home," Richard said to Pauline as all four Robinsons stepped out of the car at the cemetery. He and Claire each held a small wreath in hand.

"He didn't want to intrude on the four of us celebrating Remembrance Day as a family for the first time in a long time," Pauline said.

Richard wondered how he could make Todd understand he was no longer an outsider. Richard had asked Todd to stand up with him at their anniversary precisely because he was now part of the family. Although he and Pauline weren't married and likely never would be, Todd had become practically a son-in-law to Richard and Claire.

They walked up a gentle hill, the cold air nipping at any exposed skin.

Claire stayed close to Richard for warmth. "It was a beautiful ceremony, wasn't it?" she said. They'd attended the Remembrance Day ceremony at the cenotaph in downtown

Kitchener. "I just wish more people would attend. School and work weren't excuses this time since it's the weekend."

Richard wrapped his arm around her. "Memories of the world wars are fading as those who directly participated in them pass away."

"But war continues. We have men and women who fight today, not to mention those who've been displaced by war and immigrate here. I'm glad we devote December to peace, good-will, and fellowship."

They passed a few gravestones before finally stopping in front of the shared gravestone of Claire's parents.

Darlene Sutton nee Barton
September 13, 1922 - January 20, 1994
William Sutton
March 30, 1921 - August 2, 1984

She leaned the wreath against the gravestone. "I'm so thankful for having found that teapot. It reminded me not only of how much my father truly suffered, but also of how far he had come by the time he passed away."

After Claire stood up, Richard reached for her hand, and she leaned against his arm. "I only knew him as a kind and gentle man," he said.

"I think Mom hid a lot of his mental illness from me and the rest of the family," Claire said. "For all I know, he suppressed it around others—he didn't go out for longer than a few hours at a time."

Pauline put an arm around Claire. "That could've been one of his coping mechanisms. The medication and therapies available today might have made all that easier. It makes me so sad to hear how much Grandpa suffered."

Dawn leaned into Richard. "He always seemed so happy. But quiet."

"He did his best to be gentle with both of you," Claire said. "I think by the time Pauline was born, he realized how hard our lives had been when I was growing up. He was just too proud to say anything about it."

After a few minutes of silence, they continued to Richard's mother's grave.

Richard wished they could share similar stories about her. Although he knew his general ancestry—his family had lived in Canada since the nineteenth century—he had been raised by his uncle and paternal grandparents from the age of five. He could not remember much about his mother.

"Here we go," Richard said and lay his wreath over the stone plate tucked into the grass.

Marjorie Robinson nee Stewart
November 2, 1920 - August 12, 1944

Richard said the same thing this year he said every year, because he didn't know what else to say. "My memories of my mother are cloudy, but my uncle and grandparents told me she was a dedicated mother and volunteer. When she wasn't trying to raise me after my father was sent overseas to Hong Kong, she was sewing one thing or another for soldiers."

"How old were you again?" Dawn asked.

"Two when my father left for war. He was one of hundreds of casualties by the time Hong Kong declared defeat on Christmas Day that same year. And yet my mother soldiered on."

Anger clouded Pauline's face. "I remember my history teacher being surprised when I wrote about it. Many people didn't know we'd had troops in Asia."

"I got accused of plagiarizing, because my teacher had heard about a student writing about that topic several years prior." Dawn laughed at the memory. "Thankfully, your teacher could confirm we were sisters writing about a grandfather we never knew."

Claire hooked her hand around Richard's arm. It felt good to have this family moment together, and to feel her gentle touch.

She looked up at him. "Richard..." She paused, choosing her words carefully. "You've never visited his grave in the Sai Wan War Cemetery in Hong Kong. We have the time now."

A lump formed inside Richard that felt like a stone closing the entrance to this frightening idea. "He's nothing but stories to me. Why would I take time off work to see the gravestone of someone I never knew?"

Claire's shoulders drooped. "I'm sorry. It was just a thought, since we visit your mother's grave every year."

A dullness filled Richard's chest, and he squeezed his eyes shut. His response to Claire had been rude. "No, I'm sorry. You're speaking from your heart, as you always do."

Dawn hugged him. "I'm so glad you're more than stories to me." She reached an arm around Claire. "You, too, Mom."

Pauline joined in. "Same here. I don't know who I would've become without both my parents supporting me."

Which was why Richard had no desire to dig up his past. *This* was his family. This right here. He had a few memories of his mother, some of them probably filled in by his uncle and grandparents. But the family he cared most about was this one right here.

And he'd continue to support them as best he could.

CHAPTER 6

Richard locked the door to his car. Monday morning had finally arrived. It had been a roller coaster weekend that began with his anniversary, continued with the discovery that Claire had expected him to start travelling more, and ended with a sad goodbye to Dawn Sunday night. He couldn't wait for a little routine.

So, when he entered Robinson Realty just as one of his agents, several bags in hand, walked past him without making eye contact as he headed out the door, Richard told himself the agent was probably just going on holidays.

But his gut feeling told him otherwise, because he'd been through this dozens of times in thirty-two years. "Did Jason just quit?" he asked Terry.

"I'm afraid so, Mr. Robinson," the young man said.

"Now I have to hire two." Richard switched out his boots for his shoes, hung his coat up in the closet, and put on a cardigan. Brenda used to call him "Mr. Rogers."

Work life was never dull, even after more than five decades in this business.

Richard indicated the Poppy Fund collection box that had been sitting on Terry's desk for the past few weeks. "Make sure this gets back to the Royal Canadian Legion—and add another five thousand from our donation budget."

Terry wrote down the request. "I'll have the cheque ready before lunch."

Richard retreated to his office and sat behind his large oak desk, a gift from the previous owner when Richard had bought the brokerage. He turned on his computer.

An agent walked by his door. "Good morning, Rich."

"Hi, Preetesh. Good weekend?"

"Four viewings, one open house, six leads, no sales. Have another viewing in thirty."

"Not bad. Keep it up."

Preetesh nodded and continued on his way.

Richard glanced up at the family photos he had on the wall: his wedding portrait, a few photos of Claire and the girls at different ages in childhood, one of Pauline on the uneven bars in gymnastics, a couple of studio family shots, and a drawing of their family home by Dawn.

Richard showed his love to those wonderful people by showing up to work every day. Not only did it bring in income he could then share with them as needed, but it also kept him engaged in life and supporting his community. Helping people find a place to truly call home was what had sustained him through the ups and downs of life.

Terry knocked on Richard's door, his morning coffee and a report in hand. Richard simply found reading on paper more comfortable than on his screen and did it whenever possible.

"Your leads report, Mr. Robinson." Terry handed him the report and set the coffee on his desk. "Some were, um, assigned to the gentleman who just left."

Terry was always polite, almost to a fault. Richard had never insisted he be addressed by his last name. He'd even reminded Terry several times during his training that "Rich" was fine. Last names for your elders were common in the eighties and earlier, but Richard relaxed his management style with the times as needed.

Richard pulled a pair of reading glasses out of a desk drawer and skimmed the report.

"How are you doing without Brenda? Things working out all right still?"

Terry adjusted his glasses. "Just fine, sir. My dad always said I had a knack for organization, and Brenda left a logical system behind. She was a good teacher, and I'm learning fast whatever I still need to know."

"Great to hear. Keep up the good work. Oh—before I forget, I'd like an update on our Christmas plans by the end of the day."

Terry nodded and returned to his desk in the waiting area.

Brenda would always decorate the brokerage office with a little Christmas flair—just some garlands here and there and a small Christmas tree in the waiting area under which lay toy donations—but given its small size and the fact that not everyone celebrated Christmas, Robinson Realty never held a staff Christmas party. At the same time, Richard liked the custom of a year-end send-off. During the last week before Christmas, Richard went around to each person who worked for him to say something positive and personal and to deliver a small gift. Sometimes that included thanking a new employee for giving Robinson Realty a go, or congratulating someone on a work anniversary, or announcing their year-end results. Then, at the end, an email would be sent to everyone to share the good news.

Even though Richard frequently saw new sales reps leave within their first six months, many experienced reps had stayed for years. This year-end tradition was one reason for their dedication.

After reviewing the leads and noting which ones needed to be reassigned, Richard made his rounds through the office to say good morning to anyone who was in—agents weren't required to show up at a certain time, especially if they'd had a busy weekend. Richard had always liked to spend time in the office. He worked for many reasons, and one was to be around people.

Terry returned after Richard had sat down at his desk again, his cheeks red.

"Um…another sales rep quit via voicemail ten minutes ago," he reported. He fiddled with his fingers. "Sophie said she didn't like the hours and is going to work retail for Christmas."

Richard shook his head as he leaned back in his chair. "That's what you get for trying to take on too many newly minted agents. They do their certification while working another job, pay for all their board memberships, are eager to get started, and don't believe me when I show them the math about what their first year will probably look like." He skimmed the report again. "Sophie had a decent number of leads, too. I know the market is selling fewer homes this year than last, but this October outperformed last. I think things are picking up. She might have actually had her first sale this month." Richard instructed Terry to process two records of employment.

He watched as Terry fiddled with a thread on his shirt as though trying to formulate a question.

"If you're concerned about the health of this business," Richard said, "no need to worry. Turnover among beginners in this industry is high. It doesn't matter how often we tell new agents that they won't be working only nine to five, Monday to Friday. And they never believe our calculations when we show them a reasonable income for a first-year, hard-working agent.

It's about twenty-five or thirty thousand dollars for fifty to seventy hours a week of work."

Terry's eyes widened.

Richard smiled at his reaction. If only new sales reps believed him like that. "So, we'll be fine." *But my fifty-year marriage, on the other hand, might be heading for rocky waters.* Once he re-distributed both agents' leads, he'd be on the hook for a few himself. Claire wouldn't appreciate the extra time it might take him away from her.

At least Terry looked relieved. One potential resignation avoided.

When Terry left to continue his work, Richard logged in to the leads management program and began assigning agents anew.

After finalizing his schedule for the day, which now ended with a four o'clock viewing with a new client—the granddaughter of a client from Richard's early days—he saw the writing on the wall for *him*: he wouldn't be able to leave the brokerage to travel. What would've happened had he been gone today? He scanned the list of leads from the two sales reps and calculated the potential earnings in his head.

"We might have lost thirty or forty thousand in revenue, that's what."

RICHARD ALMOST JUMPED when Sedrick appeared in his doorway.

"I'll be right with you. Just finishing this email."

"That's the nice thing about retirement," Sedrick said, who'd finished working over ten years before. "I've got all the time in the world."

"And I'd die of boredom. Just one second…" Richard

finished updating the draft job description for new agents. This time, he aimed for those with a few years' experience under their belts. He'd try for new agents in the new year. The industry could only sustain itself if new blood joined, and he usually found training fulfilling. But with their fiscal year-end coming, he didn't have time for it now.

Richard sent the draft to Terry for proofreading, and then joined Sedrick for their scheduled lunch date.

They walked down Belmont Avenue in the chilly November air to Casimiro's, a Portuguese diner that had also withstood the test of time in the Belmont Village shopping district. Many businesses had come and gone over the years, but a few, like Claire's Tea Shop and Robinson Realty, acted as the cornerstones of the area, giving Belmont Village a healthy mix of old and new.

After Gabriel Casimiro left with their order, Richard said, "See? He's not retired either."

"He's easily ten years younger than us."

"Would still make him sixty-nine. Past retirement age."

"Plus, he's working with his wife."

They both glanced toward the kitchen, and Gabriel gave Benedita a loving kiss on the cheek. Richard and Claire were the kind of couple who helped each other at their respective businesses, but they were both too independent-minded to work together.

"Let's talk about something else," Richard said.

"Like your schedule and why you're not travelling with Claire?"

Out of the frying pan and into the fire. "I don't get why she's so disappointed. My evenings and weekends are free. Well, mostly, and that should make Claire happy. She goes out usually one evening a week with the ladies, so there's nothing to do then. They also get together a couple of times a week during the day. She's having fun."

Richard's phone dinged and he checked it. A successful sale! He texted the agent a congratulatory note as Gabriel brought them their drinks: a Pepsi for Sedrick and a ginger ale for Richard.

"Do you text your team in front of Claire like this?"

Richard shook his head. "Only during business hours, but she rarely comes by anymore. She's usually doing something with her friends." He tucked his phone back into his jacket pocket. "What were we talking about again?"

"That you're working a lot for your age."

"Your wife still works."

"To keep busy and to get out of the house. She can also book several weeks off if she wants to."

"I work to keep busy."

"But you insist you can't take a week off?"

Why was everyone nagging at him about his decision to keep working? Richard was fourteen years past typical retirement age. Wasn't it clear by now that he was going to work as long as possible?

Casimiro brought over their orders: burgers with fries on the side.

Sedrick dressed his fries with ketchup and popped one into his mouth. "So? What are we going to do while the women are in Vancouver?"

Richard drew around his plate with a fry. "Don't remind me. I suggested to Claire that she travel with Jan to get me out of hot water. I didn't think she'd actually agree to it." He bit off half the delicious deep-fried potato.

"'Absence makes the heart grow fonder' is absolutely true."

Richard ate the rest of his fry. "It's just that after she fell off that chair last year, I realized how fragile we've both become. Pauline got her hip replaced because of arthritis, and she's only forty-eight. What happens if Claire suffers another fall while she's in Vancouver? It'd take me at least twenty-four hours to get to her."

Sedrick sipped on his pop. "I guess with her recovery having gone so well, I'd forgotten about how that day affected you."

Richard never could forget the day Sedrick was referring to. He'd been showing a house out of town when he got the call from Todd about Claire's injury. He had to drive back for thirty minutes on highways, trying to pay attention while he feared his wife might go into surgery for her dislocated knee before he could see her. Richard's heart pounded just at the memory. It had been so stressful that he'd been surprised when he showed up at the hospital in one piece.

"Hey, Rich, are you all right? Sorry. I didn't mean to bring that day back for you."

Richard shook the memory out of his head. "It comes back on its own sometimes, too. It's okay." *More than sometimes, to be honest.*

"But if you're so worried about her, why spend forty hours away from her at work?"

"Thirty-five," Richard corrected. "I start at nine-thirty."

Sedrick crossed his arms. "In low season. You'll be in the office by eight-thirty in the spring."

"But that's half of what I used to work. I'm practically part time now!" Richard tried to look hopeful, but Sedrick didn't buy it. "Fine. There are so many dangers to travelling, but here she's safe. We're safe. I meant what I said at our anniversary party, that nothing should change." Richard sank into his chair. "I guess I'm just looking for reasons to keep her home. This is the first time she's doing something so rash."

"You mean the first time in a while she's dreamed so big?"

Claire's ability to dream big dreams was one of the reasons

Richard had fallen and stayed in love with her. Sedrick's words made him wonder: Who was he to stand in her way?

Sedrick studied his friend carefully. "You really are scared, aren't you?"

A shiver ran through Richard as he imagined the huge distance that would separate him from his wife.

"Terrified."

CHAPTER 7

Todd brought over a tray with tea and desserts for four: a chocolate brownie for Jan, lemon chiffon cake for Cecilia, Bûche de Noël for Claire, and toffee cake for Brenda. The women had already finished their lunches, and now it was time to indulge a little.

Claire inhaled the scent of her Assam tea. "I can't believe I've been married fifty years."

"It was a wonderful celebration," Cecilia said, but with a hint of sadness. She lost her husband earlier this year, and they'd been married over sixty years. "And I love that the tea shop is selling tea ware inspired by your love."

"Agreed," Brenda said. "And the celebration was beautiful. But Jan, your grandson! The only time I'd seen him dance before was on a YouTube video. That video brought me to tears, but to see him live? Wow. Just wow."

Jan beamed. "He practises at least twenty hours a week on top of his lessons. That he's able to keep up his marks at school despite the side effects of his anti-seizure medication... I'm totally amazed, myself."

"It has been quite the ordeal with him these past two years, hasn't it?" Claire said.

"More than any child should deal with."

Cecilia held up her teacup, ready to toast. "If it hadn't been for my family after my husband died, I don't know if I'd even be here. I honestly didn't see a future for myself. But our children got me help so I could get up every day and focus on my grandchildren. So, I'd like to propose a toast to family."

All the women held up their cups and gently toasted.

Claire cut off a piece of her cake with her fork. "This Bûche de Noël looks absolutely fabulous." She placed it in her mouth and let the buttercream layer melt. "Mmm. Simply perfect. I'll have to tell Tracy."

Cecilia bit into her lemon chiffon cake. "She and Ben have done a beautiful job with the chocolate shop. We couldn't have sold it to better people."

"Oh!" Brenda said. "Todd forgot my fork."

Claire offered to get it, but as soon as she stood up, Pauline walked over to see what was needed. She still walked with a slight limp, so it worried Claire that Pauline wasn't using a walking aid.

"Mom, what can I get you?"

"Brenda needs a fork, if you wouldn't mind?"

Pauline scanned their table to make sure nothing else was missing. "Right away, ladies." She rushed off to get one.

Jan leaned in and lowered her voice. "Is it just me, or is she pushing herself too hard?"

Brenda nodded. "I don't know her as well as you do, of course, but she does seem to be in a little pain. Is she using painkillers?"

Claire shook her head. "Unfortunately, she and I react the same to strong painkillers: we get loopy. I don't know why she's not taking mild ones, though. I should ask her."

Pauline came over with a fork, and Brenda thanked her.

As the women ate, Claire furtively observed her daughter. Pauline was working at full speed: one moment she was handling cash, the next carrying over food. If the tray was loaded, she had it perched on her shoulder, pushing her upper body to the side. That didn't seem like a wise thing to do one month after hip surgery. Pauline had returned to work just last week, and this was the first time Claire had been back in the shop.

Todd didn't appear to notice. Did he think Pauline's behaviour was acceptable? Or was Claire simply overreacting? But Pauline had suffered moderate depression with her surgery. What if this was her way of trying to forget all that and lead a normal life again? Claire could certainly empathize, but pushing too hard could still cause injury, even dislocation. Not only that, but the surgeon had made it clear that life after surgery never returned to the way it was before, or what others called "normal." Claire had certainly experienced that herself, but she'd heard many similar stories during her years of serving tea.

"So?" Cecilia said, interrupting Claire's thoughts. "You two are headed to Vancouver in two weeks?"

Jan's mouth was still half-full when she answered, her eyes wide with excitement. "I can hardly wait. I haven't been to Vancouver in over fifteen years, and it's always nice to see Dawn and her family."

"I've never visited them," Claire said. "Something I regret."

A sad look on her face, Cecilia said, "I hate regret."

Claire assumed Cecilia was referring to things she wished she'd done—or maybe even not done—when her husband had been alive. It had only been seven months since his death.

"We intend to do a lot of shopping," Claire said. "But I also hope we'll fit in some sightseeing. Aside from mine and

Richard's twenty-fifth anniversary trip, I've never been anywhere I couldn't easily drive to."

Brenda shook her head in amazement. "Don't you get cabin fever?"

Claire took a sip of her tea as she thought about Brenda's question. "I guess because I met so many people while working here, I didn't feel a strong urge to travel. I was curious about the wider world, but the thought of having to shut down the shop for a week and lose that income worried me."

Jan said, "I lost income when Sedrick and I travelled, but the memories I have, and the memories the kids have, were all worth it."

That was exactly what Claire now regretted, not having those memories with her children or grandchildren. That would begin to change with her trip to Vancouver. Unfortunately, it would change without Richard.

Cecilia shook her head. "I don't mean to tell you what to do, but you and Richard really should enjoy what you have left of life." She stared into her tea, and her voice got quiet. "Trust me: everything can change on a dime."

Exactly what Pauline had said on the weekend.

The other three offered their condolences again to Cecilia.

"You three are so wonderful. I'm so glad you asked me to join you."

Claire raised her teacup. "To friendship." The others raised their cups and toasted with her.

Life could indeed change on a dime. Until the year of Claire and Richard's marriage, a woman had to prove that her husband had been cruel before she could divorce him. With how David had treated her, it would've been impossible to do so. By everyone else's account, he was an upstanding member of society.

Then, all of a sudden, Claire was free.

"Where would you want to go?" Cecilia asked Claire. "Besides Vancouver."

"I guess it would be nice to travel to England and see where my family came from," she said. "But at the same time, Richard has never visited his father's grave in Hong Kong. He says it's because he never knew him—he had left for the war when Richard was two and sadly never came back. Family is so important to Richard, but he has no desire to travel that distance."

"Is it his fear of flying?" Brenda asked.

"It's a fear he's had for as long as I've known him, even though he tries to hide it. But I don't think it's that."

Todd came over to check on the women. "Can I get anyone anything else?"

They all shook their heads. Claire complimented him on his tea-making skills, and Todd blushed. When she'd hired him, he'd had the gumption to acknowledge that he drank bagged tea, earning her immediate respect for his honesty, even if that habit was something that had to change.

As he returned to the counter, one of Claire's least favourite customers strutted in: Doris. She looked in the women's direction, tightened her lips, and approached the counter.

In the decades since Doris had been patronizing Claire's Tea Shop, Claire had come to expect this woman would never be pleasant to deal with. Todd was the only one who could charm her—Claire watched as Pauline discreetly walked away from the cash so Todd could take over. But Doris had brought in lots of business over the years, so everyone working at Claire's tolerated her.

Doris cast Claire a side glance when she left with her order.

Within a half hour, foot traffic died down. There was often a lull between the end of lunchtime rush and after work. Pauline appeared to motion to Todd that she was stepping outside, and

Claire saw her chance to talk to Todd. She excused herself from the group and beelined for Pauline's partner.

He stopped what he was doing and faced Claire. "Is everything okay?"

Claire cut right to the chase. "She's still limping, Todd. How much pain is she really in?"

He smiled politely. "She's managing as best she can."

"Todd, I'm her mother. I'm worried about her. She was carrying that tray with sandwiches, teas, glasses of water, and desserts on her shoulder."

Todd glanced to the back room. Why was he acting nervous around his own partner?

"Todd…?"

Underscoring his unease, he rolled up his cuffs and adjusted them, a nervous habit of his. "In more pain than she was expecting to be in at this point, I guess."

"What do you mean?"

Todd pulled out a cleaning cloth and wiped down the counter. "She'd rather deal with this on her own, Claire. I'm not sure I'm the one to talk to about her."

There he went again, stepping out of the family. Claire didn't want to put him in a tight spot, but she also didn't expect that her questions would have that effect.

Claire had raised her daughters to be fiercely independent, and that had served them well through life. They'd each been successful in their own right. But ever since learning the date of the surgery, Pauline had pushed Claire and Richard away, insisting she was fine. It had taken some convincing to ensure she took three weeks off and allowed Claire to step in. "You're a part of our family, Todd. It's okay to talk about someone if you're worried for them. I'm happy to help more if that eases things for her. For both of you."

Todd shrugged hopelessly. He wouldn't say anything more.

It spoke well for him, in a way. Richard would respect her wishes for privacy, too, if someone criticized how she was handling a situation.

At the same time, when Claire was recuperating from her knee surgery, she'd immediately called in the cavalry to help out. Why was Pauline avoiding this option?

Todd placed the rag back underneath the counter. "She loves it here, Claire. She was going stir crazy by the end of her three weeks at home."

What else could Claire say? She'd shared her concerns.

The sound of the back door clicking signalled that Pauline had returned.

"Everything okay, Mom?"

"I was wondering about the Christmas tea sale and party." Not exactly the truth, but not exactly a lie either. "Do you need help with planning it? I didn't see anything up on your whiteboard while I was covering for you."

Pauline pulled down two mostly empty jars from the wall of teas behind the counter. "All planned. We already have the tea wares inspired by yours and Dad's anniversary, as I'm sure you've seen. Why don't you come to the back and I'll show you the rest?"

That sounded promising. Claire signalled to her friends that she'd be another five minutes and followed Pauline into the backroom, which served as an office and storage.

Pauline pointed to the pinboard and whiteboard on the wall that she used to communicate some of the important plans with Todd and Austin, who helped out one day a week in exchange for private ballet lessons from Todd.

"Have a look." Pauline pulled heavy wholesale bags of tea down and began filling the two jars.

Claire studied the plans, but within two minutes, she wondered how Pauline and Todd were going to accomplish everything: an extensive social media campaign, a new tea blend, restocking, and more. She knew that the restocking should happen soon, or they'd get stuck in the Christmas rush with the wholesalers.

One item in particular stood out. "You're going to be in costume?" Claire didn't know whether to be happy or worried for her daughter. Pauline didn't just slip one of those cheap Halloween costumes over her head and call it a day. She rented the full mascot-style ones.

"I'll be fine," Pauline said. "It'll be two months post-surgery by then. I don't do stunts in here, anyway, because it's too tight."

"And because you're not supposed to, right?"

Pauline nodded but avoided eye contact with Claire.

That didn't sit well with Claire at all.

CHAPTER 8

"*W*e need to talk," Claire said.

Pauline picked up one jar in each arm and pressed them close to her body so they wouldn't drop. "I know what this is about, Mom. And you don't need to worry. I'll be fine. This isn't the first time I've needed medical attention because of my performance career. I didn't get into costume until I was ready. I know my body. I'll be good."

In the past, Pauline's "medical attention" had been for ailments like a sprained ankle or pulled muscle—not having part of her thigh bone sawed off as it had been now.

Claire followed Pauline back to the counter of the tea shop.

"I just know those costumes affect how you move, and they limit your vision. I'm worried you'll trip—"

Pauline laughed. "Mom, I haven't had an accident like that in ages." She set the jars down on the counter. Todd, who had just finished serving a customer, lifted one back onto the shelf while Pauline picked up the other.

Claire continued. "It's just that when I look at all those

plans, I don't know if you've taken into account how much business increases at this time of year."

Todd gave Claire a reassuring smile. "We have everything laid out, Claire. Really, we'll be fine."

All the versions of "we'll be fine" Claire had heard these past few days were grating on her nerves. Why weren't they taking Pauline's recuperation seriously? Claire wanted her daughter to return to what she loved as soon as possible, but there were limitations.

Exasperated, Claire returned to her friends and shook her head at their hopeful glances. "They have extensive plans for the annual tea sale and party—including Pauline performing again—and I'm not convinced she's ready for that kind of workload. You should've seen it." Claire listed all the tasks she saw. "And that was just what was on the whiteboard. They've moved the shop's to-do items to some kind of program instead of a binder, so I couldn't see the details."

"Could you offer to help out again?" Brenda asked. "You've said that you enjoyed the three weeks you covered for Pauline."

"I did and Todd said no. But I'm also not sure I want to do that many hours. I miss work, but I really enjoy what we're all doing."

Jan spoke up. "Maybe that's also what Todd was thinking. What about helping out just a couple times a week? One weekday, so they can focus on administrative tasks, and Saturdays during the Christmas rush? We can arrange our activities around such a light schedule, can't we, ladies?"

Everyone nodded.

The idea sounded doable. Claire promised to talk to Richard about it.

❧

By the time Richard got into the apartment building elevator, he was sweating. He hoped a bouquet of red roses would be a good apology for coming home late. But at least he'd signed on Jaya, the granddaughter of an old client of his, and shown her two homes. He'd texted Claire a few times to give her a heads-up that he wouldn't be home until after seven. She hadn't replied, though, so she was either out having a good time or she was furious with him. On the very realistic chance it was the latter, Richard had bought the flowers.

When the elevator doors opened, he rushed to their apartment, and fumbled his keys only to have the door whipped open in front of him. She must've been waiting for him.

"Claire, I'm so—"

"Glad you're home! Come to the den when you've settled. I have something to talk to you about." She spun around and floated down the hallway, a trail of jasmine scent from her tea wafting in her wake.

Richard stood in the apartment foyer for a moment. What had he just witnessed? Claire had made it clear that she didn't approve of his still working. What was she so excited about? Then he smiled to himself. The beauty of their relationship was that, despite the years they'd spent together, they could still surprise each other.

He unwrapped the flowers, cut the stems, and placed the bouquet in a vase. He went to the fridge where he found meatloaf, baked potatoes, and boiled peas on a plate covered with a microwavable lid. Sometimes work really was the pits. It would've been nice to eat that freshly cooked instead of reheated.

His stomach growled, but he wanted to find out what had Claire so excited. He pulled the plate out of the fridge, grabbed a big spoon from the drawer, and began eating without reheating the food. The corners of his mouth turned upside down in disgust at the cold peas, but at least he would have something in his stomach before he went to discover the cause of this unexpected behaviour.

After eating a few bites of cold meatloaf and putting the plate back into the fridge, Richard followed his wife into the den, where he found her reading on her tablet at the desk, pages of notes strewn in front of her, the scent of jasmine still in the air.

He cleared his throat to announce his arrival. "What's with the, um, excitement?" What if it was that she'd found a cheap flight to Shanghai?

"No, I was right," Claire said to herself. "Here." She handed Richard her tablet while she made notes.

Several tabs were open in the browser, all about the basics of social media. "You're opening a social media account?"

Claire finished a note before answering. "No. I'm trying to better understand how social media works for businesses. If I'm going to make suggestions to Pauline about how to help her, I need to be flexible so she can't say no." She took the tablet back from him to read something on it. "But before you say anything about me returning to work, this is only temporary, maybe ten or twelve hours a week until Christmas is over. But I really think they need the help. The ladies suggested two days a week. What do you think? Does that work for us?"

"So, you're hoping to return to work?" He said this more to digest this surprise turn of events than to ask for confirmation.

"I'm hoping to help. Pauline's overexerting herself, and I'm worried she'll injure herself if she doesn't dial it back." At Richard's still puzzled look, Claire filled Richard in on everything she'd learned that afternoon at the tea shop. "I know I can do cash—that's easy. I can also serve. But I'm trying to see if there's something I can do at home for a couple of additional hours. But social media seems to require all this tech know-how. I don't think I can learn it fast enough."

Claire straightened out her papers and handed the first one to Richard. "This is a list of things I used to do—ordering food and supplies. But since Pauline moved everything to the computer, I'm less helpful there these days." Claire had always had a disdain for technology. She often likened it to a horse, something that you *could* rely on, but you had to know that had a mind of its own.

She'd never ridden a horse for that reason.

Although she'd embraced technology that helped her stay in touch with family, she avoided many other advancements. She'd even stuck it out with her very first cash register until it was an antique she could no longer get serviced.

Claire handed Richard a second list. "This one is a list of ideas for the tea sale and party."

Richard scanned the page, then turned it over to read the second side. "This is quite a bit. Are you certain they haven't planned everything by now? It's only a month away."

She nodded, still not looking up from the desk as she jotted more notes. How she managed to juggle a conversation and her own thoughts at the same time was beyond Richard. *Something she obviously learned by serving many customers at once.* Workdays could certainly leave him feeling like he'd been run off his feet, but at least he usually had the luxury of focusing on one task at a time.

"I always had all my marketing materials ready weeks beforehand. They have nothing."

"Maybe it's tucked away in a drawer somewhere?" Richard didn't want to risk appearing to Pauline as though they didn't believe in her.

Claire shook her head. "They should at least have a poster on the front door by now. I'll ask as discreetly as I can, but I'm certain they're nowhere near as prepared as they should be." She passed him another page of notes: an itinerary for the day of the tea sale and party.

Richard read it over. "You have her down as Mrs. Claus instead of a full costumed character? You know Pauline. It's all or nothing with costumes." Richard remembered that she *had* worn a regular adult costume during last year's Halloween tea party, but that was so she could keep serving with a full field of vision and bare hands. But otherwise, she always wore one of those hot, stuffy, furry costumes with the foam heads. He had no idea how his daughter spent several hours in one of those without combusting.

But he'd seen her work over the years and certainly talked to her about it a lot. She'd touched a lot of hearts with her acting.

Claire fiddled with her pen, nervous energy still obvious. "I just thought that way she could still dress up, be a character, and be safe. And since this is Claire's Tea Shop, I thought maybe for once Mrs. Claus might like to talk to the kids instead of Santa. No offence to your previous performances, of course, Mr. Claus." Claire smiled. "Afterwards was always fun."

Richard laughed at the memories of Santa's personal side. Then he paused. "But can she take kids on her lap?"

"We'll have to ask the physiotherapist what's safe. But she's not getting fully dressed up. I'm certain *that's* not safe."

Richard couldn't argue with that. He reviewed Claire's task lists. "You really think she'll let you do all this? She's as head-strong as you are."

"I'm still her mother. And she was still hurting today but both she and Todd denied any major problems. If our annual Christmas event doesn't happen, it'll be the first time in fifty-one years. Customers are expecting it. I'm hoping that talking to her about different ways I can assist will leave the choice of how I'll be involved to her."

Claire had a point. Customers loved consistency.

Customers loved consistency…and they also loved nostalgia…

"You forgot one thing," Richard said and shared his idea with Claire.

Claire smiled. "I love it when we act as a team."

So did Richard. See? Nothing had changed.

CHAPTER 9

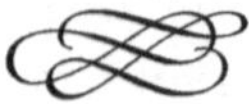

Claire and Richard entered the tea shop through the back just in time to catch Todd and Austin finishing their Sunday morning practice session in the café area.

"See what I mean?" Claire pointed to the whiteboard and the plans for the Christmas tea sale and party.

Richard shook his head in amazement. "I understand wanting to catch up after being gone for so long, but if she can't keep up with the schedule she's set for herself—"

"Everything will fall behind."

Despite the disagreement about Richard's decision to not retire, Claire sensed they were otherwise back on track with each other: finishing each other's sentences, speaking without words sometimes, cuddling before bed.

During this past week, she and Richard hadn't been able to talk to Pauline and Todd. Claire had been out with her friends one night, Richard had worked late three nights, and no one had answered the one night they knocked on Pauline and Todd's apartment door.

Today would be their opportunity as the Robinsons,

Brubachers, and Tschirharts decorated the tea shop. Though not related by blood, the Brubachers and Tschirharts were family by heart, and they regularly pitched in when it came to decking out the tea shop. The Robinsons had often returned the favour with Jan's salon, and now with Tracy and Ben's chocolate shop. It was a fun way to spend time together while doing something deeply meaningful to everyone.

"Between you overworking yourself and her not taking her healing seriously," Claire said, "I'm afraid I'll end up with a husband having a heart attack and a daughter with a dislocated joint."

Richard gave his wife a look. "This past week was a bit busier than most, but you know my heart's in excellent health." He smiled. "It's still in love with you, after all."

Claire laughed. "Always trying to sweep me off my feet."

He kissed her on the cheek. "If it gets me out of trouble." He studied the event plan in more detail. "I don't want to embarrass Pauline in front of the rest of the family, but we need to bring it up today regardless of what happens so we can all make a solid plan."

Their conversation was interrupted by an exhausted Austin. "Hi, Richard. Hi, Claire. Sorry—we thought no one would be here for at least another fifteen minutes."

"We wanted to start getting organized before everyone else arrives," Richard said. "Looking good out there, Austin."

"And we can't wait to see you in a few weeks in *The Nutcracker*," Claire said.

Austin swigged back half a litre of water in one gulp. "It's my dream come true. Todd's doing the choreography, and I'm dancing the Nutcracker Prince."

Todd came into the back room and said hello as he wiped his face with a cloth. "Time to clean up, Austin. Fast. We don't want to welcome everyone in here with—"

"Locker-room smell," Austin said as he grabbed his bag and ran into the washroom.

"Austin's improving by leaps and bounds," Todd said, winking as Claire and Richard groaned at the pun. "I'm going to go roll up the portable dance floor."

Richard and Claire followed him out to where the café tables and lounge area met—though the tables and chairs had been pushed aside for Austin and Todd. They stopped to look at the display Claire had put together with the new tea wares representing their marriage.

"Pauline thought at least one vintage tea set—this 1960s one —should be part of the collection, and the rest she commissioned from artists who took inspiration from tea sets and teapots found in our family photos."

Richard loved it. "I think our idea will fit beautifully with this concept."

"I'm glad we'll get to spend a little more time together. I'm starting to feel like I married our apartment and not you."

Richard wrapped his arms around Claire, and Claire peered up at him. "My work situation is only temporary," he said. "I'm searching for experienced agents this time." He bent down and kissed her. Claire's heart sped up. She loved the feeling of being so in tune with him.

Within twenty minutes, Austin and Todd were cleaned up and in casual clothes, and Jan, Sedrick, Tracy, and Ben had arrived. Finally, Pauline arrived, saying that her run had taken longer than usual.

Her run?!? She wasn't supposed to be running anymore. Claire didn't need to make eye contact with Richard to know they were thinking the same thing.

"So," Pauline said. "Let's get to work and make this place look like Mrs. Claus and the elves decorated!"

Claire couldn't argue with that kind of enthusiasm, but

something had to be done about her daughter's passion for ignoring doctor's orders.

They pulled out one table at the back of the café while Austin got a mop and pail. Claire couldn't help but smile as Austin danced while he cleaned.

Claire turned to Jan and Sedrick, pointing at Austin. "Remember when he was young and would lose himself in dance?"

"He hasn't changed," Jan said.

"He found himself again once the bullying at school stopped," Sedrick added. "That was so hard to watch."

"I'm glad that's over," Claire said. "He can finish high school on a happy note."

"Focused on his goals," Sedrick said.

"His dreams," Jan corrected.

Austin stopped, realizing he was being watched. His cheeks turned red and he smiled.

"Don't let us stop you, sweetie," Jan said. "Keep dreaming."

"And planning," Sedrick added.

Claire had had to resign herself all these years to Skype calls and occasional visits with Dawn's family. *Austin has been more a grandson to me than my own grandchildren*, she realized.

Tracy, Ben, Todd, and Pauline began bringing over the boxes the Robinsons had sorted through the week before. Everyone working together reminded Claire of the early days when Jan worked at the tea shop, sometimes just helping out now and then, sometimes working for minimum wage, especially as she was developing a name for herself in the neighbourhood as a hairdresser. Tracy had worked there, too, once she reached her teens. Claire's Tea Shop really was a family affair.

When all the boxes were on the table, Pauline began delegating who hung what where. The others noticed that she massaged her hip as she spoke, but no one said anything.

Maybe offering the suggestion in front of friends wouldn't be such a bad idea, Claire thought. She might have backup.

Everyone was busy with their tasks—ensuring ornaments had hooks, untangling Christmas lights, setting up the artificial tree near the front. It was now or never.

Claire jumped in. "My honey, what would you think of your father and I selling tea together on Saturdays and me helping out one extra day a week?"

Pauline could never hide her emotions, and she had always been grateful for the mask she wore as a mascot because it hid her expressions. Now annoyance briefly flashed over her face before she could cover it up with a polite smile. "I really appreciate the offer, Mom and Dad, but we'll be fine. I promise."

"Actually," Tracy said, "you two behind the counter would be really cute."

Richard looked unimpressed. "We are not cute."

"I have to agree," Sedrick said. "What's this with calling your elders cute? We're dashing, sophisticated—"

"Gorgeous," Claire continued. "Sexy."

Jan nodded in agreement. "Carefree, fashionable, whimsical."

Ben spoke up. "From a marketing perspective, I think it's a great idea to at least have Claire and Richard selling once a week, especially since your anniversary is the sub-theme of this year's Christmas promotions. It'll make for relevant social media content, and Richard's brokerage will get an extra boost. Cross-post to his accounts, and Claire's Tea Shop will experience the same."

Ben's last position before falling in love with Tracy had been as marketing director for the Toronto Peregrines, which meant he had also been Pauline's manager. To say that he knew marketing was an understatement.

Claire gave herself a metaphorical pat on the back. She'd

read last week about partnering with other companies to cross-post.

Unfortunately, Pauline doubled down instead of agreeing. "Todd and I can manage. Mom never took time off."

"I most certainly did."

"Two days if you were super sick."

Todd laid a reassuring hand on Pauline's but addressed Claire. "Thanks for your concern, Claire. We really do appreciate it."

Pauline mumbled something under her breath, and Claire felt her blood pressure rise.

"Think of it this way," Ben said. "Romance sells really well two times during the year: at Valentine's and Christmas. And there's nothing more romantic than a romance as long as your parents'."

Pauline let out a short sigh. She was caving; Claire was sure of it.

Richard added, "If you let us help—I can schmooze with the ladies when I'm in, and your mother can run things as she usually has—it'll give you and Todd time to prepare for the tea sale and party."

"It's a smart plan," Ben said. "You've seen athletes come back to the game too soon after an injury. You really need to slow down, Pauline."

"You're not my boss anymore."

"I'm speaking as a friend, which I hope has more sway."

Pauline stared at the table, and Claire knew it was time to change the subject. Maybe giving Pauline time to consider the idea while everyone—including Pauline—had fun decorating would help.

Claire held up a freshly coiled string of lights. "So, who gets to hang these up?"

Pauline yanked them out of her hands. "I do."

Claire's jaw dropped. "Should you be climbing? Especially after going for a run?" She could no longer control the accusatory tone in her voice: Pauline was going too far with her pretending that life was back to normal after major surgery.

Pauline answered in a tight voice. "I'm fine."

Todd had returned from the back room carrying a ladder just in time to hear Pauline's reply. Claire noticed a fleeting look of worry on his face like ones she'd caught before. She added that to what he'd said last week when she'd tried to talk to him about Pauline, and it confirmed to her that everything with her daughter was not fine.

"Maybe Austin can —" she started.

"I'm fine."

Pauline climbed the ladder to string Christmas lights across the ceiling. She appeared comfortable. Was Claire overreacting?

Then she noticed Todd emerging from the back room with an ice pack. He discretely handed it to Pauline and she promptly held it against her hip. His automatic behaviour—Pauline hadn't asked for anything—suggested that whatever Pauline was feeling had been going on for a while.

"You know," Jan said as she evaluated which decorations to lay on the shelves. "I've noticed over the years that more and more people love supporting family-run businesses. Having Claire in during the week and then both Richard and Claire at the counter on Saturdays during Christmas would probably communicate exactly how much of a family business this is. Parents running the shop with their daughter and her partner. I think it'd help with sales."

Ben held up the large red bows and quickly set them aside. Claire chuckled inwardly.

"You're not wrong," Ben said. "Our sales took a hit when Mr. Gisler's loyal customers stopped coming because he wasn't there on a regular basis. No one knew me or Tracy." Mr. Gisler was Cecilia's late husband and the former owner of the chocolate shop.

Tracy put her arm around Ben. "Things are finally picking up for us, a year later."

Ben was thirteen years younger than Tracy, and yet somehow, it worked. Claire couldn't imagine being with someone that much younger than she was. At her stage of life, he'd still be working.

Oh, wait. He still was. Apparently, age didn't make a difference in matters such as retirement these days.

Jan and Sedrick now had an arm around each other, too. "We all care about your well-being, Pauline. Your parents and us, we didn't make it this far without looking out for each other."

Pauline sat down in a chair and stared at her lap. Todd placed a hand on her shoulder. Was that his way of trying to calm her down? Richard had a similar gesture for Claire—a simple, light touch that said he supported her, but that calming down in the moment would serve her better. Claire's passion for life and for doing the right thing could sometimes get her riled up a little too much for her own good.

Austin smiled as he surveyed the room. "I hope my next boyfriend is my lifelong love. Would be cool to be married fifty years."

Tracy unhooked herself from Ben. "Not so fast, young man. Don't you want to be a major ballet star? You'd have to find someone willing to tolerate your practice schedule."

Austin's smile fell. "The other guys in my ballet class have girlfriends. I feel left out."

"No need to deflate his hope," Claire said. "Never give up on your dream of love, Austin."

Tracy looked at Todd. "You didn't rise to stardom by focusing on boyfriends."

Todd laughed. "No, I didn't."

Tracy covered her eyes and burst out laughing. "I mean girl-friends."

"Since I'm standing next to my partner and in the company of her parents, no comment."

Pauline gave his hand a kiss. "At least someone's in my corner."

"We're all in your corner," Claire said. "That's why we're pushing on this. It's clear your hip still needs time to heal." Claire chose her next words very carefully, as though her daughter were her toughest customer. "You want to live your fullest life, but you also have a lot to plan for the tea sale and party. Plus, I'm sure you'd like to have a pain-free Christmas. With me dropping in once during the week, and me and Dad here Saturdays, you and Todd will have some time to breathe."

Pauline sighed. "All right. Fine. Work. But Todd and I will still be here."

Richard gave Claire's waist a gentle squeeze.

"We're looking forward to it," she said, her voice as calm as a summer evening.

CHAPTER 10

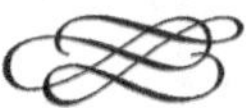

If there was one thing Richard hated more than anything else in the world, it was interviewing job candidates. He had to choose a select few—sometimes only one—and let the others know they were not suitable for Robinson Realty. Running a business obviously included team turnover, but he'd never forgotten the disappointment of not getting a job in his youth.

He waited two minutes after the current candidate had left the office and then planted his elbows on his desk and his face in his hands.

He had conducted four interviews this morning and still not a suitable candidate was to be found.

Terry knocked on his door and Richard lifted his head to see Terry's concerned expression. "Are you okay, Mr. Robinson?"

Richard nodded. "My next interview is in fifteen minutes. I think I'll just stretch my legs."

"Actually, he called and said he was lost in the city. He couldn't orient himself because of our messy road-naming conventions."

Richard laughed. If you knew Waterloo Region—which included the cities Kitchener, Waterloo, and Cambridge, and several townships—you knew that you couldn't navigate according to the street names. King Street, for example, ran in all four directions: mostly East and West in Kitchener and North and South in Waterloo. There were also funny situations like Victoria Street South and Highland Street West running parallel to one another because they'd been named in relation to the major street they crossed: King Street West and Queen Street South, respectively.

If Richard had been expecting out-of-town friends, he'd have had no issues with them getting lost. But what good was a real estate agent who didn't first study where he was going? And where was his GPS?

Terry seemed to be reading his mind. "His message said that his phone was on five percent, so he couldn't talk any longer than to just say he'd be late."

"Which means he forgot his charger at home and has never heard of a map as backup."

Terry shrugged. "He didn't say."

Out of respect for that candidate's time, and on the gamble that there was something, as Claire would say, "magical" about this man, Richard would keep the interview. He asked Terry to show the candidate in as soon as he arrived.

As Terry left, Richard's phone rang. It was Claire. He closed his office door. "Hi, my Darjeeling."

Claire laughed. "You're going to scare off that new assistant if you answer the phone like that."

"He's lasted a month so far, and apart from the fact that he won't address me by my first name, he's working out well. Is everything okay? How's Pauline?" Claire had gone into the tea shop this morning to discuss her new role.

"Mmm." Ah. Claire couldn't talk. That was right: there was nowhere private to go at the tea shop.

"Understood," he said.

"I thought I'd check if you had time for a late lunch? I'll be finished here at one. I could bring sandwiches over and we could eat in your office. Something nice and quick."

Guilt filled Richard's heart. He could see an olive branch when one was being offered: Claire was trying to find more ways to spend time with him while still respecting his schedule. Unfortunately, his schedule for today was full.

"I'm really sorry," he said. "I've got a job candidate coming shortly—he's already late—followed by two more after lunch. Then two viewings later this afternoon."

"Oh."

He hated disappointing Claire. He checked his calendar and a knot formed in his stomach: the only lunchtime he had free was at the end of the week. "Would Friday work?"

"Um, yes, sure." Then her voice brightened. "Okay. I can do Friday."

"Great!"

He entered the date into his calendar immediately so his office staff wouldn't book anything at that time for him. After saying goodbye, Richard took a walk around the brokerage to see how everyone was doing. Business was slow overall according to the numbers, but those who'd received the other agents' clients were excited to have the opportunity to close a deal.

Not bad given they were short three agents.

On his way back to his office, a commotion in the waiting area caught Richard's attention. The next job candidate, probably so flustered from being—Richard checked his watch—twenty minutes late, had tripped over the boot trays. Which were well away from any walking path.

The man looked up, his cheeks bright red. Richard gave him the benefit of the doubt and assumed his cheeks were rosy from the frosty winds outside.

"Um, hi," the man said to Richard and Terry. "I'm here to see Rich?"

Late and inappropriately informal.

Richard smiled, hiding behind his professional manner. "I'm Richard Robinson."

Now the man's entire face turned red.

Maybe Richard should have cancelled this interview and enjoyed lunch with Claire.

CLAIRE HAD TRIED to sound upbeat on the phone. Richard was obviously busy.

Less busy would be nice, she thought. *We only have just over a month until Christmas, and Jan and I are flying out on Sunday.*

"Everything okay, Mom?" Pauline asked.

Just like Pauline couldn't hide her emotions from anyone, she could tune into others' feelings easily.

"I was just hoping to have lunch with your father. We're done here for now?" Claire happily changed the subject.

Pauline nodded. "But just remember, if you and Dad can't make it on a Saturday, just let us know. We'll be here anyway."

Claire simply nodded at the offer—no point in debating things—and called up Jan to see if she wanted to join Claire for lunch. They met at Claire's apartment, where they had privacy from prying ears.

It was just as well that Richard didn't have time today. This week was another anniversary for Claire, one only Jan knew about, and Claire wanted to ask her best friend about something that had been on her mind since the day before.

Claire hung up their coats in the front closet. "I'm wondering if it isn't time to finally talk to Richard about my first marriage."

Jan slipped out of her boots. "You know my feelings on that. I think it's been wrong to keep Richard in the dark all these years."

Jan had urged Claire many times to tell Richard about what had been such an important part of Claire's life. But Claire could never bring herself to do it aside from saying that she'd been married before and her husband had died.

Claire unwrapped their sandwiches and placed them on plates. "I wanted to keep David out of my marriage to Richard, but he was also responsible for who I've become. So, in a bizarre and unfair way, he's responsible for the tea shop. How can I explain that to Richard without hurting him? He's supported me so much, and to give any credit to another man has always seemed wrong."

Jan helped herself to water, but Claire declined anything for the moment. They sat down at the small dining table.

"But you haven't been able to let David go either after all these years."

"It's true when they say hate hurts."

"Then why now?" Jan took a bite of her egg salad sandwich.

"All this denial from Pauline, her trying to keep up appearances for some reason or other... It just got me thinking: Am I denying Richard something by not telling him?"

"So...the pain you're feeling from Pauline hiding herself from you has you questioning if Richard might feel the same way about you?"

"That about sums it up. I just feel like a hypocrite if I expect my daughter to open up to us, but I haven't opened up to my husband in all these years."

Jan shook her head and smiled. "Claire Robinson. Always thinking things through."

Claire returned her best friend's smile. "Jan Brubacher. Always feeling her way through."

They finished their sandwiches, so Claire offered to make them both tea. They chose a sweet-tasting sencha: something Claire called a light and simple tea that's perfect for best friends. They curled up with their mugs of tea on the couch.

"I looked up all the tea shops in Vancouver," Claire said. "I can't wait to go."

"Should we pack an extra suitcase and share the cost? I'm looking forward to the arts-and-crafts scene."

Claire laughed. "We may just have to!"

They each took a sip of their tea before continuing the conversation.

"I take it Richard still hasn't expressed any interest in joining us?"

"No. He's chin-deep in work. I tried scheduling lunch with him this week, and the best he can give me is Friday."

"Ouch."

"It's starting to feel like that teapot Pauline found: a promise made, a promise broken. I thought we'd do everything in life together. Apparently not."

"What do you mean? What teapot?"

Claire retrieved the Royal Delft teapot and quickly explained its history. "Dad had said he'd bought it from a man who'd needed help, and so every time we used it, I believed we were helping this stranger. I guess I'd assumed that if Santa was watching us, so was this man. Then...Mom just packed it away."

"Do you know why?"

Claire shivered. "Dad was part of the Canadian battalion that liberated a transit camp in Holland. He witnessed the worst of humanity there. It was the first time he'd ever seen children in captivity."

Jan's hand flew to her mouth. "So that teapot brought back those memories?"

"Mom told me after he'd passed so I'd finally understand my childhood."

Both women sipped on their tea for a few minutes. Claire remembered how her father's eyes would sometimes stare at something—or nothing—without blinking, or that he'd cover his ears at the sound of something normal like the kettle whistling.

Jan broke the silence. "He wouldn't let you out of his sight the entire time you lived at home, would he?"

"Mom explained it was because of all the harm he'd seen. Grown-up Claire understands that now, of course, but Little Claire didn't back then. I couldn't wait to get married and move out of the house."

"Where things went from bad to worse."

"At least my father loved me and did his best to get better. I can't say the same for David."

Jan's eyebrows knit together in thought. "And if I recall, you didn't recognize your father when he first arrived home from the war."

Claire shook her head. "Mom told me this as she got older: She spent the years Dad was away showing me their wedding photo so I would recognize him when he got home. But he came home dressed in fatigues and had his hair shorn. It took I don't know how long—a year?—before I stopped fighting him every step of the way. I was only three, and yet for some reason, I didn't trust him. And then the teapot situation a year later... I guess I wasn't happy to have him home. It must've broken his heart to be rejected by his only daughter. I'd certainly feel that way."

Jan nodded slowly, clearly lost in thought herself.

Recounting everything filled Claire with regret. On one hand, she didn't know what she would have told her own daughters if they'd been in a similar situation. How do you explain to a young child that their father had seen children in deplorable conditions? On the other hand, she wished her parents had handled it differently so she could have had a better relationship with her father. Things had improved with time, but it had required a lot of struggle to get there.

Jan finished the last drops of her tea and set her cup on a coaster on the table. "Then I don't think you need to give David credit for who you became."

Jan's statement took Claire by surprise. "I don't understand."

"Your father was the one who made you an independent woman. You had to find your own ways of breaking free of his mental illness. The situation with David may have forced you to speak up more as an adult, but it was your father who planted the seed for Claire's Tea Shop: family, healing, and a strong voice standing up against anyone who crossed your boundaries."

Was Jan right? Had Claire held on to anger toward David all these years for no reason? If so, that also meant she'd been giving him credit where none was due. Reviewing everything she'd ever told herself about who she was from this new angle made Claire both uncomfortable and excited. To let go of those beliefs and anger opened up a new story for who Claire was: a woman solely created through her family. That included sadness and pain but also the many happy times she spent having tea with her parents and grandparents.

She'd always credited her family for her love of tea, but never for the tea shop.

"What you're saying," Claire said, "is that I can tell Richard about my ritual because David has nothing to do with the shop." The sense of relief brought tears to Claire's eyes.

"Our childhood feelings sometimes need to say hello," Jan said gently. She handed Claire tissues from the coffee table, and Claire dabbed her tears away.

"So if I've been unaware of how war has affected me all these years, how has it affected Richard?"

"It's Christmastime, a time for peace. Maybe also time to find out."

CHAPTER 11

*R*ichard had always hated what war had done to his family, and what better way for life to throw him another punch by making him show a client the home he'd lived in with his uncle and grandparents.

"I love old homes," Jaya said. "Just think of all the Christmases that happened here, all the gifts that were given."

But all Richard could think of was maintaining a professional smile while his childhood Christmases without his parents played in his memory.

He focused on his client to push those memories aside. "This home doesn't have a bathroom on the main floor. Will that be an issue?"

Jaya said it wouldn't. "Besides, we might put on an addition in four or five years. But we've always wanted to start with an old house." She winked. "The benefits of being married to an architect."

Richard had dreaded this viewing from the moment he'd seen the address. But he'd do anything to help a client buy a house. After all, why should memories over half a century old still affect him?

He followed Jaya upstairs and shivered: the stairs creaked in the same spots they had in his childhood, only louder.

"I love a house that makes noise," Jaya said. "Friends of mine have said creaky stairs are useful for knowing when your kids sneak back in the house."

"That's true!" Was that too cheerful? Nothing worse than a real estate agent appearing too eager to help a client buy a house. But he remembered sneaking into this very house.

When they reached the top, Richard could almost hear his uncle's heavy footsteps as he lumbered to the bathroom to get ready for bed after coming home late from his second job. Even though Richard was supposed to be asleep by then, he had spent many nights awake, praying for someone to give him back his parents.

His uncle had slept in the largest bedroom.

Jaya began with the smallest. "Oh…this is perfect for our son."

How had Richard ever fit in this room? It seemed so tiny.

He checked his notes. "This one is, um, ten feet by ten feet, five inches. It won't be too small for him?"

Jaya smiled. "He'll be fine in here. He doesn't need a gymnasium to sleep in."

Richard laughed. "That's true!"

Jaya glanced at him, and Richard would've covered his eyes if it wouldn't have made him look silly. Why should this house have this much of a hold on him? Too many good things had happened in his life—these uncomfortable memories shouldn't have been surfacing.

"The next largest room is ten-five by eleven." Was his grandfather still snoring in there? *You're not hallucinating, you're remembering. Get your act together, Rich.*

By the time he finished showing the home, his coat and scarf were open in an attempt to stop sweating.

"Are you all right? You look tired," Jaya said.

"It's been a long day. You know when you get to my age..." Richard smiled reassuringly. He hated using his age as an excuse, but better than saddling a client with a story about a five-year-old spending all Christmas Day staring out the window, hoping Santa or God would deliver his mother alive, after an asthma attack had taken her life, and a father who looked like the man next to his uncle in the photos on the hearth.

What good would travelling to Hong Kong to see his father's grave do? It might make him start questioning all over again how his life might have turned out if his parents had lived. His uncle and grandparents had loved him, he had found the most amazing wife the world could possibly offer him, and together they had raised two stupendous daughters.

Had he just thought of the word *stupendous*? Yes, he had. Because that was the most accurate word to describe how his life had turned out despite all the tragedy in his childhood. Tragedy he'd rather bury away again.

Richard pulled himself out of his memories. "Do you have any other questions about this house? Anything you'd like to see again?"

Jaya glanced around one more time and shook her head.

"Let's have a look around the outside." Richard couldn't be happier to get some fresh air. He led Jaya outside, but to his dismay, Doris, Claire's long-time customer walked by. *She* lived in this neighbourhood?

As usual, Doris dispensed with the niceties. "Ah, it's you. I need you to tell Claire something for me."

Jaya blinked.

"I'm in the middle of a showing," Richard said. "We're on a bit of a schedule."

Doris didn't seem to hear him. "The problem with that tea shop is that your wife no longer runs it. A lot of people aren't happy. Someone has to tell her."

Not now, Doris, Richard thought. "I'll pass along the message. Now, if you wouldn't mind, I do need to continue here with my client." He indicated the backyard to Jaya, but Doris continued talking.

"Your daughter has made too many changes to a place so full of tradition."

What changes? Nothing had really changed since Pauline had taken over last year.

"We really must go," Richard said.

But Doris wouldn't stop, and Richard worried if he walked away from her, she'd start spreading word about his "rude" behaviour. She was, unfortunately, that kind of person.

"You need to know what people are saying," Doris said.

FOR ONCE, Richard was home on time. Claire would be happy, and he needed her happiness right now.

"Hi, my Darjeeling." He closed the door behind him, slipped off his boots, and hung up his coat in the closet.

Claire spun around from the stove and her eyes lit up when she saw him. Richard loved coming home to that kind of joy. He took her in his arms and hugged her tight, inhaling her subtle rose-and-peaches scent. So comforting.

Claire giggled. "What's this?" When they separated, though, she studied his face. "Oh, no. Something's wrong. What is it?"

Richard sighed. "I ran into Doris today. We need to talk about her." As he set the table, Richard told Claire what had happened, but left out the detail about his history with the house he had been showing. *It's not relevant*, he told himself.

"I don't know how you ever put up with her," he finished.

Claire placed a pork chop on each of their plates. "She hasn't always been like this..." Claire said, thinking for a moment. "She's always had an edge to her, but this excessive rudeness only showed up maybe six or seven years ago. Her husband died somewhere around then, and her children are too busy to visit. That has to be sad. And she moved into her parents' house when they died. Memories everywhere but no family around to share them with. I've learned to tolerate her by reminding myself that her life hasn't been easy." But she quickly corrected herself. "Though I won't anymore. She can't just take her issues out on my family like that. She really believes the tea shop has changed for the worse under Pauline's guidance?"

"She said people are talking. Has there been a dip in business?"

Claire brought the carrots and mashed potatoes to the table. "Well, Todd told me on my last day that business had increased while I was filling in for Pauline. He didn't say those words exactly—he just referred to 'the last few weeks'—but now that you mention it, that was the timing."

Richard began serving them both. "Doris wouldn't let me go until she made sure I fully understood how she and *everyone else* felt about the changeover. I also didn't want to appear rude to my client by walking away from someone talking to me. It was infuriating...and embarrassing." Richard's blood pressure began to rise again at the memory.

Claire sat down. "I'm sorry you had to go through that. Maybe I should've kicked her out of the store a while ago."

Richard let out a laugh. "Then she might've kidnapped me out of revenge."

Claire held up her glass of water. "There is definitely truth to that. Let's drink to honesty helping us make it this far."

A hint of guilt nudged Richard. He should tell Claire about the house itself. But why? What point was there in rehashing events from his childhood?

None. Although he would always be thankful for having landed in the house of his loving extended family instead of an orphanage, he owed most of his success to his own choices. He thought of himself as a self-made man. After all, he'd been living on his own since he was seventeen when his uncle wanted to try for economic prosperity up north in the mines. Richard was content to stay on his own in Kitchener.

They clinked glasses and Richard continued on their current topic. "Doris did give me an idea about what might be ailing Pauline. Do you think she's finding it difficult to live up to you?"

Claire scoffed at his question. "Pauline is a very self-confident woman. I don't see what I have to do with anything."

"I just mean that you're part of the foundation that has built this community. Pauline, on the other hand, moved away after university and didn't come back until last year."

"You think they see her as an outsider? That's ridiculous if that's what's happening. Why do people think everything about my family is their business?"

Richard set down his cutlery. "But you have to admit, some of your regulars—like Doris—think everything that happens at the shop *is* their business. It's their very bizarre way of saying they love the place. I just wonder if a loud minority is telling Pauline what they don't like, and she's feeling it. And if Pauline noticed the correlation in the drop in revenue… I had one rude run-in with Doris because you weren't around. If Pauline's had to deal with that for over a year, I can only imagine how that must wear on her."

Claire put a piece of pork in her mouth and chewed in silence. After fifty years of marriage, Richard recognized her need to think for a minute or two before speaking, so he waited.

Claire sat back in her chair and sighed. "If Pauline's been bothered by these comments for so long, how did we as her parents not notice?"

Richard didn't have an answer for that.

CHAPTER 12

Claire dreaded this particular Wednesday.

But at least it was starting on a good note: she'd found a way to spend a little extra time with Richard. Their car needed its snow tires installed, so Claire was accompanying Richard to Mayumi's garage.

They parked their car outside the two-bay garage and entered the office and waiting area, where another woman was seated.

Mayumi, the owner and only car mechanic of her business, greeted them. "Good morning, Mrs. Robinson and Mr. Robinson." She checked her computer. "Perfect. Right on time." She said something in Japanese to the woman, who looked at Claire and Richard and smiled and nodded while Mayumi spoke.

"This is my mother, Kazuko Enomoto."

"Hello," Claire said. "Very nice to meet you."

Kazuko nodded and smiled again. "Very nice to meet you, too."

Mayumi explained, "She's nervous about using English—

she studied to become an English teacher but then gave up her career when she married. That was normal back then."

Kazuko nodded again.

"Please don't be nervous," Claire said. "I certainly don't speak Japanese." She smiled and Kazuko laughed.

"Thank you," she said.

Mayumi processed the paperwork for their appointment. "My mother is looking after my daughter after school while I deal with busy season. Then we'll all fly back to Japan while my daughter's on Christmas break."

"That's wonderful that you can spend that time with Mayumi and your granddaughter," Richard said.

Kazuko nodded again. "I like to travel, and I love my family."

"Your daughter recommended my newest employee." Richard faced Mayumi. "Terry only told me yesterday that you were the one who told him about the position."

Mayumi smiled. "I was happy to hear he got the job. We met when my father was transferred to the auto plant here for a few years when I was a teen. We lost touch when my family moved back home. Several years later, I came back to Canada on exchange to study auto tech at the local college, where Terry and I reconnected." She handed Richard a work order to sign. "I fell in love with and married Charlotte's father, but Terry and I have stayed in touch."

Mayumi's mother's disposition changed, and a little sadness showed.

"You miss her," Claire said, empathizing.

"Yes, I do. But she's very happy here. She has her own business. She's very successful."

"She looks after our car really well," Richard said.

Richard handed over the keys and had taken a step toward

the door when Claire announced her plans to travel to Vancouver next week.

"You'll love all the different tea stores," Mayumi said, and explained something in Japanese to her mother.

"I love tea, too," Kazuko said. "Have you tried Japanese tea?"

Claire felt her cheeks warm. "I do enjoy gyokuro and sencha, but I'm afraid I brew them English style." She smiled, slightly embarrassed, because she didn't want to insult Mayumi's mother and because brewing tea properly was a source of pride for her.

Kazuko briskly waved her hands. "It's not a problem! There are many different ways to make tea. If you come to Japan, I can show you how we brew tea."

Claire's initial instinct was to politely say she'd never travel that far. But here was a woman a little younger than her who had no apparent problem flying that distance.

Could Claire and Richard fly to Japan? Or to China to visit the tea gardens there? They could also visit Richard's father's grave. Ideas came fast and furious, expanding possibilities for Claire. Given how highly the Robinsons respected Remembrance Day, it would be the right thing to do. That man died during the war, never knowing how wonderfully his son had turned out.

Claire nodded to Kazuko. "Thank you. I would be very interested."

"If you go when the cherry blossoms are in full bloom in the spring," Mayumi said, "many of the cities will have festivals. It's so beautiful."

That sounded like the same time she and Richard planned to fly to Vancouver. *If I'm already all the way across the country, what's one more flight? Richard would never agree to come, anyway.*

Kazuko smiled. "You can both come. We have lots of friends

in Tokyo, on Hokkaido…you can visit almost anywhere and we know someone."

Richard let out a nervous laugh. "I don't think I could. Spring is the start of high season at the brokerage."

Claire smiled politely. "It is a busy time for Richard." Hopefully, she'd concealed her disappointment. She didn't air personal grievances to people she barely knew.

Mayumi told her mother what Richard did.

"Then Claire-*san* can come alone. I fly alone."

I could fly alone, couldn't I? Claire thought. *Or would Jan, or Cecilia, or Brenda join me? Travelling would be more fun with someone.*

Kazuko looked to her daughter. "You can bring Claire-*san* back some nice tea from Japan."

Mayumi smiled. "That sounds like a great idea, *okaasan*. We can give her a taste of Japan. I'll bring some Japanese sweets, too."

Claire shook her head. "Oh, I couldn't possibly—"

Mayumi interrupted her. "Lesson number one about Japanese culture: it's very rude to refuse a gift."

Claire smiled and nodded. "Thank you for your generosity."

As they were about to leave, a car on one of the hoists pierced Claire's daydreams of cherry blossoms and Japanese tea: it was a perfectly restored 1962 Corvair.

The same model as the car driven by a man who'd told Claire repeatedly she'd never amount to anything.

Of all the days to see it, it had to be today, the anniversary of David's death and the day she planned to finally tell Richard everything.

How would Richard react? Claire had always been upfront about being widowed and Richard had never pressed her for more information. But she knew that sometimes when you opened up the proverbial can of worms, unexpected emotions came out. The impending conversation and its possible outcomes had floated through her mind for the past few days, and most versions of the daydream ended with Richard leaving the room in frustration, angry that she hadn't trusted him enough to tell him sooner.

Although David had had a short temper while they were dating, Claire had just assumed he was a man being a man. After all, her father had similar personality traits, and men were, in general, more outspoken back then.

David's true nature had shown itself after they were married: all he wanted was a beautiful woman to serve him. Claire had tried to change this dynamic, but when she started a friendly conversation in the car—they'd had many while they had been dating—he would say, sharply, "Can't you see I'm driving?" And it was always David who drove. He said Claire wasn't allowed behind the steering wheel.

"Claire? Claire?" A hand was gently shaking her. It was Richard. "Are you all right?"

Mayumi and Kazuko looked concerned, too. "Mrs. Robinson?" Mayumi said. "Maybe I should call you a cab to take you home. I'll pay for it, since I don't run a shuttle."

Claire shook her head. "I'm fine, thank you. Sorry. Just lost in thought for a minute. Japan sounds like a wonderful idea."

Richard pulled out his phone and began texting. He couldn't stay away from work long enough to drop off a car and walk home with her?

"What now?" she asked.

RICHARD WASN'T BUYING Claire's reassurance. Something was up with the way she'd been staring at that car, completely oblivious to the calls from all three of them.

"I'm just letting Terry know I'll be an hour late." He tucked his phone away and offered his arm, which Claire took, thankfully.

"That's not necessary. I know it's important to you to show up on time."

They gave their thanks to the Enomotos and left.

Outside in the bright winter sun, Richard turned to her. "Claire, we'd been calling you for a full minute."

She patted him gently on the arm as they walked to their apartment, only about five minutes away. "Honestly, my Darjeeling, I'm fine. My mind was just occupied by something. You know I tune things out sometimes."

Like mother, like daughter. He'd press further once they were home so she had the walk to think a little.

In their apartment, Richard calmly took off Claire's coat first and offered to make them both a tea. "Earl Claire?"

Just then Claire's phone rang. She answered it. "Hi, Jan... I saw the car today... Yes, I'll be fine... I think I will now... We'll talk later." She hung up.

"What was that about?" Richard asked, hanging up his coat. "Claire, please, you're worrying me. I can't go to work knowing you're not okay."

"We do need to talk." She paused, as though in thought again, and then disappeared into the den.

We do need to talk was never something you wanted to hear from the woman you loved.

Claire returned holding...a box of bagged tea? Since when did Claire own one of those? In her other hand was a small, yellowed newspaper clipping. Claire's face had become white, almost as pale as when she'd been recovering from her surgery last year.

What was this about? Richard's pulse sped up. She spoke her next words so quietly he could barely hear her.

"It's about time I told you something."

Claire moved quietly into the kitchen and began boiling water. She handed the clipping to Richard who read the headline: "Man Dies in Snowy Crash." The paper was decades old, but the day and month were the same as today.

With a sudden shock, Richard realized he held the article about Claire's first husband in his hand.

He read the short piece while she brewed them both cheap grocery-store black tea. This wasn't the Claire Robinson he knew.

"His name was David Harris?"

Claire nodded.

Richard read the rest, though it was just the usual details: It had snowed several days in a row, and the driver had lost control and hit a light pole. Dead at the scene. But the car description was included: the same make and model that had been on the hoist at the garage.

Claire was mechanically dipping tea bags up and down in mugs of hot water.

"Shouldn't you take those out? I thought tea bags were thirty seconds?"

Claire shook her head. "The worse it tastes the better. The only tea he'd let me buy was this junk. I do this every year on this day."

Richard's chest compressed just a bit. She'd had this ritual—drinking something she abhorred—their entire marriage, and he'd never known? He guessed from the quick phone call that Jan had known all this time. It would make sense. They'd been best friends since high school. But this new truth still hurt. He wanted to punch this David Harris. But what did you do to someone who'd been dead fifty-four years?

Patience, he told himself. Abuse was never a straightforward situation.

Claire took the clipping from Richard, read it herself, then removed the tea bags and took a sip. She grimaced. Richard couldn't recall the last time he'd drunk bagged tea that'd been steeped this long. He took a sip, too. All he could taste were the bitter tannins.

Claire closed her eyes and took another few sips. Richard could do nothing but watch as the sadness from so long ago returned to her. She tried to squeeze back tears, but they trailed down her cheeks. Richard stepped in and wiped them away. It was the only thing he could think to do.

Claire whispered, "He was so cruel."

SHE COULDN'T HOLD back the tears as soon as she felt Richard's gentle touch on her face. Claire had never cried during her ritual. She always got angry, drank a few sips, and poured the rest down the drain. David had left scars on her life, permanent ones, and November twenty-first was the one day a year she acknowledged they existed and how they affected her. Then she tried to ignore them for another year.

But as she thought about Jan's revelation—that her father had been the first man to cross her boundaries, thereby pushing her to stand up for herself—she wondered how much energy she had been wasting on this abusive man all this time.

Richard wrapped his arms around her and she tucked her head into his chest. It felt so good to finally share this with him. He didn't say anything, just passed her tissues and stroked her back.

Claire had imagined this outcome, but voices told her no man would be this understanding. She should've known better.

After several minutes, when Claire had finally calmed down, Richard said, "I am so, so sorry you had to go through that. You are my one true love, Claire. Any time you want to talk about it, I'm here for you."

She loved this man so much. He'd stood by her side through all these years and never once pushed her to talk about her first marriage. That took the patience of a saint.

She guided him to the couch, wiping away the last of her tears. He deserved to learn why she'd kept this to herself for so long.

"I honestly believed all this time that I owed David some gratitude for giving me the strength to open my own store, when you're the one who's supported me all these years. At the same time, I didn't want him to take up any space in our marriage." She played with a tissue. "This little ritual was my way of letting off the steam, if you will, of remembering the hurt, the insults, the condescension…" Her chest shook as she inhaled. "Of feeling guilty for being happy when the police officers told me he'd died. Then I could move on for another year."

Richard glided his hand over her hair. "If you've been carrying this pain inside you all this time, Claire, he *has* been taking up space in our marriage. And you've been alone with it. I would never want you to shoulder so much pain on your own. Ever."

He pulled her head to his, and they touched foreheads for a moment, the silence of the apartment allowing Claire to experience only his love for her and share hers for him.

Claire Sutton becoming Claire Harris had meant more than a name change. It had meant a change in voice, from an outspoken one to a silenced one. When she opened Claire's Tea Shop, she had to continue using Harris publicly so she wouldn't shame her family by rejecting his family's name. She had at least changed a few private documents back to her maiden name for her own sanity. Taking on Richard's name was one of the happiest days of her life.

Richard pulled Claire on top of him, and Claire happily gave him a tender kiss. He tucked her hair behind her ears. "I love you with all my heart, Claire Robinson. And I always will."

Claire began undoing the top button of his shirt, and Richard reached for her blouse.

As Claire kissed down Richard's neck to his chest, an image of the car on the hoist flashed into her mind, reminding her that she had never put her dreams on hold for anyone. But what had happened to her dream of doing everything together as a couple? Would Richard accept her decision to fly to Asia while she still could? She wondered if love could exist when lives began to diverge.

The soft touch of Richard's hand down her back convinced her it could.

CHAPTER 13

Claire, Jan, Cecilia, and Brenda showed their tickets to someone standing at the entrance at the Art Gallery of Ontario and entered the main area.

Jan studied the brochure. "I want to see the Käthe Kollwitz exhibit first. The emotions in her work are so intense."

"I don't know if I can look at those drawings right now," Cecilia said. "I think they'll remind me too much of my husband."

Many of the drawings appeared dark, and some even depicted death. Claire wasn't so sure she wanted to see them either.

"I'll go with you to see something else," Brenda said.

"I might join you, too," Claire added.

Jan feigned hurt. "You're going to leave me alone with Kollwitz? What if I get lost in my own emotions? I'd need someone to pull me out."

Claire smiled. "All right, all right, I'll join you."

The women split ways, agreeing to meet in two hours at the Group of Seven collection.

"I can't help but wonder if I should be staying home to help Pauline and Todd more," Claire said. "When I helped out at the tea shop Wednesday, I could tell they were overwhelmed. They tried to hide their bickering by keeping it in the back room, but I could hear it from behind the counter."

Jan pointed in the direction they needed to go. "What could you be doing?"

Claire shrugged. "Without them allowing me to help more, I don't know. But maybe handing out postcards—if they had any —or hanging up posters—if they had any. Maybe reminding them of all those things?"

"And becoming the nagging mother no one wants?"

Claire sighed. "I know, I know. But what else am I supposed to do? That event can't be skipped, and Pauline still has to be mindful of her healing."

They entered the Käthe Kollwitz exhibit. Jan's eyes opened in wonder as the work drew her in, but Claire shuddered. The artwork was dark, scratchy, sometimes aggressive, sometimes sad.

She would even call it ugly.

She caught up quickly to Jan. "I'm really not in the mood for this. Why don't we go to the Group of Seven exhibition early?"

"You're looking at this like someone whose first tea is pu-erh and declares all tea disgusting."

"When the first picture you see includes a depiction of death, what do you expect me to think? I don't need a reminder that the Grim Reaper is waiting to get my address. I have too many dreams still to fulfill."

Jan read the brochure quickly, glanced around, and then beckoned Claire to follow her.

"I read up on this one online. What do you make of this one?"

The description beside it read, "The Mothers, 1919. Lithograph on paper."

The drawing was of mothers holding babies tightly to themselves, and pulling older children in, as though wanting to protect them all. Claire guessed it was drawn with dark pencil — or was that charcoal? She never purchased art unless it cheered up a room with colour.

The darkness of whatever medium the artist had used to make this drawing added to its sombreness.

Claire took in a deep breath. The drawing somehow reflected how she felt about Pauline right now: something was still bothering her daughter after the surgery, and Claire just wanted to hold her tight, tell her she'd protect her, and that everything would work out with just an ounce or two of patience.

She shared her observation with Jan.

"This drawing reflects how I felt when Tracy was dealing with not only Austin's epilepsy diagnosis, but also all that bullying in grade ten."

"I can see that."

"That's what I love about this," Jan replied. "In one drawing, so much emotion despite it only being in shades of grey. She's drawn it in such a way that the faces are generic, but her style is unique. So you know it's her work, but it could be about anyone."

Both women stared at the drawing a little longer.

"Like the artist for that teapot," Claire noticed. "It's a common style of pottery in Holland, but I'm sure if we studied it in more detail, we'd get to know the artist. I just wish its memory didn't create so much sadness in me."

Jan pointed to a collection of sculptures and they headed there. "But it must awaken happy memories, too."

Claire tried to push past the negative associations she had

with the teapot. "I loved Sunday teatime, and my earliest memories of it are with that blue-and-white teapot. My grandparents often joined us. Sometimes we had friends over. The memories are all vague, but they're there."

"What you described Monday was two men—your father and the Dutch man—overcoming trauma. But from what you've just told me, it also means family and friends bonding over tea."

That was what Claire loved about her friends: their ability to help her see a different perspective.

They spent another hour studying Kollwitz's artwork. Although the work conveyed much of the artist's sadness—Claire had learned that Kollwitz had lost an eighteen-year-old son to war—many of the pieces also depicted people supporting one another.

"I love looking at work like this because I think it's important to become comfortable with all emotions," Jan said. "Otherwise, depression can set in."

Depression can set in. Pauline did seem overly happy nowadays, even though she'd experienced moderate depression around her surgery. Could Claire's daughter still be depressed but was just hiding it? No, that didn't make sense. Pauline had worked with people from all walks of life in her last career. Her degree in psychology also acted as a buffer against all the sadness she encountered when acting for special groups. She had said so herself in the past. The depression around the surgery had been temporary, hadn't it?

Claire shared her thoughts with Jan as they finally headed for the Group of Seven exhibit. "If she's still depressed, why haven't I noticed? She wears her emotions on her sleeve—always has."

"But she's still a performer at heart. She may not be able to hide her immediate reactions, but if she shares any personality with Austin, she can probably hide depression quite well if she wants to. It took us a while to even realize he was being bullied."

Maybe "moderate" depression around the surgery was putting it mildly. If Pauline could no longer hide her state of mind, then even that depression could've been more severe than Claire and Richard had thought.

They stepped into the elevator and rode it to the next floor. Once there, they were greeted by the colourful, uplifting nature and historical paintings of Canada's most famous group of painters. Claire's mood lifted. A minute later, Cecilia and Brenda joined them.

They came up to a painting by David B. Milne called "Outlet of the Pond, Morning." Many of the trees were whited out, as was the pond. This was likely in order to show winter, but in an unnatural, almost childlike way. The trees were shaped like pines, but the colours that poked out from under the snow were reds, purples, and golds, with a few strokes of black for outline.

"This is what's going on with Pauline," Claire said. "These trees are uniquely colourful, bright, cheery. Not what you'd expect from a pine."

"I see oak trees," Jan said, "but I'll accept they could be pines."

"I see maple," Brenda said.

Cecilia smiled as she shrugged. "I see trees."

Four people, four interpretations. Claire loved their different perspectives. "At the same time, none of those trees has purple leaves—or needles—and whatever these trees are, they've retained their colour under a blanket of snow."

The other women nodded, indicating they were following along.

"But snow has a range of experiences for us," Claire continued. "In this painting, the snow is peaceful. It's just lying there, hiding the colourful trees beneath it. So, if we were to visit this beautiful place covered in snow, we'd think we were in the most peaceful place in the world."

Jan drew in a breath. "We'd think we were fine—when that blanket of perfection is covering up everything. For all we know, those trees could have some kind of fungal infection."

The others laughed at Jan's assumption of the underlying malady. Claire would've described it perhaps as leaves drying up early, or some of the branches having no needles or leaves, but Jan was still right.

"I don't know many performers," Cecilia said when Claire explained more about Pauline, "but they do always try hard to put on a good show."

"Her feelings and needs have always had to come second to the people she was entertaining," Claire explained. "She could only break character in an emergency. I don't believe that ever happened, thankfully."

"And now that level of performance has become habit," Cecilia finished.

A mild weakness overcame Claire as something dawned on her. She sat down on one of the benches, and Jan asked if she was okay. "I'm fine." She smiled at the potential irony of the statement. "I mean it. I just realized something and need to...sit with this for a moment."

The other women joined her on the cushioned bench. Although Cecilia and Brenda tried to offer comfort, Jan indicated to them to wait.

She knows me as well as Richard, Claire thought.

Sitting among all these beautiful, colourful, vibrant works of art for the first time gave Claire the strength to express her regret.

"How long has my daughter been grinning and bearing it?

How long have I been seeing the snow instead of the true colours? How long has she been suffering?"

Jan nodded, taking in Claire's concerns. She set her purse to the side and placed both her hands in her lap. "I'm going to be harshly honest with you right now, but it's only because I care and want you and Pauline to sort this out."

Claire nodded. What good was a friendship as old as theirs if they couldn't speak openly with each other?

"You'd said when we got here that you worried you should've stayed home today. But I believe being home today wouldn't have changed anything for Pauline because she learned from you and Richard, but especially from you, to grin and bear it. It helped make her an extraordinary performer, but it's…harmful in other situations."

Surrounded by all this art that was reflecting her feelings and emotions, Claire could no longer ignore the truth in front of her. "Because I never took a day off except in emergencies."

Cecilia patted Claire on the hand. "We all did that."

Brenda nodded.

Pushing through pain and discomfort was the Silent Generation's way. It was how they got through harsh times before government support existed. It was also how they got through wars.

"Any time I had to close the shop, I was losing money. I even breastfed at work because it was cheaper than paying for formula." Claire took in a deep breath and let it out. "Richard and I have to help Pauline realize that there's another way, one that won't drain or hurt her more. I just hope we can do it."

Her group of friends wrapped their arms around her in encouragement.

CHAPTER 14

Richard had always loved how Pauline and Todd's apartment reflected their relationship. It was decorated with both ballet and sports memorabilia. He wondered if the Christmas tree would look the same.

"I'm sorry I'm late again," he said as Todd welcomed him in. "I've hired two new agents, but one can't start until the new year. We're still looking for a third one."

Todd smiled as he extended an arm toward the seating area, which now had an artificial tree with lights already installed standing off to one side. "No worries. The tree isn't going anywhere."

Pauline gave her father a welcoming hug. "Work's important. We get it, Dad."

Richard felt guilty for not having pulled his and Claire's own small artificial tree out of their storage locker yet. But he'd been too tired at the end of each day.

Pauline handed Claire a small box. "I found these in a box we didn't get to the other weekend. Could you take these to

Dawn? They were either ones that she made, that were given to her, or that I think might be meaningful to her."

"I'd be more than happy to."

Claire set the box by her purse so she wouldn't forget it on the way out, and Pauline added a small pile of wrapped gifts next to it.

Claire rubbed her hands together. "So. What's the plan? Have the two of you already begun some kind of Christmas-tree-decorating tradition? Or do we just throw things at it and hope they stick?"

Richard was happy to see Claire's light-hearted mood. After what she had shared with him two days before, he'd been worried that Claire would find it difficult to have a good time this evening. Based on what they'd discussed at lunch today, it seemed that her trip to Toronto yesterday had done her some good. He'd spent his evening in a bidding war, which he'd lost, so he hadn't gotten home until after she'd gone to bed.

He didn't like this growing feeling that they lived separate lives. *But you're not going to think about that right now*, he thought. *You're here to enjoy what's right in front of you.* Claire had made Richard promise at lunch to not discuss Pauline's hip this evening. He had agreed. Besides, a festive mood filled the apartment, and he didn't want to spoil it.

"Can I get everyone drinks first?" Pauline asked.

"I can look after that," Todd said. "Why don't you get started with the decorations."

Todd took drink orders as Pauline placed a box of decorations on the couch by Richard and Claire, and another beside her. "No tradition, no plans. It's a free-for-all," she explained.

Many of the ornaments brought back Christmas memories from when the girls were young. Some had been made by the girls at school, others purchased as gifts to mark milestones in the family's life.

"Oh my!" Claire held up a big, round, red ornament with paint flaking off that still read "Baby's First Christmas 1970." She smiled from ear to ear. "You had it! I was so sad last year when we couldn't find it!"

"Dawn's is in her box. I thought she'd like to have it."

"I know she will," Claire said.

Todd held one up to Pauline, also a milestone ornament: two bears hugging each other. Underneath it said, "Our First Christmas 2017." They exchanged a quick kiss before Todd hung it on a branch.

"Doris dropped by the shop today," Pauline said. "She was not in a good mood. Insisted on talking to me."

Richard's throat closed. He'd take great pleasure in selling Doris's house for her if she moved out of town.

Claire asked what had happened.

Pauline sighed. "She was angry because she asked if Dad had told me whatever it was he was supposed to pass on, and I said I hadn't heard anything yet."

Richard sat up. "She said that to you?"

"Even I couldn't calm Doris down," Todd said.

"What did she say to you, Dad?"

Richard glanced at Claire, who shook her head.

"Nothing important. Doris was just being Doris."

"If it's just that she doesn't like whatever changes I've implemented, I can take it. She tells me almost every time she comes in."

Richard had had his share of rude clients over the years, too. One couple had cleaned the house so rarely that he'd recommended a cleaning service before the house went on the market. They expected him to pay for it. Another demanded he sell their home for a flat fee that equated to maybe one percent of the list price. When he explained how commission was split between agents, the client said that a few thousand dollars for signing a sales contract should suffice.

He hadn't minded losing that client.

"You can always ask Doris to leave," Richard said, and Claire nodded.

Pauline shook her head. "Seriously, I've taken my share—more than my share—of rudeness over the years. I used to get groped in costume, remember? At least that doesn't happen anymore."

Richard's stomach did a double flip. "That doesn't mean you have to tolerate it,"

Pauline shrugged. "Not a big deal."

A statement equivalent to "I'm fine."

Claire paused for a moment—she clearly understood the same thing—and then continued hanging ornaments.

But Richard couldn't leave this alone, no matter what he'd promised Claire. "Pauline, you keep saying you're fine but your mother and I can tell that you're not."

Pauline's lips tightened—she was beginning to lose her calm. But Richard couldn't make out Todd's expression. Ambivalence? Confusion? Overwhelm? Any of those could describe it. Todd stood as though frozen in place.

"We just wish you'd talk to us," Claire added. "You're still in pain—"

"You know I can't take painkillers."

"You can't take strong ones. You're fine with over-the-counter medication. But you should also be using a walking aid."

"I'm not old."

The room fell silent.

Pauline looked away. "I'm...I'm sorry. That's not what I meant."

But Claire's boundary had been crossed. She either didn't

hear or believe the apology. "Do you mean to tell me that within the hundreds of thousands of people you encountered while a mascot, only 'old people' used a walking aid?" Claire used air quotes around "old people."

Staring in her lap, Pauline shook her head.

What Pauline had said was hurtful to Claire, who used a cane after her surgery, but Richard was certain she didn't mean it the way it sounded. He gently touched Claire's hand. "Maybe we should leave them alone, my Darjeeling. Pauline's had a difficult day."

Claire positioned her cane in front of herself and stood up.

"No, Mom, Dad, please stay. I'm really sorry."

Todd placed an arm around her. "We were hoping to decorate the tree with you tonight as a way of saying thank you for all your help in the past month."

Still standing, Claire replied, "That comment didn't come out of nowhere, Pauline. What's going on?"

Pauline fidgeted with her fingers as she whispered, "I said I'm sorry."

Then—to Richard's amazement—Claire sat down and nodded. Normally, she would've kept pushing Pauline to admit what was troubling her. Richard understood Claire always tried to put an end to any of her daughter's suffering by trying to solve the problem, but insisting Pauline tell her had never helped.

Something had changed, but now was not the time to discuss it.

"So, Todd," Richard said, taking a deep breath. "What do you recommend Claire see in Vancouver?"

Claire took the hint. "Do you know of any good Japanese restaurants? Mayumi and her mother have me interested in Japanese cuisine."

Japanese cuisine? Claire? She hated fish. The Japanese ate

more than fish, of course, but Richard had eaten in a few Japanese restaurants over the years with clients. That had involved a lot of fish.

As Todd and Claire attempted to make conversation, Richard began wondering what was happening to his family. Pauline's usually exuberant personality lay dormant, many aspects of his and Claire's life together were beginning to diverge…and now she wanted to try Japanese cuisine for the first time?

What was next, that trip to Asia he'd been fearing?

BACK IN THEIR APARTMENT, Claire pressed her hand to her chest as she leaned against the apartment door. "I wish I'd been calmer with her, but I can't handle seeing her in pain. We've really harmed her."

Richard gently took her hand in his and brought her over to the couch. "Are you thinking again about what Jan had said yesterday?"

"We raised workaholics, Richard, because *we* were workaholics."

Richard ran a hand over his head. They'd touched on this topic at lunch today, and Richard thought differently on the matter. "I still don't know if I'd agree with her on that."

"Why not? We both worked sixty to seventy hours a week most of our lives. How do you not call that workaholism?"

"That's what happens when you run your own business. A thirty-five-hour work week is unreasonable. I don't recall Jan working just thirty-five hours when she owned the salon."

"No, but she only worked extra-long hours during busy times, like Christmas and right before summer vacation. Plus, she closed the salon once or twice a year for family vacations."

Claire was playing the "what if?" game. Richard refused to play it in any part of his life. "We made the decisions we did for the sake of our family. It was good for the girls. They walked to the tea shop after school, learned how a business runs, did their homework there… So much good has come out of both of us owning our businesses."

"But look where it's gotten us: one daughter moved so far away we barely see her, and the other doesn't trust us to help her. I'd have happily sacrificed business success to have my family in one piece."

Richard needed to get Claire out of this mood. You couldn't change the past, only the future. That painful lesson Richard had learned as a child.

"Tea?"

Claire straightened out her blouse and hair, as though she were expecting someone. "Why not? Crème oolong, please. I need something sweet and relaxing."

Richard filled the kettle with water and pulled tins of tea from a kitchen cupboard, including a ginger black tea for himself. "Dawn moved out West for love, not to get away from us," he said. "And Pauline trusts us, she'd just rather do everything on her own. I think her comment was more a reflection of her own fears of aging, not a comment on our age." He spooned tea into tea baskets.

"I suppose that makes sense. But don't we show how exciting life can be at our age?"

"I thought so, too. But not only is Pauline not us, she also had a much more active career. We don't know how long she kept performing with her sore hip. I'd always assumed her tenacity to keep performing had to do with a love of her career—and I'm still sure it did—but maybe she also fears aging much more than you and I have." The kettle beeped when the water was near boiling. He filled Claire's cup and set the kettle back on its base to bring the water up to a full boil for his tea.

Claire's forehead creased with worry. "It's just that…what started as a necessity for us—both earning our keep and contributing to our family—became a way of life. I'm wondering if I should cancel my trip to Vancouver so I can be close by in case she needs more help."

Richard removed the tea basket from Claire's cup just as the kettle beeped to announce it had sufficiently heated up his water.

"No. Go." He surprised himself as those words came out. "We now know that the daughter we live down the hall from isn't telling us everything. I know our two girls are very different—"

"But if Pauline can hide something under our noses, maybe something's going on with Dawn and we have no idea."

They agreed Claire would still fly to Vancouver with Jan.

Richard brought their teas to the couch and set them on the coffee table.

"I'm also worried about Todd," Richard said. "Unlike Pauline, he hides all his feelings well. I can't figure out what he thinks about all this."

Claire picked up her tea, blew at it, and took a sip. "I think he's so like you, you don't see it." She smiled at Richard. "He is concerned, but he's also trying to protect her dignity." Claire set her cup down and picked up her parents' Royal Delft teapot and snuggled into Richard. "I wonder…"

"Wonder what?" Richard loved the feeling of Claire leaning against him, something he always viewed as her subtle way of saying she trusted him.

"I wonder if there's something that's affecting Pauline like this teapot did my father."

That sounded plausible.

Claire's face lit up. "I'll bet it's all those photos she has at the tea shop and in her apartment of her career. Think of it, Richard. Reminders of the stunts she used to be able to do..."

"And all the families she helped. But we can't take all those down. I understand your father's situation, but I think Pauline's will pass."

Although Claire agreed with Richard in principle, she had to wonder: How long did a "temporary" low last?

She returned to her tea. "Maybe Dawn might be able to talk to her?"

Richard's gut feeling told him that would be a mistake. He shook his head. "I think she'll feel cornered. My guess is that the only person she truly trusts right now is Todd. We need to talk to him without making him feel like he's betraying his partner."

As Claire continued to think up ideas to help their family, Richard sat back and admired her bright, inner sunlight. But in a few days, they'd be separated by thousands of kilometres. What happened if that sunlight began to dim? He wouldn't be nearby to help.

But he'd agreed to the trip. As with everything else in life, Richard would simply find a way to deal with the situation.

So long as Claire didn't want to fly to Japan.

CHAPTER 15

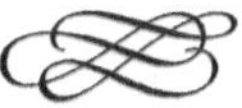

*R*ichard checked in the mirror to make sure his Santa Claus hat was on straight.

"I'm old enough I only need a fake beard now." He chuckled. "But I'm glad I don't have to wear those suits anymore. They were so hot." The last time Richard had played Santa was probably ten years ago. With a fake beard and wig, of course.

"You're hot without one," Claire replied, her eyes twinkling. "The light snow we're finally getting should put people in more of a Christmas mood."

What he wouldn't give to rechristen the back room at the tea shop to its earlier days, when he and Claire used it as…a room away from home. *That* would put him in the Christmas mood. But the store opened in ten minutes.

"Okay, you two love birds," Pauline said, as cheery as the morning sun. "Ready?" It was as though last night had never happened.

Her ability to focus on her work no matter what had always amazed Richard. In Pauline's previous career, she'd had to stay in character regardless of whether fans whispered to her they were heading for a painful divorce, had a loved one in hospital, were still sad about someone who'd passed away a few months ago, or anything else. She'd even been called to hold the hand of children at the end of their terminal illness. A few hours later, she'd be able to get an entire stadium on its feet, cheering.

She must've had a way to deal with all that sadness, but Richard didn't know the particulars.

Pauline pointed toward the front of the shop. "I think we should open early. Take a look."

A lineup had already formed outside.

"Because of us?" Claire asked.

"Todd and I gave you a big push on social, and…" Pauline studied the crowd a little. "I think that's a lot of regulars."

Regulars. Perfect. Exactly the clientele Richard and Claire had hoped for.

"Sure, let's start early," Claire said. "Regulars almost always buy one-hundred-gram bags. It'll be a good boost to the morning."

Claire and Richard took up positions behind the counter, and Pauline did her best to hide her limp as she walked to the front door to unlock it. Customers headed straight for the counter, and those who stood in line marvelled at the interior décor, especially the lights draped across the ceiling and the small tree by the front corner decorated in tea-related ornaments.

"Oh my god, you have those, too!" someone called out as they pointed to the big red bows prominently attached to the food display case.

Richard and Claire laughed. Given how much of a reaction those bows had garnered from all the family, they assumed customers would feel something similar.

"Our daughter, Pauline, thought big and bright belonged near food," Claire said.

The first few customers didn't recognize Claire or Richard, so the long-married couple processed their orders in a friendly way, and explained who they were and what they were celebrating. Those customers left happier than an elf at Christmas.

Ben had been right: romance did sell.

An hour later, Richard recognized the next person in line: Sandra was the wife of a retired mortgage broker he'd sent a lot of business.

She greeted them with warm smiles. "It's so good to see you both," Francine said. "Makes it feel like old times, doesn't it?"

There it was: "like old times." The euphemism of someone who lived in a rosy past.

"It was Pauline's idea that we celebrate our fiftieth anniversary through the tea shop," Claire explained.

"Ah." The customer gave a side glance at Pauline, who was serving tables.

Sandra was the kind of customer Richard and Claire had in mind.

"When she proposed it," Claire said, "I first thought, who'd want to celebrate with us? We're just another couple in this region of over six-hundred-thousand people. But thanks to Pauline's idea, this morning started with a lineup out the door."

Claire and Richard had agreed they'd tell people the idea was Pauline's. A little white lie never hurt. She'd had to approve it, anyway, so she had been involved in the decision.

"People are just eager to see the two of you."

"Which is flattering," Richard said. "But we're also assuming they're eager to support a family business that's been around long enough to pass on to the next generation."

Richard forbade himself from smiling at Sandra's silence.

"So?" Claire asked. "What can I get you?"

Sandra requested Tea of Joy. "It's your original blend from your first year? My mom had that at home."

Claire smiled and nodded. "The very one. Black tea with cinnamon."

As the morning wore on, Richard heard several customers say that it was too bad Claire had sold the tea shop.

The rudeness of people, especially at a time meant to celebrate peace and family.

But each time, he and Claire set the customer straight. Pauline had the heart and desire to continue what Claire's Tea Shop had always been about: giving a voice to each person, one package of tea at a time.

Close to lunch, a young woman—she looked maybe twenty—who'd followed a regular said, "It sounds like you two are famous, but—I'm sorry—I don't know who you are." She blushed.

"We've just been around long enough to know lots of people," Claire said. "That's all. How can we help?"

"I was just passing by when I saw the rainbow flag in the window."

"Anyone who believes in love is welcome here," Claire said.

"*All* kinds of love," Richard added.

"I just came out to my parents this week. It went well so I just want to show them my appreciation for their love and support. But I can't afford much. They like tea, so I thought maybe a tea of some sort?"

Claire indicated to a jar for Richard to pull down. "I call this one Dawn's Delight. It's named for my younger daughter, who lives in Vancouver. She's straight but I added the different colours in it—"

"The rainbow."

"Yes, I created this blend to remind her of the sunrise. Every day begins with the promise of something new. Here…" Claire opened the jar and tilted it toward the customer, who inhaled and smiled. "I'll take a small package of it."

Claire immediately packaged up two fifty-gram bags, but the young woman protested. "I just need one. I don't have enough for two."

Richard knew what his wife was doing and punched in one at full price and one at full discount.

"The second one's for you," Claire said. "On us. My best friend's grandson is gay and I know that life can…sometimes be difficult." She pointed to another jar on the shelf. "His is the Nutcracker Prince, a rooibos blend because he can't drink caffeine." She handed the two bags of tea to the young woman. "Hopefully, this will help you gather strength to face whatever comes your way."

The young woman smiled. "Thank you so much."

Pauline and Todd insisted on dealing with the lunchtime rush, and Richard and Claire agreed. This was the first Saturday Richard and Claire were helping out and it was going well so far. Pauline seemed to be in a good mood, and their plan of selling Pauline's value to the customers along with the tea and tea ware appeared to be working.

"But there's one thing I noticed," Richard said quietly as he ate a cold roast beef sandwich in the back room. "The way Pauline's hand clenched whenever someone complained about her. So, it's not water off a duck's back the way she makes it seem."

When Todd came back to thank them for all their work so far, Richard raised the issue of how Pauline was dealing with all the complaints, saying that he and Claire could plainly see that the negative comments were hurting her.

"We've both dealt with rude comments our entire profes-sional careers. This is nothing new."

"But I can *see* how she's reacting to it," Claire said.

Richard glanced back out to the front. Pauline was smiling

at something a customer was saying. That looked like a favourable conversation.

"Thank you both for your concern. We do really appreciate it. But she dealt with far worse as a mascot, and so did I as a ballet dancer. At least drunk customers aren't groping her, and married women aren't draping themselves all over me." He smiled at the last comment, apparently hoping it would come across as a bit of a joke.

Pauline brought back the jar for Dawn's Delight and handed it to Todd. "This one's suddenly selling like hot cakes. Do you mind refilling it?"

Todd pulled a wholesale bag off the shelf and began scooping it into the jar.

"How are you holding up?" Claire asked her daughter.

Pauline gave the answer they expected: "Fine."

As more people sat in the café, Pauline and Todd rushed between taking orders at the counter and serving food. From the back room, Claire and Richard noticed that Pauline frequently tried to massage her hip muscles with her hand when she thought no one was looking.

"They wanted us to take an hour for lunch, but..." Richard said.

"...let's get back to helping them," Claire finished for him.

When they approached the counter, Todd tried to insist they take the rest of their break, but Claire stood her ground. Her voice was quiet. "Look at your partner, Todd. Her limp is getting worse. She needs to rest."

Todd clenched his jaw. "I know. But I'm not going to go against her wishes to ease my discomfort."

So, his happiness *was* an act.

"When it comes to a person you love so deeply, sometimes you have to override their wishes," Richard said.

A quick glance between Richard and Claire told Claire to

leave the two men alone, so she joined Pauline behind the counter.

"This can't be easy for you to watch," Richard said.

Todd shook his head, his eyes on the woman he loved as she carried a tray full of food and drink to a table.

"You need to step in."

"But—"

"What she's doing is harming her more than any backlash you'll have to deal with."

Todd watched Pauline a little longer. "I'm just trying to show her support. She's dealing with so much criticism, she can't block it out anymore."

"So the comments *are* getting to her."

Todd's nod was barely noticeable.

"You're a good man, Todd. But focus on alleviating her pain, not following her orders." He smiled gently. "You'd be surprised how far that gets you."

Pauline returned to the counter, carrying a full tray again, so Todd rushed out to help. That resulted in a glare, but at least she wasn't carrying ten pounds of teacups, saucers, teapots, and garbage.

Richard returned to the counter to help Claire.

Claire pointed to the front window. "I've been so busy inside that I hadn't noticed outside."

Snow was coming down in big flakes.

The next customer explained: "That snowstorm that was supposed to hit Buffalo tonight? It's here instead."

Claire turned to Richard. "I hope my flight tomorrow isn't cancelled."

"Technically," the next customer said, "the weather people did say there was a twenty percent chance of snow here." She laughed. "Because those percentages are worth something."

"Might as well be a coin toss," Richard added.

"They're now saying we will get a huge dump of snow this afternoon."

Richard looked over the customers' shoulders and out the window. Cars outside were already draped in snow while the air was what traffic reports would call whiteout conditions. He processed the two customers while Claire pulled Pauline aside. Within five minutes, Claire returned to inform Richard that they'd be closing in an hour.

"Pauline is updating social media. Our job is to serve as many people as possible."

But not barely ten minutes later, they heard Pauline call out, "I'll be back soon!" as she rushed out the front door.

Claire and Richard continued processing orders. After half an hour, the snow had mounted up, but the café didn't seem any emptier. Had the customers not left?

Todd joined them. "Pauline went to the other stores in Belmont Village to see if there were any out-of-towners. Since we live just up the street, we can get home whenever. But most of the shopkeepers don't live that close."

Pauline, her cheeks rosy red from outside, came up behind Todd and leaned on the counter. "We're not going to charge for food either."

"Not only will the highways be congested now," Richard said, "but the roads to the outlying townships will have even worse visibility. It's good you brought them here."

Pauline set two unlabeled canisters on the counter. "Tracy and Ben gave me some of their hot chocolate mixture. They're heading downtown to help make sure everyone gets inside. They recommend adding two creamers," she said. "It'll taste even better."

The snow outside continued to come down hard. Snow-plows likely wouldn't come by for quite some time: they'd be busy clearing the main roads first.

When Richard went to the back room for some fresh cloths to wipe down the counter, Pauline was holding an ice pack to her hip while Todd stood beside her, concerned.

"Are you okay?" Richard asked.

She only nodded, but Todd said, "She'll be fine."

Richard's fatherly instincts said otherwise, but they needed to give a unified front to all the customers in the café, so he wasn't going to risk adding tension to the afternoon. He grabbed some cloths and left them alone, promising himself to keep an eye on Pauline.

CHAPTER 16

Two hours into the storm, Claire's Tea Shop had about thirty people enjoying each other's company. With the lights on, it invited anyone in who couldn't get home.

As Claire served, she noticed she hadn't seen Pauline in some time. At first, she'd assumed Pauline was taking a break, but then she realized Todd had also quietly disappeared.

"I should go see how they're doing," Claire said to Richard.

He laid a gentle hand on hers. "I suspect she's in a lot of pain. Otherwise, she'd be out here."

Claire agreed. Not only had Pauline gone outside several times to find people caught in the storm, but she had also shovelled the sidewalk in front of the tea shop each time on her way back.

Claire's gut told her to go look after her daughter, but last night still played in her mind. Pauline had lashed out in frustration, that much Claire now understood. Would she still welcome an inquiry into her well-being after that?

"Do you think she wants privacy? After last night…"

Richard cast a glance toward the back room. "If we want to

show her that we respect her wishes but can also run this shop on our own for a few Saturdays, it's probably best we let them do their own thing."

Claire remembered the drawing at the art gallery, the women clutching their children, protecting them. How could she ignore a child in pain when that child was a mere twenty feet away? But if she invaded that child's privacy, she might push her fiercely independent daughter another twenty feet away. Or twenty thousand feet.

"If they need help, they'll let us know, won't they?"

"I hope so."

But as another hour passed and the snow kept falling, the customers were getting restless, and Claire impatient. Maybe being understanding toward Pauline's situation wasn't working. Claire and Richard's eldest daughter thrived when she was needed.

"We have two world-class performers back there," Claire said. "They understand that the show must go on. If they want to keep pulling the hours they expect to, despite her condition, they need to understand what that means."

Claire marched into the back room to talk to Pauline. What she saw, though, punctured her resolve within a fraction of a second.

Pauline, seated with her back to the door and an ice pack still on her hip, was weeping quietly while Todd knelt to one side, one arm around her in a tight embrace, the other stroking her hair.

Nothing proved to Claire more than that moment of pain and caring that they needed her and Richard's help, but neither of them was an entertainer. The two with that job title were sitting in front of Claire, unable to perform.

Claire quietly stepped back then entered again, announcing her arrival with louder steps so they could be forewarned. Todd immediately stood up to block Pauline from view.

Why all the lies to conceal Pauline's condition? Did they really believe they could hide her pain and depression from her parents? But now was not the time to discuss this. "Do the two of you want to head home? Richard and I can stay."

Without looking at Pauline, Todd shook his head. "We've already talked about it. Pauline's just taking a short break, and then she'll be out."

Claire didn't mention that this "short break" had already lasted for well over an hour. "Well, if you need anything, or if you want to go home, we can hold down the fort. This won't be the first time I've done it."

Todd thanked her.

"And?" Richard asked when Claire returned to the front.

"I should've gone back there earlier." She filled him in.

Richard let out a sigh. "That they haven't come to us says they don't want our help. We should leave them alone so they can deal with things on their own."

"But how many times in our marriage have you insisted on helping me, only to be right? Sometimes you have to push a little. Our daughter's in pain, Richard, and she won't accept our help to alleviate it. That bothers me."

They both glanced at the front window that looked like it'd been painted in artificial frosting. The clickety-clack of ice now pelting against it served as a warning to stay indoors.

Claire admired her daughter's desire to help as many people as she could, but how did she expect to keep helping people when she wouldn't stop abusing her body? Even right now, Pauline had a chance to make lots of people happy, but not in her condition.

"We need to get her mind off the pain," Richard said. "The

drugstore's closed, so that's out. But just sitting back there, focused on her pain won't do anything for her."

A few moments later, Claire hit the counter. "I've got it. We're going to put on a show."

~

"I'M NOT GOING OUT THERE." Pauline lifted an arm to her face, her back still turned to her mother.

Her pain broke Claire's heart. "The people out there don't know you. There's no shame in showing your face."

"I'm just taking a break."

Todd rubbed her back. Claire could now clearly see that he was fully engulfed in her pain, too. She couldn't blame him: Pauline's big personality, the one that let her communicate through mascot costumes, could also pull you in if you weren't careful. You had to pull yourself away to figure out how to help her, something Todd probably hadn't learned yet. After all, they'd only been together a little more than a year. Some things required time to learn.

But Pauline kept insisting she was "just taking a break." Claire needed a new tactic.

"Please freshen up. Your father and I can last maybe another ten minutes, but then we really need a break. We've been working steady for five hours now."

That got Pauline's attention. She turned around, tears still on her cheeks. "Oh, of course, okay. I'm sorry."

Claire's heart jumped for joy, but she did her best to look relieved.

In truth, Claire enjoyed helping as much as everyone else in her family. She had enough energy to do another five hours. But at this point, she'd say anything to get Pauline out of the back room.

"Thank you. We only need to take a rest for maybe a half hour, then we'll be good until the roads open again."

Now she just needed to find a way to separate Todd from Pauline so she could ask him to dance. If Kevin Bacon could dance in eighties prom clothes in *Footloose*, Claire assumed Todd could do a ballet solo in business casual.

"While you're freshening up, maybe Todd can come out?"

While Claire waited for Todd, she explained her idea to the customers gathered in the café. It had turned out that among the patrons waiting for the storm to subside were two children taking dance lessons, three men from a farm who were part of a cover band and happy to sing *a cappella*, and a woman who was a choir director. She said she'd lead the café customers in some carolling. Another customer offered their access to a music streaming service, so they could play whatever music they wanted over the store's sound system.

Todd joined her a few minutes later and immediately noticed the change in surroundings. Some of the patrons were congregating with others in the lounge area, a man was running through a dance routine with his children, and three men were quietly rehearsing songs.

"Yes, I lied," Claire said. She explained what was happening. "I need you to prepare something, too."

"I'm not sure Pauline's going to like this," Todd said cautiously. "She doesn't want the attention."

"She'll probably hate it at first," Richard admitted. "But she's spent her life entertaining others to get their mind off life's painful moments. It's time she lets us—and others—entertain her. That was Claire's reasoning behind this idea, and I think it's marvellous. We thought maybe you could do that Nutcracker Prince's solo by...Ka...Ki..."

"Kudelka. James Kudelka." Todd looked down at his

clothes. "This will be interesting." But he smiled. "There's definitely never a dull moment at this place. Sure. Why not?"

Todd offered to help move a few tables and chairs quickly before stealing away to a corner where he began stretching while everyone else helped with the rest of the transformation.

When Pauline emerged from the back room, the professional smile on her face transformed into surprise and then anger.

But Claire placed a hand on her daughter's arm. "It's time for everyone here to entertain you."

"I'm not up for this." Pauline tried to turn around.

When all else failed in your attempts to help someone who really needed it, you had to resort to punching below the belt. "The kids are looking forward to showing you—the woman who invited them in here—their dance. They'll leave greatly disappointed if you don't let them."

Pauline took a seat. When she caught sight of Todd stretching in the corner, her face positively lit up.

It didn't matter to Claire how the rest of the evening passed: Pauline had, for a moment, been pulled out of her grief of transition. Taking over the tea shop, moving in with Todd before the family home had sold, losing the family home, and dealing with changes in her physical abilities... Pauline had been through a lot in the last year and a half. *Add to that all the criticism*, Claire thought. No wonder Pauline was trying to act normal: it was probably the only way she could cope.

Should Claire fly tomorrow, weather permitting? Or would Pauline talk to her tomorrow if Claire stayed home?

As though reading her mind, Richard whispered, "I'll keep an eye on her. Go check in on our other daughter. Make sure we're not missing something with her, too."

CHAPTER 17

Claire stared at all the people around her at Toronto Pearson International Airport. "It's busier than I remember."

Thankfully, the storm had stopped by late evening yesterday, and Claire and Jan were flying out on an early afternoon flight from Toronto, because the single flight from Waterloo Region Airport had been fully booked. But that meant that instead of enjoying the quietness of a box-sized airport, they began their journey in Canada's largest one an hour away.

"Don't worry," Jan said. "I'll get us through this. Follow me."

As Claire followed Jan to the ticket counter, she thanked the stars for such a good friend. But Jan had advised her to pack as light as possible, whereas Dawn had said to dress for cold, wet weather.

"As though your early spring and late fall were one season."

Spring and fall on the edges of winter required a myriad of clothing options. So, Claire packed for the weather, buried several packages of Dawn's Delight between the layers to protect them, but made sure she could carry her luggage herself.

Claire allowed Jan to go first every step of the way. She was appalled by how intrusive security was, but heeded Jan's warnings to not complain, make any jokes, or use any kind of vocabulary that could get them pulled aside.

"Just answer their questions directly," Jan said.

The flight was relatively comfortable, but about an hour before landing, Claire saw the most beautiful sight she'd ever seen: the Rockies from above, stretching as far as the eye could see. The jagged snow-capped peaks sent shivers down her spine.

Claire couldn't take her eyes off the window as they approached Vancouver. With the mountains on one side and water on the other, it reminded her a little of a teacup. Jan agreed.

Claire had already fallen in love with Vancouver by the time they reached the gate.

They texted Richard and Sedrick that they'd landed safely, headed to the baggage claim area, and about thirty minutes later, Claire found herself surrounded by her daughter and her grandchildren—Daniela, Dave, and Destiny.

Jan and Sedrick got this kind of welcome from Austin and their other grandchildren every week, if not multiple times a week. Claire could only enjoy these hugs once or twice a year.

What had she been thinking, never once closing the shop to fly out here?

I wouldn't have come without Richard, she thought. They always did things together because they'd spent so much time running their businesses separately. She would've felt like she was leaving him behind if she'd flown out West on her own.

Claire felt a little like that right now.

"Okay, okay, you three, help Grandma and Jan with their

luggage," Dawn said. The kids peeled themselves away from Claire to grab what they could, and Dawn opened her arms wide. "I can't believe you're actually here."

The embrace felt tighter than usual, but it was probably just the excitement of the moment.

"Where's Dean?" Claire asked.

"The movie has moved up its deadline, so he's pulling huge overtime. You must both be exhausted from the flight. Let's get you to your hotel."

Claire admitted she was. She hadn't realized that just sitting in a plane could be so draining.

But she was so happy she'd come. She just wished Richard could be here to enjoy the trip with her.

RICHARD TURNED up "You Can't Always Get What You Want" to drown out his fears, sat back down in his armchair, and stared out the window at the sky.

Numerous disaster scenarios had flown through Richard's mind since Claire had texted that she wouldn't be able to contact him again until they landed: ice forming on wings, a sudden wind gust throwing the plane out of the sky, the plane flying too low and crashing into the Rockies…

Part of Richard knew his fears were baseless, but he'd heard enough randomly bizarre, scary stories over the years about plane crashes that he figured anything was possible.

The phone rang.

"What?" Richard asked.

It was Sedrick. "Turn down your music!"

Oops. Richard did. "Sorry about that."

"You're depressed already and she hasn't even been gone three hours."

"I told you I can't stand being parted from her like this. What if a gust of wind throws the plane out of the sky?"

Sedrick laughed. "Why are you catastrophizing? You and I have a little freedom for the next few days. We should enjoy it!"

Richard had never understood the ball-and-chain and related metaphors. He'd willingly and joyfully entered into the compromise that was marriage. Why would he want to spend time apart from Claire when he'd agreed to stay together with her?

"I'll be fine," Richard said.

"I can hear what you're playing in the background. If you're not dressed for going out, get dressed now. I'm coming over."

Richard groaned. "I'm really not in the mood for visitors, Sed."

"You're already acting like your daughter—everything is not fine with you, even though Claire's only in BC. We're going out to plan what we're going to do each night they're gone."

Richard groaned again. "I'm really not in the mood. I'm too tired from work as it is."

"All you're going to do is mope around, lament that there's nothing in the fridge, wonder if your Claire is okay, and blare that song. We've been friends too long, Rich. I'll be over in fifteen. Clock starts now."

"I don't know..."

"Fourteen minutes and fifty-three seconds."

"I don't have to let you up here."

"I'm sure Todd and Pauline will be happy to let me in if it keeps you out of their hair every night, given what you've been telling me is going on with them. Fourteen minutes and eight seconds."

Richard groaned a third time. "Fine."

Ready in time, Richard waited for his best friend outside to save him the trip up.

Sedrick looked both ways on Belmont Avenue and turned right toward Waterloo. "The two of you have an amazing relationship, but it's not healthy that you're this afraid of being alone from her once in a while. You need to see how enjoyable a little time alone can be."

Richard wasn't convinced.

FULLY REFRESHED after a long nap at their hotel, Claire and Jan said almost nothing on the ride with Dawn through Vancouver—the city's architecture took their breath away. No wonder Dawn loved it here: it was as beautiful on the ground as from the air.

"We're now in my neighbourhood, Mom. Yaletown."

Nothing like Yaletown existed in Waterloo Region. It was almost exclusively modern-looking high-rises with a few matching townhouses stuck in between. Despite the high-density housing, though, trees and greenspaces abounded.

"And here's our home." Dawn pulled into the driveway of a narrow townhouse.

Claire and Jan needed a moment to appreciate its beauty: stone-and-window exterior and a flat roof. With the lack of snow in Vancouver, a sloped roof probably wasn't needed. Claire had seen photos of her daughter's house, but standing in front of it was a different experience.

If she was this much in awe of her daughter's house and neighbourhood, Claire could only imagine what it would be like to stand in front of beautiful Asian architecture.

Inside was even more gorgeous: contemporary whites, beiges, and greys in a very open-concept space. Abstract art decorated the walls.

The house of artists.

Then chaos startled Claire and Jan.

Daniela yelled from somewhere on the second floor that Dave needed to turn his tablet down and let her study, while Dave insisted she was being too sensitive and should buy "big, fat headphones" to keep the noise out. "I live here, too!"

Destiny stomped to the foot of the stairs and shouted that they were both being too loud. She returned to the open-concept living room and turned up the TV.

Dawn shouted for everyone to be quiet and then smiled at her mom. "Kids."

"You and your sister weren't much different. Pauline would be jumping all over the house and you'd just want to doodle quietly in a corner."

"The twins always ganged up on Tracy. Drove her nuts," Jan added.

"See?" Claire tried to comfort her daughter. "This is normal." Though in truth, it wasn't. Claire didn't know her grandchildren to be this rude to one another, and Dawn looked too frazzled to know where to start dealing with the situation.

"It's the devices..." Dawn said.

"Like your Sony Walkman and ghetto blasters?" Claire asked. "Also no different."

"That's not the same thing, Mom."

"It's not identical, but if you and Pauline wanted to skip chores, you used art class as an excuse and turned up the music so you wouldn't hear me calling for you, and Pauline insisted she needed to go jogging with her Walkman. By the way, where is your artwork?"

But the children were getting louder again, and Dawn excused herself.

Claire lowered her voice as she spoke to Jan. "I'll be the first to suspect perfectly well-behaved children of hiding something, but the way they speak to one another? Something's not right."

"Maybe Dawn and Dean tell them to be on their best behaviour around guests?"

"Could be. But I'm their grandmother. Hopefully they feel comfortable enough around me to be themselves."

After five minutes, Dawn still hadn't returned, and Claire wondered if she should start on supper. An open cookbook on the counter divulged Dawn's supper plans: something fancy that would take at least ninety minutes to complete.

"She can't cook this," Claire said, "not with the kids ready to kill each other and Dean at work."

"How can I help?" Jan asked.

By the time Dawn returned to the kitchen, another ten minutes had passed, and Claire was cutting up potatoes while Jan was sautéing onions.

"Oh my god, no, Mom, Jan, I didn't mean for you to start cooking! Great. Now I've ruined your first night here."

Claire turned away from the cutting board. "You're my daughter, and right now, you look completely drained. We're cooking."

Claire and Jan insisted Dawn could go do whatever she wanted until supper was ready.

Destiny ran down the stairs, her eyes bright with energy, her hands behind her back, as though she was hiding something. She reminded Claire of Pauline at the same age.

But as soon as Destiny wanted to speak, she became quiet. Claire recognized that sad sign of a girl's social development. Last year, Destiny had had no problem saying what was on her mind. But once children entered this age, they became too aware of themselves. For girls, it could lead to slouched shoulders and hiding behind their long hair. Claire could only hope that Destiny would outgrow this phase with her exuberance intact. If she visited more often, maybe she could help with that.

"What is it, Destiny? You know you can talk to Grandma about anything."

Destiny nodded but looked at Jan.

"I think I need to use the washroom." Jan asked Destiny to point her in the right direction, which she did.

Destiny began to squirm. Definitely Pauline's energy, cooped up by the beginnings of puberty.

"What do you want to show me?"

Destiny pulled out a drawing from behind her back. It was of Pauline as Perry the Peregrine, her last and most successful mascot role. The drawing had Pauline's face but Perry's body.

"Mom said Aunt Pauline isn't doing too good so I thought this could help. I thought maybe if she had a picture of a time when she helped lots of kids get through their sicknesses and surgeries, she might feel better."

Claire wiped her hands on a kitchen towel before she accepted the drawing. "Destiny, this is beautiful. You clearly have your mother's talent for art."

Destiny stared at the floor. "Will Aunt Pauline like it?"

"She'll love it." But an uneasiness welled up in Claire as she said that: it felt like a lie. With everything the elder Robinsons and Brubachers had pieced together so far, Pauline's depression was running deeper than anyone had anticipated, and Todd was left with the job of trying to help her hide it. If Claire and Richard were right, and the constant reminders of Pauline's past career were contributing to her depression, then this drawing might not be welcome.

But you won't know until you give it to her, Claire thought. *Maybe a drawing from a niece who loves her dearly will help lift her spirits.*

"Do you have an envelope I could put it in so it doesn't get ruined?"

Destiny opened a drawer in a desk in the family room, pulled out a large envelope, and slid the drawing inside. Claire asked her to lay it by her purse so she wouldn't forget it.

Supper began with apologies from the children for their behaviour, which Claire and Jan accepted, and soon filled with the children's stories. *This* was what Claire wanted to experience, and it would make her even happier if their grandfather had been able to join the meal.

Dawn appeared to be relieved about something. Whether it was because of the children's apologies or something else, Claire couldn't tell. But after what had happened when she'd pushed too hard with Pauline, Claire would hold back this time.

CHAPTER 18

erry knocked on the door to Richard's office.

"Jaya has to cancel her one o'clock appointment: the flu's going around their house, and she'd rather not pass it on to you."

Richard appreciated the caution. The last thing he wanted was to welcome Claire home with a Rudolph-like nose.

"Would you like me to call your wife for you to arrange for lunch?"

Terry's attention to detail impressed Richard, but Richard also hadn't told anyone Claire was in Vancouver—work was supposed to be a distraction, not a reminder that his wife was thousands of kilometres away, out of reach.

"Thanks for the offer, Terry, but I'll just pop into the café instead." He had, after all, promised to look in on Pauline.

It figured that the week Claire was gone, Richard's schedule had calmed down a little. They could've spent more time together.

When lunchtime came around, Richard headed out. It was a dreary, warm November day. The snow that had fallen during the storm not two days before had begun to melt, and the grey clouds teased everyone with the snow—or rain—they could drop at any moment if they wanted to.

Which they probably wouldn't.

The shops in Belmont Village, though, had enough Christmas cheer to make up for the weather. The light posts had their customary green-and-red tinsel Christmas trees affixed high up. Some of the natural trees, now leafless, had lights threaded throughout their branches. They looked beautiful once the sun had set, which was getting earlier by the day. Many storefronts showed off a local artist's handiwork with snowy drawings in their windows.

Richard entered the tea shop and was delighted to see a bit of a lunch crowd. Mondays used to be quiet, but thanks to Pauline and Todd's efforts, business had seemingly picked up.

Richard approached the counter.

"Dad? Is Mom okay?"

That was how rarely he'd dropped by the family business during the day in recent times: Pauline automatically assumed an emergency.

"No, no, Mom's fine. So far as I know." He checked his watch. It was only just after nine in Vancouver. Claire was most likely awake. What was she up to? "I just thought I'd grab lunch here for once. I've been working so much over lunchtime, but today my one o'clock cancelled, so I figured I'd drop in." He ordered a roast beef sandwich. "How are you?"

Pauline smiled. "Much better. Rest does wonders, as you know." She patted her hip. "Those kids Saturday night were so cute. But the highlight, of course, was seeing Todd dance again. He only does maybe an hour at the barre a few days a week at home, and he and Austin don't like it when I visit." Her gaze floated to the love of her life as he was signing a photo for some customers. "He still gets a few fans dropping in. That gives him a lot of joy."

Maybe Pauline really was doing better? But she'd started Saturday with the same cheeriness, and her condition by the evening was clearly not good.

Pauline passed her father a sandwich, and Richard pulled out a card to pay.

"Don't worry about it. You and Mom have been amazing. It's my way of saying thanks."

This was definitely a performance.

"You know I'm happy to support your business."

"It's all good, Dad. I'm sorry I overextended myself Saturday. I learned my lesson. Won't happen again."

Another customer came up behind Richard, so he moved off to a table.

Had she learned her lesson? She had had a day off yesterday. Maybe that was all she needed to feel better? Maybe she'd taken some painkillers to help her rest?

Richard watched that customer pay.

Wait. Pauline hadn't entered his order. How else would they keep track of stock if she didn't enter it with its full discount? Maybe she'd do it later? But then the time stamp on the transaction would be inaccurate.

Richard observed the café as he ate. Within ten minutes, he saw that some napkin holders were empty, and Pauline and Todd weren't keeping up with cleaning the tables before the next customer came. Half the jars on the shelves also stood empty. Pauline and Todd only filled them when someone appeared to ask about stock. But how many would've ordered had those jars been full? Was this business as usual for the two of them? Or was something else going on that Richard and Claire hadn't heard about yet?

Richard knew where he'd be spending lunch a couple more times this week.

~

DRESSED FOR RAINY, cool weather, Claire and Jan stepped outside after a lovely—and very expensive—hotel breakfast. It was after nine, and they wanted to get a good start on the day. They had brought their own compact umbrellas, not realizing the hotel supplied each room with a sturdy, full-sized one.

"These hills looked smaller from Dawn's car," Claire said as she looked up the hill they were about to walk. "I never really gave much thought to mountains producing a hilly city."

"I thought Kitchener-Waterloo was hilly."

But Claire wasn't going to let a few steep streets stop her from enjoying herself. "On to Robson Street to do some shopping?"

"Yes!"

Robson Street was Vancouver's equivalent to Toronto's Yonge Street and promised to have lots of stores. They reached it in twenty minutes, out of breath.

"My lord," Jan said. "It's probably a hundred times longer than Belmont Village."

The green lights were flashing, so Claire and Jan waited for solid greens. To their utter surprise, though, people passed them and crossed. Jaywalkers? But when Claire looked at the pedestrian lights again, they showed the white walking figure. Since when did you cross the road on an advanced green? They crossed with everyone else and continued on their way.

"Claire, look—no lights for the other cars."

The intersecting streets had stop signs only.

Vancouver was indeed a strange place, but at the same time, discovering all these minute differences excited Claire.

EVERYONE in the bar jumped up and cheered as the Toronto Peregrines scored a goal.

Everyone, that is, except Richard.

Whose head was propped up by his hand.

His chicken wings and beer hardly touched.

His eyes staring at his phone on the table.

Sedrick gave him a whack on the back that almost knocked Richard out of his chair.

"How can you feel this down with all this energy? The Peregrines may have lost the cup last season, but they're still doing fantastic this season. Everyone's predicting that this could be Evanoff's best season yet!"

Richard picked at his chicken wings. "There's a reason I chose that song for her at our anniversary. I really can't get her off my mind, Sedrick." He picked up his beer and set it back down, not in the mood for a drink.

Twenty-four hours without his Claire and he'd left the house without brushing his teeth, driven past the brokerage's driveway—twice—and almost hired the wrong sales rep.

She might as well be in Asia, he thought. That's how far away she felt to him.

"HOW'S DAD DOING?" Dawn asked as they perused the menus in an upscale Japanese restaurant. Dean, once again, was working overtime hours.

"I texted him earlier today, and he said he's doing fine."

Jan giggled.

"What?"

"Does he really think Sedrick isn't going to report back? He's absolutely miserable without you, Claire."

Claire lay her menu down on the table. "He is?"

"The Peregrines won the game tonight, the entire bar—"

"My Richard went out to a bar?" Claire could hardly believe her ears. Furthermore, she didn't know if she should be happy he was going out or angry that he was always too tired to do something with her but apparently not with Sedrick.

"No need to get jealous," Jan said. "Sedrick's trying to get him out so he doesn't get depressed while you're gone. Don't tell me you didn't foresee this."

Dawn propped up her chin with her hand, her eyes inquiring. "Yes, Mom. Tell us you didn't think Dad would be forlorn without you there."

"Um, well…"

"Does Grandpa get lonely without Grandma?" Daniela asked, her eyes looking for a romantic story.

"I don't think Grandma and Grandpa have been separated this far or long from each other before," Dawn answered. "Right, Mom?"

Guilt suddenly filled Claire's heart. Maybe she shouldn't have left her husband alone like this. But then who'd be out here, checking in on Dawn? Dean's overtime hours were perfectly understandable to someone who had worked excessive hours pretty much her entire adult life, but Dawn appeared more tired than usual.

No, it was a good thing Claire had flown out.

"Really?" Dave asked. "Like, never? In fifty years?"

"This is the first time."

"I can't imagine being attached at the hip to someone for that long," Daniela said. "That doesn't sound like very much freedom."

Dawn shot her daughter a look, but Claire indicated it was

okay. "I like honesty, you know that." She turned to Daniela. "Your grandpa and I ended up working so much, but we were never apart from each other for any great length of time or distance."

If Claire wasn't mistaken, she could've sworn she'd seen a hint of jealousy in Dawn's expression. "Grandma and Grandpa have a rare kind of love. It's something most of us will never experience."

Jan quietly touched Claire's leg, and Claire understood: something was up with Dawn's marriage but it wasn't something they could discuss in front of the children.

"Tell Sedrick I say thank you for looking after my Richard," Claire said. She picked up the menu again and asked about a few items. She soon discovered that almost everything was either fish—often raw—or seaweed. Tofu, rice, expensive steak, and some vegetables were the only items she recognized.

"Miso-marinated egg yolks...? Well, I'm going to try it."

Dawn cocked her head. "Do you even know what miso tastes like?"

Claire shook her head as she laughed at herself. She was indeed a traditional Canadian family cook. But if she was thinking about travelling to Japan, she would have to try out their cuisine. Should she tell Dawn that she'd been thinking about travelling more?

"Promise not to tell your father this. I'm not sure about it yet, but I will talk to him soon after I return. Just please don't tell him while I'm here." She looked at Jan. "And nothing to Sedrick either. I still need to think this through."

Dawn nodded, her face serious. "What is it?"

"Is everything okay?" Jan asked.

"I'm considering taking a trip. To Asia."

Jan threw up her hands in excitement. "That's *amazing*, Claire!" She then looked around nervously. "Sorry, everyone," she said quietly. Then back to Claire, "You've never dreamed so big before. This is terrific!"

Dawn's eyes were wide. "You want to fly across the Pacific?"

Claire nodded. "I think so. I mean, I don't know how I'd get around and—"

"Seniors tours," Jan said matter-of-factly.

"That's true. And Mayumi's mother said she'd introduce me to some friends in Japan. Plus…I want to finally pay respects to your paternal grandfather."

After a moment of silence, Dawn smiled. "I think you should do it. But will Dad join you?"

Claire shrugged. "If I make such a large trip, I'm going to be gone for four to six weeks. He won't take that much time away from the brokerage. I don't think he'll even want me to leave."

Was Claire attached at the hip to Richard? That didn't sound like the woman she imagined herself to be—independent and free-spirited.

Was her granddaughter right?

CHAPTER 19

*R*ichard opened their customer relationship management software to see the current state of leads for the entire brokerage.

Not good. Numbers usually fell around this time, but with the loss of the three sales reps, those numbers had sunk even lower. Robinson Realty's own advertising channels only did so much.

He spent the next hour searching online listings for the clients he'd taken on. Maybe he'd missed possible homes to show them.

"Ah! Found one!" It'd be perfect for Jaya. An older home with a main-floor bathroom already installed. But before Richard could get too excited, he realized it was being sold independently. He understood a homeowner's desire to save the commission, but did they understand that many real estate agents hesitated to take their clients to those homes if the seller wasn't going to pay the buyer half of the commission? Selling homes was hard enough and they didn't want to give away their services for free.

But before Richard closed the listing, he noticed it had been on the market for forty-seven days. Either something was wrong with the house, or the homeowners were having difficulties with the entire selling process. For starters, if they both worked full time, that would reduce the hours they could show their home. If buyers found something else, they'd move on.

How many other independently listed homes were out there having a tough time selling? Richard wasn't going to do his sales reps' jobs for them, but he needed to know if his hunch was right, so he continued searching.

Huh. There were quite a few.

Christmas was just under a month away. Too soon to guarantee the sale of any house, but far enough away that he felt comfortable attempting a bonus plan. Not only could it motivate his sales team, but if they did sell a few more homes before the end of the year, Robinson Realty could increase its donation budget. Terry had reported earlier that more charities than usual were requesting support this year.

He walked out to Terry's desk and explained the plan: a fifteen-hundred-dollar bonus to any sales rep who could convince one independent seller to sign on with the brokerage.

Terry smiled and confirmed he'd have the wording for the email ready in thirty minutes. Richard then headed to the shop for lunch.

"Do I *really* have to wear this, Sedrick?"

Richard felt full of confidence at work in his slacks, dress shirt, and cardigans or blazers. They gave an air of professionalism, the impression that he was going to look after his clients, and indicated a certain gravitas to his employees and sales team.

He felt silly in shorts, a T-shirt, white socks, and runners.

"I haven't worn these running shoes in fifteen years."

Sedrick wrinkled his nose. "It's gross you've kept them around that long."

"They're still in good condition."

What else was Richard going to wear to play pickleball?

Sedrick patted him on the back. "We've got a half hour before my friends come." He moved to the other side of the court and began explaining the rules.

Surprisingly, the rules were simple. But hitting the ball with a paddle was a bit of a challenge for someone who hadn't touched a racquet of any kind easily since…maybe since high school.

"Okay, Rich. Let's try serving!"

Sedrick held the ball up just above hip level, dropped it, and hit it from underneath toward Richard, who was standing kitty-corner from him on the other side of the net to receive it.

Looked easy enough.

Or not.

Every time Richard tried to serve, his ball landed out of bounds. He thankfully had more success when they practised hitting the ball back and forth.

After playing for twenty-five minutes, they took a short break while they waited for Sedrick's friends, former colleagues he'd stayed in touch with.

"So?" Sedrick asked.

Richard laughed. "At this point, I think I'll have an easier time selling ten houses in the next month than I will getting that ball to land where it's supposed to."

Sedrick laughed along with him. "You'll get the hang of it, and then you won't be able to give it up."

Two fit-looking men in their sixties came onto the court: Henry and Adam.

"This is not fair," Richard playfully complained. "You're pitting me against men clearly years younger."

"Oh, don't worry. They've promised to go easy on us."

By the end of the game, Sedrick's friends had not gone "easy" on them, but Richard hadn't felt so exuberant in a while. Tired, yes. Even exhausted. And…jolly? Yes, he actually felt jolly.

"That was, as I think Austin would say, some serious fun," he said as all four men toasted the end of the game by clinking their water bottles.

"We need to send photos of us to Jan and Claire," Sedrick said. "Make them feel jealous at what they're missing out on. When was the last time Claire saw you in shorts?"

Henry used Sedrick's phone to take pictures of Sedrick and Richard leaning against each other in feigned exhaustion, slouching against the wall, lying prone with their extremities splayed, and then laughing. Sedrick sent the pictures to Richard before everyone parted ways for the evening.

Richard selected three of the best photos and typed, *Tried pickleball tonight. Young women knocked us out.* He hit send.

Sedrick laughed. "You're actually having fun!"

"I always have lots of fun," Richard said in protest.

"You've been mopey since Sunday. This is the first time I've seen you smile since she left."

It was true. And it was true that Richard had had a good time despite losing horribly.

By the time they reached the locker room, though, he hadn't received a response from Claire. Would Claire be angry that he was out having fun without her? After all, he always complained he was too tired after work to do anything. Would she think he really had been out with young women?

"They might be out in the middle of a forest somewhere without reception," Sedrick said. "Don't worry about it."

In the middle of a forest? Without reception? There were bears and cougars out there.

Sedrick clapped Richard on the back. "Or shopping downtown. Rich, they'll be fine. Let's go shower."

By the time he was dressed in his more comfortable slacks and shirt again, his phone dinged.

Richard burst out laughing the moment he saw the photo: Claire and Jan sat collapsed on the couch, covered in shopping bags overbrimming with…stuff.

You wouldn't believe all the young men who helped us carry our bags.

He really didn't have anything to worry about.

Richard had tucked his phone into his pocket when it dinged again.

Two new photos. One of Claire hugging Dawn, and the other of Claire with her arms around the three grandchildren.

Why was he playing pickleball when he could've been in Vancouver visiting his family?

"You okay?" Sedrick asked.

Richard tucked his phone away again and grabbed his bag. "Would be nice to be there with them."

Sedrick held open the change room door. "Not too late to grab a ticket. You could fly out tonight."

Richard walked through, and the men headed down the hall. "Too much to take care of at the brokerage. I just started a bonus program today, and I need to be there to monitor it."

Sedrick grabbed Richard's arm and stopped him. "Rich, how can you not be filled with regret by now? You hit retirement age before Destiny was even born. You could've played an active role in her life. And Daniela and Dave wouldn't remember life without you and Claire. One of these days, you need to stop working. Are you waiting for a major life event to happen like it did to Claire before you retire? And why?"

Richard couldn't answer him.

He studied the last photos while Sedrick drove him home. "Maybe I'll at least see if I can join Pauline and Todd for supper."

"That, my good Richard, sounds like a plan."

CHAPTER 20

After another day of shopping and sightseeing in rain, followed by a much-needed afternoon nap, it was time for Claire to have supper with Todd's father. Jan stayed back at the hotel.

Michael Parsons lived in Kerrisdale, one of the very upscale neighbourhoods in Vancouver. It was full of artistic homes, often large, but usually on small lots. Shrubbery appeared to be the preferred privacy fence.

"Palm trees in Canada?" she asked Michael as they drove by one home.

"Bamboo, ferns," he said with a knowing smile. "You don't see them too often, but the climate here is much more conducive to plants you usually associate with hot spots or consider house plants back in Ontario. And those shops we drove past are called Kerrisdale Village."

Claire laughed. "It was a lot bigger than Belmont Village."

Claire fell in love with the Parsons home as soon as they stopped out front: a two-storey brick-and-stucco house with a small balcony on the second floor supported by pillars over the main entrance. Michael let Claire off so he could park the car in behind the house.

"We have lanes here," he explained. "I don't like bringing guests in through the back. It's not as nice."

Some of the old neighbourhoods in Kitchener had lanes behind homes, too, but for whatever reason—space?—almost all Waterloo Region homes had the usual driveways-at-the-front design.

Michael opened the front door from inside. Claire stepped into a clean entranceway with family photos hanging in wide wooden frames. Only a couple pairs of men's footwear stood by the doorway. Michael's wife had passed away a few years ago, and Michael was between Claire and Richard in age.

"I know it's too big for me," Michael said, "but my other two sons come by at least twice a week with their families for supper, more often during hockey season to watch Peregrines games."

Claire wasn't much of a sports fan, but she'd sit through a game here and there if it meant hanging out with her family. When the girls had lived at home, she and Richard had spent a good deal of time driving them around to lessons and friends' homes (ostensibly to "study" together, although Claire had always doubted much studying got done). Then there was all the cooking.

The closest thing they had to tradition was Sunday afternoon tea, but even that happened less and less frequently once Claire's mother had moved to Toronto. ("Kitchener's too boring for someone my age," she'd said.)

Claire took off her coat and Michael hung it in the sparse closet. She left her shoes on a boot tray. "In your famed Peregrines Nest, I assume?" She was referring to what Pauline had called a "man cave for Peregrines fans who'd died and gone to heaven."

He blushed. "I was starstruck when I learned Pauline was their mascot. And then embarrassed." He laughed. "I get silly around those characters."

Pauline had once shown Claire a video from two summers ago when Michael and his two other sons, dressed in Toronto Peregrines swag from head to toe and with painted faces, were doing the "Chicken Dance" at a game while Perry the Peregrine — Pauline — covered them in spray confetti.

"I try to never argue with someone who's young at heart," Claire said.

Michael laughed again. "Todd told me you're always polite — unless someone crosses you. Any chance you'd like to head up the training of our customer service department?"

Claire blushed at the compliment. "I know tea and how to run a small business, not tools and a multinational franchise. I have a feeling many of your customers who call in would 'cross me.' You'd lose customers faster than nails spilled from a container."

Michael led Claire to the kitchen, but she paused to look at a family photo that hung at the end of the foyer: their mother had one arm around young Todd and the other around Michael, while Michael was reaching his other arm around his other sons. The family could have posed in many different ways to show they accepted each other, but Michael back then couldn't support the thought that he had a son who loved ballet.

Father and son had since reconciled, but that photo still left a bitter taste in Claire's mouth. As unique as Pauline's career trajectory had been before she'd assumed control of the tea shop, Claire and Richard had always supported her. It'd been her dream to bring a smile to thousands, and she'd done just that.

Michael noticed Claire studying the photos. "Betty loved whatever the kids loved — ballet, sports, all of it." He paused.

"As you know, I wasn't as...accepting...of Todd's career. Something I deeply regret."

Claire may not have approved of his parenting choices, but she'd also made mistakes, some just recently, and understood that admitting them was the first step to fixing them. "I'm dealing with some regret now, too. It is a hard pill to swallow, isn't it?"

"Sometimes I choke on it."

In the kitchen, a casserole dish on hot plates sat covered on the table. Claire didn't need that cover lifted: she could smell lasagna.

"It's Betty's recipe," he explained. "Since we're basically family—if that's not too forward of me to say—I thought I'd have our chef prepare this."

A chef? How did Claire probably work as hard as Michael and end up with one tea shop, when he had a national home improvement chain and a private chef?

"I'm looking forward to it."

Michael served the lasagna with wine, and they immediately dove into talking about their children. Claire was surprised to learn that Michael had offered to pay for extra care for Pauline so she could take more time off and they'd be financially sound.

"Please don't take this the wrong way, Claire, but I had a feeling they were struggling."

Claire held up a hand. "There's no need to apologize, and your offer to help my daughter is very generous. Todd made a comment to me while I was helping at the store during her time off that sales increased while I was there. So they may be having problems with sales, as well. Plus, there are now two of them needing a full salary. And they don't even have benefits yet. I'm volunteering twice a week until Christmas to help them. If I'm to be honest, it's for me, too. I enjoy my friends, but I miss my business."

Michael raised a glass. "Here's to sticking our tongues out at old age."

Claire laughed as she toasted with him.

He took a sip before continuing. "So they're still in a growth phase and could use a little help? I guess my history with Todd still hurts him from time to time." Michael took the next forkful slowly, a pained expression on his face.

"I'm certain it's not you. Pauline is fiercely independent, so I'm worried she's pushing Todd away." Claire filled Michael in on Pauline and Todd's extensive plan for the tea sale and party, including her suspicion that they hadn't started any of the tasks yet.

Michael repeatedly shook his head in disbelief.

"The reason I wanted to speak to you since I'm in town was to see if you had any advice about how I approach Todd. His loyalty to Pauline is admirable, but I think he's protecting her instead of helping her, and I can't tell if he's doing it because he wants to or because he feels he has to."

Michael set his cutlery down. "Todd said they were fine."

"You have no idea how often Richard and I have heard that phrase in the past few weeks."

"Then there's more at play than just independence?" Michael tapped a finger on the table. "There's no easy way to say this so I'll be blunt."

"My preferred kind of honesty."

"It sounds like Pauline is in a deep depression."

Michael's comment caught Claire off guard. "Deep" depression carried a sense of foreboding with it that "moderate" and "temporary" had not. Maybe he was exaggerating?

"May I show you something downstairs?"

"Anything, if it'll help me convince them she needs to take it much easier."

Michael let out a short, embarrassed laugh. "Just please promise not to think of me and my other two sons as weird."

Confused, Claire accepted. After they finished eating, Michael led Claire down to his Peregrines' Nest.

Claire's jaw dropped at the entrance. The room looked gaudier than interior décor that'd gone overboard on seventies psychedelia or eighties effervescence. Her awe stemmed not only from the respect she had for anyone who could spend more than fifteen minutes in this room, but also for how much time and money must have gone into decorating it.

Even the couch was covered in Peregrines fabric. How on earth had Michael sourced that?

There was only a small corner dedicated to Todd's ballet career.

And Richard was suggesting that Pauline was an outsider at home. This is what an outsider looks like.

But Todd did speak highly of his father now, and he was certainly very much in love with Pauline, who still watched all Peregrines games.

Michael turned red. "This normally wouldn't bother or embarrass me, but since a great many of these pictures are actually of your daughter..." He laughed nervously to finish his sentence as he pointed to what was apparently a Perry the Peregrine shrine and proceeded to point out exactly which photos were of Pauline and which of other actors.

Like a child in a theme park.

"All this requires a lot of dedication." Claire smiled, unsure of how else to react. She hadn't owned an equivalent in teas in their family home. A tea-themed room, yes, but she'd tastefully decorated it.

Michael went on for an hour about everything Pauline had accomplished in her three years as a mascot actor for the professional men's hockey team: the community service she had done, how she had raised so many people's spirits, was maybe in part responsible for the team winning their first cup since 1967 because even the players began believing in themselves.

"She even convinced me to match donations for the children's hospital fundraiser last year. I can't underscore enough how critical her role was in the millions that were raised that night."

Claire had seen some of this ability to inspire firsthand when Pauline used to rent a costume for an event at the tea shop, or when Pauline acted for her university and the local junior hockey team. Pauline had also told her some of these stories. But hearing them from a mega-fan warmed Claire's heart.

"I understand you never saw her perform with the Peregrines because of her non-disclosure agreement," Michael said.

"She wasn't allowed to tell even family about her job there."

Confidentiality was common in the world of famous mascots, from what Pauline had told her family. But her contract with the Peregrines had gone too far, forcing Pauline into silence. Discovering the truth had hurt Claire deeply: it had prevented her from sharing in Pauline's joy.

"I'm sorry you and I belong in the same club," Michael said. "I also didn't get a chance to see Todd perform before he retired. And the Peregrines rarely played on a Sunday so I'm not sure you would have been able to attend while you were running the tea shop."

Claire wanted to declare herself in a different club from Michael—she'd embraced both her daughters' dreams—but his comment about how many hours she used to work hit home. "I'd have been too tired to drive down to Toronto on Sundays."

Claire's heart felt heavy as the realization sank in that she might not have chosen to leave work to see her daughter perform. Pauline would've shared many happy stories of her escapades as Perry—Claire had missed out on that because of that ridiculous contract—but would Claire have really gone to watch? Given that hockey season took place mostly during Claire's busiest times—fall and winter—she wasn't sure she'd have been able to go. Maybe once or twice, which was more than nothing, but to be a true supporter of your child, you watched them perform often.

Didn't you?

Her daughter's NDA had been a convenient scapegoat all this time for the truth: Claire had put work ahead of family far too often. Yes, she'd needed to support her family. Yes, Claire's Tea Shop had provided both her daughters with early work experience. Yes, it now provided Pauline with a new career.

But would any of that be different if she had occasionally closed for several days to visit her family? Even just set regular holidays? Would it have really hurt that much? Jan's hair salon had been successful despite the closures for family time.

"Claire?"

"I'm sorry, Michael. Just lost in thought." She gathered herself together. "No. This is all wonderful, thank you. Richard and I had begun suspecting that Pauline missed this career, but more in the sense of missing her abilities to perform as opposed to the world her career had created for her. She keeps saying she's happy at the tea shop, but her hip surgery has limited some of her abilities."

"That's what I'm actually getting to, but I'm giving you the detailed version. I think it's more than that. Mascot actors of her calibre get a powerful high from performing for thousands of people. Many become depressed during the off-season."

Claire had never heard this before.

"Don't beat yourself up about it," Michael said. "It was only after I'd started seeing media reports about Todd Parsons having disappeared that I took notice. That's how engrossed I'd been in my work." He picked up a photo from the little ballet display. "This one's from when Todd was in Madrid for a season."

Todd wore what looked like a snug-fitting blue velvet jacket decorated in brocade, with golden epaulettes. His legs were covered in perfectly white tights, and he wore black boots clearly made to allow him to dance. He was standing in a lunge while holding a woman in what Claire could only describe as a graceful nosedive: Her face was precariously close to the floor, but her legs extended behind her and past Todd's shoulders in a shape that reminded her of a checkmark. The only thing that seemed to keep gravity from pulling her right down was the *single* arm Todd had around her. His other arm was extended toward the ceiling.

"He loved wowing audiences. The bigger, the better," Michael continued. "These women are maybe only a hundred pounds, but he used to be able to hold them above his head with one arm. Unfortunately, with his back spasms now, Todd can't do these sorts of lifts anymore."

"I'm afraid I don't follow. Austin doesn't lift girls in his class because of his seizures, but he's still dreaming of a ballet career."

"Austin's also about thirty years younger." Michael set the photo back in its place. "You and I both know the importance of branding." He pointed to the photo. "Every elite dancer also has a brand, some more well known than others. Todd's personal brand was the male dancer who could do it all. When—shall we say—more *demanding* members of his fanbase believed they started seeing cracks in it, they hammered those cracks wide open."

Like Doris and other regulars at the tea shop. Were Todd's experiences causing him to empathize too much with what Pauline was going through?

Michael continued. "Austin's creating a personal brand for

himself that he'll be able to live up to, one that doesn't involve lifting. I suspect his advocacy for epilepsy will help with that."

That made sense. "And Pauline's personal brand is to be the person everyone relies on for help."

"She probably feels her diminishing physical abilities are affecting that."

"Which is ridiculous, because she will be able to help others in so many ways, including performing again. She just has to be a little careful."

"Just like Todd danced for the hospital fundraiser with Austin last year."

"He actually danced in his work clothes the other evening to bring a smile to Pauline's face."

Michael's eyes lit up. "He did?"

Claire nodded. "I have to admit, I may have—what does Austin call it?—fangirled a little? When the person you know as an employee shines so brightly when he's doing what he loves, you can't help but keep your eyes on them."

Michael indicated the Perry shrine and smiled. "I have an idea of what you're talking about."

Both shared a friendly laugh, and Claire studied the other photos of Todd—some as a boy in his dance uniform, like Austin, and others in full costume and stage makeup. "I think you're right. I've never appreciated how much a performing artist's mental health can fall when they can no longer perform."

"It can drop quite deep."

Could a realtor's depression fall just as deep if pulled away from his career? The thought frightened Claire. What good would Richard's retirement be if he spent it in a dark hole? Michael was still working full time, too.

But he also finds time for family, she noticed. There was a middle ground that Claire and Richard were missing.

But for now, her focus had to be on Pauline and Todd.

Michael and Claire spent the rest of the evening discussing ideas on how to help their grown children, including how to suggest they both seek out professional help. But understanding that retirement could affect Richard in the same way as it had their daughter kept nagging at Claire.

CHAPTER 21

*R*ichard slept like a log Tuesday night, the first good sleep he'd had since Claire's departure. In fact, he arrived at work ten minutes late, feeling a little embarrassed.

By mid-morning, the first sales rep he'd hired was sitting in his office, proving himself. He'd hit the ground running yesterday, knocking on fifty doors and finding someone to sign on.

"Look for the ones that have been listed for at least sixty days," Richard said. "There's a greater chance they'll have tired of attempting to sell."

The rep asked if he'd get the same bonus for each house. Richard thought about it. The goal was to increase the donation budget through the increased revenue, but this bonus could end up eating into the donation budget if these homes didn't sell.

Another problem Richard foresaw was reps getting excited by the quick cash—this one had just earned himself fifteen hundred dollars in twenty-four hours and could probably do it again. He might start ignoring his clients.

"I'll extend the bonus to three homes that you find between

now and Christmas. So choose ones you believe you can sell." It was a gamble, but real estate involved some risk.

The sales rep nodded and headed back out.

That was the type of realtor Richard wanted. Of course it helped to have a little success at the beginning of your career.

Hmm...maybe this idea of an incentive for the first few clients wasn't such a bad one? Sales bonuses usually happened after someone had sold a certain number of homes, the idea being to motivate them to keep reaching such high numbers. But without the initial hit of those first sales, there were no future sales.

Which meant the system automatically rewarded those who'd been selling forever and had an established client list, network, and reputation. But what about those who wanted to get started, couldn't get a foothold, and still had a family to support? Real estate agents in the beginning of their career didn't make a lot of money. After they'd received their half of the commission from the sale of a home, all business expenses were taken. That included everything from brokerage fees to cell phone bills to gas. Not to mention taxes. And if you were new to the market, the continual rejection could be disheartening.

Richard immediately wrote a draft announcement about the change to the Christmas program. He'd hammer out the details of the permanent program later.

The ultimate goal, he wrote at the end, *is to increase our donation budget by increasing sales. The more homes we all sell, the more money Robinson Realty can donate to charity. So you'll not only be helping your family but also others in our community.*

Claire wanted him to give this up? If he fully retired, he'd be on a fixed income, unable to increase the amount he could give in a year. He and Claire were well off, but not so much that they could donate over a hundred thousand at Christmas every year.

As a business owner, Richard could keep contributing to the community.

~

THE MORE CLAIRE and Jan shopped in Vancouver, the more excited Claire had become about "being Grandma." When they bought gifts for their grandchildren in Christmases past, Claire and Richard had to be mindful of delivery costs and suitcase allowances. Either way, they could never enjoy watching everyone open them.

This evening would be different.

But this evening wasn't just about giving more gifts than a grandmother usually would. Claire was going to help her younger daughter, if possible. It'd become clear during Claire's stay that Dawn, too, was hiding just how difficult life had become from her parents.

Claire and Jan stepped out of the taxi—Claire insisted on a taxi this time to save Dawn the driving—with bags of wrapped gifts in their hands. Her grandchildren's eyes shimmered like stars when they learned the content of the bags.

When Claire handed Dawn the box of ornaments from Pauline, Dawn immediately teared up. "I'm sorry I don't have a tree up yet."

"Don't fret about something like that," Claire said. "I'm here to enjoy time with my family, not stare at a tree. Your sister just wanted to make sure you had these." In truth, a decorated tree would've been nice, but Christmas was still about a month away and Dawn looked overly occupied with other matters. "Dean had to work late again?"

Dawn held up her phone to show a message that he'd be at work "until whenever" tonight again.

"Hollywood studios need their CGI on deadline—or companies like Dean's don't get the next contract."

"Surely there must be other work that suits family life?"

"Says the mother who worked non-stop." No sooner had the words escaped Dawn's lips than she apologized for them. "I'm just under a lot of strain lately, Mom. I'm sorry. You and Dad worked hard to support us and we're grateful."

Jan had been right: a family of workaholics only developed because the parents set the example. *Cat's in the cradle,* Claire thought. She had never understood what the chorus to that song meant, but the song had somehow come true in her family.

She was going to make up every spare minute she could with her family. Starting now.

Claire and Jan got all three children to help with dinner preparation and insisted Dawn could run a few errands.

"I've got homework!" Dave complained. The tone in his voice was like one Pauline had used all too often in her early years of high school. It usually meant someone was trying to avoid work.

Claire handed him carrots and a peeler. "What subject?"

"Science. What do I do with this?"

Fifteen and he didn't know how to peel carrots?

"What are you studying in science?"

Claire got Destiny to wash the potatoes and Daniela the lettuce before returning to Dave to demonstrate how to use a peeler.

"I don't know."

"You don't know? Or you don't have homework?"

Dave shrugged.

"He doesn't have homework," Daniela said. "He just plays on his phone. He's failing half his courses." Her tone wasn't the caring tone Claire wanted to hear from a family member. It was the bickering and "I'm better than you" tone of sibling rivalry.

Claire did her best to take all judgment out of her voice. "Dave? Are you having difficulties in school?"

The middle child slammed his carrots and peeler onto the counter and marched up to his bedroom.

Jan immediately offered to try to talk to him. "Sometimes a stranger is more comforting than family. And with everything we've been through with Austin, I might be able to help a little."

Claire's best friend had a heart of gold. "Thank you."

Jan washed her hands and headed upstairs.

His sister, on the other hand, needed a lesson in empathy and real life.

"Daniela, stop what you're doing and look at me, please."

Daniela turned toward Claire, but she kept her gaze lowered.

"No, I said look at me."

Daniela looked up.

Claire had to be careful what she said: Destiny was listening.

"Do you think your brother is proud of his failing marks?"

"But he doesn't study! That's his fault!"

Claire kept her voice even. "Do you think he's proud of them?"

"He should be studying more. Then he can get higher marks."

Claire spoke in a firmer voice. "You're not answering my question. Do you think he's proud of them?"

A quiet "no" squeaked out of Daniela's mouth. "Then why doesn't he study?"

"There can be many reasons, and I'll discuss them with your mother. But if you're going to be an endocrinologist, you're going to be dealing with people—including teenagers—who don't take their medicine like they're supposed. You can't treat them that way."

"But Dave—"

Claire cut off the protest. "Dave is your brother. And you're the oldest by three years, already in university. It's time to act like the adult I know you can be."

Daniela nodded.

"I don't act like that," Destiny said.

"You do, too!" Daniela retaliated.

Claire slapped the counter. "Girls!"

Her granddaughters jumped.

To Destiny, she said, "You don't ever need to brag about how you act. Just act and let your helpful actions speak for themselves." To Daniela, she said, "You don't need to prove everyone wrong to make yourself look right. In fact, it has the opposite effect. Now, let's get back to work or there won't be Christmas dinner, and if there's no Christmas dinner, there won't be any Christmas gifts. I still have the receipts and can return everything tomorrow."

The girls stared at her in disbelief. Had no one ever threatened to cancel an event on them because of their behaviour?

If Dawn didn't tell Claire this evening what was going on, Claire would have to ask. She was flying back tomorrow.

About ten minutes later, footsteps down the stairs told Claire that Jan and Dave were returning. Claire turned around to delegate a new task to Dave since she'd finished the carrots, and saw his sadness. Jan didn't look happy either.

"Is everything okay?" Claire asked.

Jan shook her head.

Claire didn't want to cause any more stress than was already happening. She knew what always helped in such situations. She took a deep breath. "Jan, could you please boil some water?" To the children she said, "Let's all take a pause. Where does your mom keep her tea?"

Destiny eagerly pointed to a cupboard. "Aunt Pauline's tea is up there, too!"

In the cupboard stood box upon box of tea. She didn't expect her daughter to buy only from the family store but boxed teas? She pulled them out and noticed that many had expired, some over two years before.

She set Destiny on the task of properly composting expired teas, found boxed peppermint that was still good, and made peppermint tea for the children and Dawn's Delight for herself and Jan.

"I'm old enough for caffeine," Daniela complained.

"Not in that mood, you're not." As calming as the L-theanine in tea could be, the caffeine could aggravate emotions, too. Claire felt sad that she didn't know her grandchildren well enough to guess how the older ones would react to her favourite beverage.

"Don't you want to know what Jan talked to me about?" Dave asked as he skimmed over the recipe for the salad dressing. His voice communicated challenge—the "I'm going to keep information from you" challenge. This was not an invitation to talk.

"If you want to tell me, I'm here for you, Dave, and happy to listen. I'm glad you at least spoke to a trustworthy adult, but Jan won't betray the trust you've shown her unless you're in serious danger."

Seeing Jan shake her head slightly, Claire moved to get everyone refocused on their tasks.

"Jan and I will take care of the garlic and onions but if I hear another complaint, that person will have to cut an onion. Understood?"

Claire did her best to guide conversation into peaceful topics while encouraging her grandchildren to drink their tea. She didn't know what she would do if they refused to go along with her rules. She wasn't their mother.

But it worked. When Dawn returned home an hour later, the kids didn't even rat each other out to her. Claire was just finishing turning over the last breaded chicken breast she was frying at the stove while Jan washed large dishes that wouldn't fit into the dishwasher. Everything else was ready to go at the table.

Dawn hugged her mother and Jan, grateful beyond words for the help.

Supper was a success, although it took work. Claire, with Jan's support, led conversation to keep everyone civil. She couldn't hang from ceiling rafters or do gymnastics tricks in head-to-toe costumes to distract the children, but she knew how to listen and converse.

If only she could do this with Pauline.

The highlight of the evening—the Christmas presents—was everything Claire had dreamed of. It was wonderful to watch them open their presents, even those they tried hard to show appreciation for, like clothes.

When they had opened all their gifts, Destiny approached Claire, smiling nervously and letting some of her hair fall in front of her face.

"She has our family Christmas card for you," Dawn explained. "She drew it."

Destiny had drawn a lovely picture of the family.

Without Dean.

What was this about? An impending separation? Anger toward her father?

Claire smiled, said it was a beautiful card, and hugged Destiny. "You're a gifted artist, just like your mother."

Dawn looked at the card and her face fell. She quickly indicated to Daniela and Dave, who worked together to carry a large wrapped flat rectangle of a gift to their grandmother.

"Oh! I don't know how I'll get this home!"

"I had it picked out before you said you were coming, so I was going to ship it, anyway. But I wanted to give you your present in person."

Claire unwrapped it to discover a print of a painting by Emily Carr, an acclaimed Canadian artist who painted scenes of British Columbia.

Claire's hand flew to her chest. "My goodness. This is so lovely."

Dawn smiled. "She's always reminded me a bit of you: ahead of her time, sometimes needing to be accepted by men before society would accept her…but she always retained her own voice."

Claire's throat tightened. How could her daughter be this perceptive? Starting the tea shop had been difficult: Claire's father needed to sign for an initial loan from the bank so Claire could put a deposit down on the store unit. It took a good amount of convincing the landlord to rent to her, too, but he did. She also couldn't publicly give up her first husband's name after his death without causing pain to people she loved. What was worse, she'd decided back then to never remarry. Had she not met Richard, she didn't know how long she would've lasted as Claire Harris. But when Richard became her agent to help with the commercial unit rental, something in her heart had changed. She had changed.

He'd made her feel heard.

After hugs all around, Claire asked Dawn if she could talk to her. Jan saw her cue and offered to clean up with help from the kids.

"You mentioned earlier about my working so much," Claire began.

Dawn immediately sat up straight, an apologetic look on her face. "I'm so sorry, Mom. That just slipped out. I know you and Dad worked hard for our family."

"But you're right: we did work too much, and now we've raised two daughters with the same work ethic." Claire placed her hands in her lap. "Which means I'm concerned about what's happening here in your home. I have yet to see Dean this week, and running a brokerage entails a lot of work. Please tell me what's going on."

That was all it took for Dawn to break into tears. "I don't know how much longer I can last. Dean's new job pays really well…but he's never home. That's why Destiny didn't draw him on your card. She's angry with him for suddenly disappearing. He's usually out the door before she's up for school, and he usually comes home after she's gone to bed. I should've checked that card before she gave it to you, but I'm barely holding myself above water with my business. How did you do it all?"

Claire swallowed. Hearing her daughter's voice crack as she tried to explain everything made the pain almost unbearable. Claire embraced her daughter in the tightest hug she'd given her in a long while and began to cry, too. How had both her daughters become skilled at hiding such important matters from their parents?

Of all the times she needed Richard in her life, now was one of those times.

And he was thousands of kilometres away.

CHAPTER 22

Claire's thoughts felt like their flight: seeing the destination—the airport—but circling around it, unable to land.

"I'm really unsure about Asia now," she said to Jan.

"Don't decide yet. Lots can change in the next six months."

"Or get worse… If Pauline's depression is as deep as Michael thinks, then she's not going to come out of it soon. And with Dean's work schedule, Dawn's almost drowning in her own responsibilities. I could use that time and money to fly out to her more often, like Mayumi's mom does. You were right about our family legacy of workaholism."

Jan shook her head. "Don't be so hard on yourself. Both girls are also grown, independent women. Once you've helped set them on the right path, they'll take over."

Claire stared out the window at the lights below—it was only after six in the evening, but it was already dark. "Dawn needed my emotional support on this. But how to tell Richard everything? 'Hi, my Keemun! So nice to see you again! Guess what? Our younger daughter is overwhelmed and can barely keep herself together, and you and I were too occupied with our own lives to see it.'" Claire shrugged. "Or, 'Hi, my Keemun! I think our older daughter has been in a much deeper depression than we realized, and Todd's been shouldering all the responsibility himself. How was work?'"

Jan took Claire's hand in both of hers. "I trust you'll make the right decision, whatever you do. You and I have both been around the block more often than we care to admit. That's got to count for something."

Claire placed her free hand on Jan's. "Your trust means the world to me."

The intercom dinged and the captain came on. "Ladies and gentlemen, thank you for your patience. We've been cleared for landing."

Worry and excitement grew in Claire at the same time. She didn't know how she would explain everything to Richard, but she couldn't wait to see him again either. As amazing as Jan had been on the trip, she wasn't Claire's husband of fifty years.

THANK god for texting and video calls, Richard thought as he paced back and forth in the apartment. But not waking up beside her? He had to remind himself every morning that she was neither in the hospital nor dead.

Pickleball with Sedrick had been fun, Richard had to admit. The men and women at the racquet club were collegial, and he could see himself enjoying time with them. He didn't think Claire would join him—due to her knee. But maybe she'd come and watch on occasion and then hang out with everyone afterwards?

Richard laughed. "Sure she'd come. To laugh at me when I serve." But one of the many benefits of having been in love this long was the sense of humour they had with and about each other.

He checked his phone in case he'd missed a text from her announcing that she was almost home. Nothing yet. He picked up the apartment phone to test it in case she buzzed up to get help with her luggage.

Dial tone. It wasn't broken.

Richard had eaten at the café every day. Tuesday, he'd even dropped by after work to see if he could help with anything. By that afternoon, Pauline had understood why Richard was hanging around a lot and had become impatient with his inquiries.

He'd kept good on his promise, though, and found that he and Claire had been right. Pauline wasn't faring well and was trying to cover it up. It hurt to see her refuse his help. But she was an adult. Best to let her make her own decisions. That's what he had learned over the years.

He stepped into the bathroom to check his appearance again. He had gotten his hair trimmed today to make sure it looked absolutely perfect when they saw each other. His collar on his golf shirt was straight. His slacks had a nice crease in them.

Maybe he could manage two weeks away in the spring to visit Dawn and the family plus take some time for just himself and Claire.

Who was already an hour late. Richard couldn't handle it anymore and texted her to see where she was.

Almost back. Miss me already? she replied.

"More than you realize," he said aloud in the empty apartment.

～

THE ELEVATOR DOORS closed in front of her. Claire pressed the button for her floor number and waited.

She'd promised herself to tell Richard everything right away. They still had an hour before bedtime, and she'd be awake another two at least because of the time change. She had a day to recuperate before she and Richard worked at the tea shop on Saturday again.

But Richard needed to know everything as soon as possible.

When the elevator doors opened, Claire pulled her luggage behind her, reached her apartment door, stood the luggage up on its legs, and opened her purse. But as she searched for her keys, the door flew open, startling her. Her husband pulled her in, grabbed her luggage, let the door shut behind them, and wrapped her in his arms so tightly she could barely breathe.

She kissed him deeply in return, her arms reaching around his back and pulling him in. His lips caressing hers were impatient, wanting. Hers desiring as much love as they could absorb.

They kissed and embraced, then kissed and embraced some more. Claire found herself against the wall, which gave her the support she needed to pull him in tighter.

When Claire woke up in the morning, it was past ten. Richard had left for work almost an hour before. She hadn't brought up everything she'd learned after their reunion: their passion and desire for each other had needed breath.

Now loneliness and sadness settled in fast. What had made her think she could spend six weeks away from Richard? These few days had been fun, but when she had spent time with Michael to brainstorm ways to help their grown children, and when Dawn had surprised Claire with her news, the first person she'd thought of was her husband.

Had she been selfish to leave him alone and travel so far away from him?

An old voice inside herself said no. When Claire had asked

her mother in her later years how she'd survived her father's outbursts and moods, her mother had answered, "Loving myself, my pumpkin. You need to have love for yourself first before you can give it to others."

Claire was filling her soul with all the new discoveries she was making in retirement. It was giving her the strength to move forward with both daughters.

Which meant that Claire needed to figure out a way to visit Asia *and* still care for her family.

CHAPTER 23

*B*y evening, Claire had her plan laid out. Richard had to work late, which was just as well. Armed with Destiny's drawing, she knocked on Pauline and Todd's door. It took a minute for Todd to answer.

"Good evening, Claire. I hope Vancouver was good?"

Claire walked inside without waiting to be invited in—she and Michael had agreed that the time for respectful parental distance was past. Pauline's surgery had been more than a month before and she was still in pain, possibly from over-working herself. She'd admitted once to going jogging, but Claire assumed that wasn't the only time. Plus, watching Pauling stay on her feet all day, trying to calm her discomfort with ice packs had proven to Claire that her eldest wasn't taking care of herself.

The first step of Claire's plan was to convince both Pauline and Todd to let her and Richard work Saturday alone so Pauline could finally take a break—but not be by herself. Pauline was the consummate extrovert, so being alone with her depression while her family tried to get her professional help could harm her more.

But there was no sign of Pauline in the apartment even though the shop had closed an hour ago.

"She has a few last-minute things to tend to," Todd said in answer to her question, his smile wavering ever so slightly.

Claire jumped ahead to the part of the plan where she'd talk to Todd alone. Michael had recommended cornering Pauline by talking to Todd first, but that had made Claire uncomfortable. She'd hoped to start with Pauline, or with both of them together. However, since Pauline wasn't home and time wasn't on Claire's side, Todd it would be.

"I'm worried about her, which is no secret —"

Todd's lips barely moved. "We're fine."

"That's the last time I want to hear that sentence. My daughter is suffering, and you don't want to stand between a mother and her hurting child. Especially me."

Michael had reminded Claire that the more they had pushed to help, the more the younger couple had probably interpreted their actions as an attack, no matter how well intended they were. Claire and Richard's frustrations had been born out of love for their daughter, so if Claire's ultimate goal was to get them to start looking after each other and themselves, she had to set her frustrations aside. She'd be firm to make it clear that doing nothing was no longer an option, but she wouldn't get frustrated.

She continued. "I'm sorry if I sometimes come across as too strong. Please know that Richard and I love having you in our family. Pauline couldn't have fallen in love with a better man."

Todd's smile relaxed.

"We are here to support you both, and your father wanted me to tell you that he's also there for you if you need him."

"The Robinsons are different from the Parsons. *You've* always supported Pauline."

So Todd still harboured anger toward his father. Given everything Claire had seen in their family home, and the extent of regret Michael had expressed to her, it didn't surprise her.

"I met with your father while I was in Vancouver, and he explained some things I'd never thought of. I appreciate that retiring is hard, but I never took into consideration the *difference* between serving a thousand customers in a month versus in one night. Or what might be a year's worth of customers in one night for Pauline. Your father helped me see how much your performing careers have meant to you and how much you both might be missing them." She let out a little laugh. "And I saw the Peregrines' Nest."

Todd chuckled. "I'm sorry. Interior design was never my father's strength."

"He knows how to use tools. It's the decoration materials he doesn't know what to do with. But looking through that Nest with your father showed me a side to my daughter I knew about but had never experienced in such…intensity. I've seen the joy on people's faces when she performs, but no one's ever talked to me about her for an hour, and I imagine your father isn't the only super-fan out there."

The corners of Todd's mouth lifted slightly. "The easiest way to describe performing to someone who doesn't do it is that it's a natural high. A thrill. You're scared about messing up in front of everyone, but you love the attention and accolades. You thrive on that tension."

Todd's phone dinged from the kitchen counter, and he excused himself.

Claire sighed. She had almost reached him.

He replied to the message and then asked, "Can I make you a tea, Claire?"

That was her answer: whatever happened next, Todd was willing to talk to her more.

Claire smiled. "What would *you* recommend?"

Todd blushed. "The only thing more nerve-wracking than waiting for the curtain to open is recommending a tea to Claire Robinson."

Claire shook her head. "You know I drink almost anything of good quality. I love how you recommend teas. You have a way I'd never have thought of in a million years."

Todd thought for a moment and then explained. "Someone we care about isn't faring well, but that's almost any story."

"So, what makes ours unique?"

"I think of *Giselle*, actually. It's a sad ballet, but several characters die from dancing too much. Giselle herself doesn't—she kills herself because she's been misled to love a man who's betrothed to someone else."

Was he about to recommend depression-in-a-cup? Claire would prefer something a little more uplifting. "Are all ballets this sad? I mean, other than *The Nutcracker*?"

Todd smiled. "No. But I rarely take narrative ballets literally. This one is about a person who has been deceived, and so her hope is gone. Those who loved her are saddened by this loss of hope, and the new friends Giselle acquires—these fairy-like beings who force you to dance until you die—exact revenge on her behalf. She tries to protect the mortals from them, but she's only somewhat successful. To me, this ballet is about what happens when you lose hope."

Claire wasn't expecting such a sad story, but she understood Todd's interpretation of it. "I guess hopelessness can beget hopelessness."

Todd nodded. "*Or* you need something very powerful to pull someone out of it. For me, it's one of your most basic tea blends: Love's Labour's Tea. Roses for love, black tea for strength."

"Really? I'd never thought of that tea in that way."

Todd smiled. "Maybe after years of Jan buying it for… personal reasons…it would be hard to see it as anything else."

Claire had to laugh. "Fair enough! Jan is open about being amorous. Yes, I'll take that."

Pauline opened the door just as Todd handed Claire her tea.

"Hi, Mom. You're back from Vancouver? Nice to see you." The lack of enthusiasm at seeing her mother rang in Claire's ears, even though Pauline tried to cover it up.

"I'm happy to see you, too. I'm trying Todd's recommended tea."

Pauline slid out of her boots and put her coat, hat, and mitts in the closet. When she spoke, she didn't even try to face her mother. "I can smell it. The one for losing hope. Great. You were talking about me, I assume? Look. I can take care of myself. You and Dad can stop babysitting me."

Todd answered before Claire could even think about how to respond. "We're just worried about you, that's all. How was the shop?" He pulled an ice pack out of the freezer, indicating this had become their usual routine.

"Fine. Did some bookkeeping." Pauline eyed Claire's tea. "I guess you're staying?"

The annoyance in Pauline's voice hurt, but Claire had to work through it. *Not dance around this sadness until I die*, she thought grimly.

"Since I've been gone all week, I wanted to come by to see if there was anything specific you wanted me and your father to take care of tomorrow."

Pauline hobbled to the kitchen and took the ice pack out of Todd's hand. "Todd and I can look after everything. You and Dad can just smile and talk to people."

As Pauline limped to the couch to sit down, Claire looked at

Todd. He shrugged, unwilling to contradict Pauline in front of Claire. Claire had to respect that.

But that meant she was on her own. She reminded herself of the plan she and Michael had discussed. "You're not going to work tomorrow. Your surgery is little more than a month behind you, and you're still in pain."

"It's fine by morning."

"Repeatedly injuring your body like this won't help you in the long run. You know that."

"How do you think I got through my last year at the Peregrines?" Pauline turned on the TV and landed on a crime drama, something she knew her mother wouldn't like.

Claire saw the power bar. *And it had an off-switch. Click.*

"Mother! You had no right doing that!"

"I'm here for a visit. I'd very much like to see the daughter I haven't seen all week."

"You see me all the time. I'm sure a break must've been nice."

Claire blinked. "Why would I want a break from one of my daughters? Why would you say that? I don't understand where all this is coming from."

"I just want to relax with my partner on a Friday night."

Despite her outer façade of steel, Claire's heart ached at seeing her daughter like this. Normally if Claire did something Pauline didn't like, she would've directly said so—but without the sting in her voice.

Focus on empathy, Claire reminded herself. Of course, Destiny's drawing.

She retrieved the envelope from her purse, pulled out the beautiful piece of artwork, and handed it to Pauline.

"Would this help lift your spirits?"

Pauline glanced at the drawing and then tore it to shreds.

Claire gasped. "Destiny drew that for you! What is wrong with you?!"

Pauline held her breath for a moment—was it regret?—then pushed herself up from the couch and limped into her room, slamming the door behind her.

Claire covered her mouth as she grasped the seriousness of her daughter's despair, her own regret at her reaction seeping through now.

"She didn't even pause to see who'd drawn it," Claire said, her voice low.

Todd spoke quietly. "She can't stand anything to do with that character. The only reason the photos are still up is because Austin and I know all too well that disappearing into a black hole by erasing everything you love doesn't work. I wasn't going to let that happen to her."

"This change in her life is killing her on the inside," Claire said. "The new hip has changed how she's allowed to move, and movement was not only her bread and butter for thirty years, but also her coping strategy since she'd been a teen."

"She's allowed to do weights," Todd said, "but she does that mostly to release anger and to stay in shape. To get rid of her pent-up energy from having to stay still all day, and to clear her head, she needs to jog. But she can't. And she's not allowed to do backflips anymore either: the impact of the landing would be too hard on her prosthetic hip." His weak voice told Claire he also knew that Pauline was trapped in a cage.

Michael had been right.

"You know," Todd said, interrupting Claire's thoughts, "when I first met her, she couldn't sit still. Her leg was always bouncing and she'd even step outside more often than a smoker."

Claire smiled. "She knew I didn't like it when she was all

bouncy in front of the customers. It made people nervous and they'd buy less. She hasn't done that in ages, has she?"

Todd shook his head. "And she used to make these little slip-ups, like 'Don Quicksoat' for Don Quixote or 'What's-His-Name' for Nureyev." He let out a little laugh. "But she's so careful around customers—and even me sometimes—with what she says. It's like she's afraid to take any risks."

So there had been signs. Pauline was the biggest risktaker in the family: she lived life to the fullest and never let anything hold her back. "I thought she was just her controlling her urges more, and all this time it's been her growing depression."

Todd continued. "She feels like all she does is sell tea. When those customers put on that performance during the snow-storm...she wished she could do that again, make people as happy as they had made her that night."

Maybe passing the tea shop to Pauline hadn't been such a good idea. But she'd wanted it. Claire had always hoped one of her daughters would take over, but she had been careful not to push it on them either.

"Why didn't you come to me and Richard? Or go to Dawn?"

Todd glanced toward the bedroom door. "She didn't want anyone's help. She wanted to do this on her own. I love her." He shrugged as if to suggest the rest was obvious.

"When your love is so strong for someone, sometimes you have to do something they don't want you to do."

"But I don't want to disrespect her wishes."

"Which proves just how remarkable of a man you are, Todd. But you must know as much as I do that she needs professional help, don't you?"

Todd nodded, the sadness in his eyes no longer hidden.

Pauline needed someone with her right now, but it definitely could not be Claire: she'd burned her bridges with Pauline for at least the evening. "You fought your own depression when you were thrown out of your career. You know what she's going through. Talk to her. Love her. Show her there's a way out—starting with the two of you not coming in tomorrow. But first and foremost, listen. Don't make the same mistake I've made. Again, actually." *When will I ever learn to not jump into discussions so fast? It's just hard when someone you love is in pain*, she thought.

So that portion of her and Michael's plan hadn't worked, but Claire believed Todd had finally accepted he couldn't support Pauline on his own, regardless of what Pauline said.

Claire took Todd's hand in hers. "You're the perfect man for her, Todd. Please don't ever doubt that. But she needs someone to pull her out of her head. She's so used to flying high above the clouds, she can't yet imagine what it's like to glide below them, where you can actually see more."

"I never though of it that way."

"I saw Pauline's career from high up, like when we flew to Vancouver and were above the clouds. Magical, yes, but you can't see anything. Your father helped me see the details, like the landscape you finally see once you're below the clouds." Claire patted his hand as she let go. "Can Richard and I do a little cooking so you have food in the freezer for nights when she needs more attention from you?"

"That's a kind offer, Claire, but we'll be fine."

Claire laughed. "I never want to hear that word again. So…?"

Todd smiled as he shook his head. "Your daughter said to never cross your boundaries. So, yes."

"Give me some containers, and I will cook up a storm on Sunday."

CHAPTER 24

"Where have you been? Is everything okay?" Richard asked. Claire had barely stepped into their apartment, and he'd already wrapped his arms around her. He still missed her from her absence during her Vancouver trip. "I tried texting you."

She kissed him quickly. "I had my phone on Do Not Disturb. It was necessary. But you and I need to talk."

Richard couldn't make love when a pronouncement like that hung over their heads.

"Is everything all right?"

"I'm sorry," Claire said, pulling away. "I didn't make supper tonight. Sandwiches?"

Claire looked…off. Her face was pale, her smile didn't hold the warmth and energy it usually did. Had she realized something in Vancouver? Did it have to do with him?

"You look exhausted. Let me make them. Why don't we just start talking?"

Claire gave him a quick peck on the cheek, and Richard tried to contain his relief. Any kiss was a sign that they were still all right. He and Claire had survived some tumultuous times over the years, and at those times she did not kiss him. That had hurt and frightened him, but he had learned to appreciate her honesty. Those horrible times meant that he could trust a kiss in situations like this.

She sat down on the couch and lifted up the Royal Delft teapot. "Todd told me something this evening that surprised me."

Richard pulled ingredients from the fridge. "Oh?"

"You know how Pauline still has photos up of her as a mascot in the café? And a few in their apartment?"

"Yes." Richard popped slices of bread into the toaster.

"Todd and Austin are forcing her to keep them up, to remind her of what made her happy."

"So, like your father's teapot, they *are* making her sad. We were right."

"Only half right. They're actually making her deeply depressed."

Richard stopped what he was doing. "Deeply?"

Claire shared with him what she'd learned from Michael Parsons and what Todd had admitted just before, and about how performers can fall to such depths if they don't get "a fix." Richard told her a bit of what he'd seen in the café all week.

When they finished, Richard had their sandwiches on the table. "We'll need to make sure she sees a psychiatrist, too. Let's add that to your plan." Having a plan to move forward always made things better.

Claire nodded, but as she stood up, Richard held up his palm. "You eat. I'll get it."

He returned with Claire's list of ways to help Pauline, and Richard added *psychiatrist referral.*

He sat back down. "In the meantime, we're going to have to do the best we can to support her. Referrals can take forever."

"I wonder…what if we asked Todd to help her find a sports psychotherapist? I think her physiotherapist specializes in athletes, so she might be able to recommend someone. At least Pauline could do *something* to improve her outlook on life while we're waiting for the medical system to kick in. I think that would give her hope."

The news that his oldest daughter was in such a dark place saddened Richard. At least they had a more effective plan of attack to help Pauline. The hardest part would be getting around her pride, but Richard was confident they could manage that, especially now that Todd appeared to see things more realistically.

"But that's not all," Claire said. "It seems like both our daughters are avoiding us."

Richard's hands froze, holding his sandwich just in front of his mouth. There was more?

"Dawn's completely overwhelmed with Dean's new work hours, and the children are feeling it. You wouldn't have recognized them. Angry with each other, shouting all the time. You and I both know siblings often don't get along, but this was past that."

Richard had somehow eaten his sandwich by the time Claire had finished telling him about their younger daughter. As much as he'd missed Claire while she'd been in Vancouver, he was now glad she'd gone.

"How have we failed as parents?" she said.

Claire's sadness became his sadness. He wanted to tell his wife that they hadn't failed, that they simply couldn't have seen any of this coming. But his intended words of comfort stuck in his throat because he wasn't sure if they were the truth.

"Richard?" She reached out across the table to his hand, and he enclosed hers in both of his. He still couldn't say anything. "How could we not see both our daughters fall into these dark holes? Dawn was just here not two weeks ago, and we live down the hall from our other daughter. It's like distance doesn't make a difference, when it should. Todd mentioned tonight that Pauline had stopped her jitteriness a long time ago, but I'd assumed she simply had better control of it. What other clues have we missed? And why?"

At least the answer to the last question came out easily. "Because we've been too occupied with our own lives to pay attention. Jan was right."

Claire pulled her hand back and sat up. "How are we supposed to fulfill our dreams while watching our children all day, every day?"

"We chose to have them. We need to take care of them. Our lives come secondary."

Anger arose in Claire although she controlled her tone. "But we're also people. I have needs. So do you."

"Those needs get pushed aside when children are in the picture."

Claire shook her head. "By answering those needs, we build our strength to help those around us."

"By just digging deeper, we find that strength."

"At some point, that strength runs out. Trust me. I've been there."

"You don't think I have?" As soon as the words left Richard's throat, he regretted them.

Claire's eyes narrowed. "I have no idea what you're talking about, unless you were also previously married and repeatedly lied to, threatened, thrown down on the bed because that wouldn't leave bruises, and told to shut the hell up."

A pit formed in Richard's stomach. David Harris had done *that* to Claire? How could anyone…? He had meant his childhood, but talking about it would add no value to this life. He would have to push the memories back into their box again.

"I'm sorry. I didn't mean to compare my life to yours like that."

Richard took their plates to the kitchen and put them in the dishwasher. Time to return to the actual topic at hand. "I'm certain our children hid their problems on purpose out of pride." Suddenly the truth hit Richard square between the eyes. He faced Claire. "What kind of fool was I to declare that I hoped nothing would change? Everything is changing, just as you said."

"I have to admit, it scared me to hear you say those words."

"And it probably scared our daughters, too."

"What do you mean?"

But Richard now knew what he had to do. He grabbed his coat but explained quickly. "To Dawn, we're a reminder of the kind of parents she wants to be—working excessive hours while raising children. Pauline is continually told how she's not like you."

"Where are you going?"

He pulled on his boots. "To the brokerage. I have a phone call to make."

"Make it from here."

"The paperwork's there." Not wanting to worry Claire, he walked over to her, squeezed her shoulders, and pressed his lips to hers. "I love you and I'm doing this for our family. I'll be back in an hour or so."

"WHY DIDN'T you tell us things were going this badly for you?" Richard asked his youngest daughter, who was on the other side of the screen on their video call. It was late afternoon in Vancouver.

Dawn cast her gaze down and shrugged.

Richard leaned into his screen. "Dawn, your mother and I love you. We'll do whatever we can to help you through this."

"Thanks, Dad."

For the umpteenth time, Richard stared at the contract that lay on his desk: the sales contract he'd signed over thirty years before to purchase the brokerage from his former boss. But his proposal to Dawn was the right one. It would let him continue working without the stresses of management.

"What would you think about merging our brokerages?"

Dawn blinked. "I...I never thought of that. But won't that mean more work for us?"

"The merger itself will be a lot of work, but once we have processes sorted out, I think it'll be less. My salesforce always floats around twenty or so. I think you have eight?" Dawn nodded. "So managing the sales teams might feel like more work to you at the beginning, but you talked about different programs you use to save you time."

Dawn's eyes lit up. "You'd be willing to implement them?"

Richard took a deep breath. "Thanks to Jan, your mother and I realized that we've raised two girls who work as hard as we did, when that's not necessary. I don't know if I'm willing to learn new programs at this point in my life—I feel like I have better things to do than fight with computers." Dawn laughed. "But I just implemented a bonus program for new hires that you might find interesting."

Dawn let out a breath and dabbed a finger under her eyes. "That idea hit me hard. Wow. I...I need to talk it over with Dean, of course. Would you be willing to hire a sales manager? That would also help take the strain off us."

Richard nodded. "And one of our office staff should be promoted to manager, too. Operations manager, if you will. Assuming the budgeting works out." Change was happening all around him. He needed to stop ignoring it. "There are four things I can't live without: your mother, my two children, and my career. I can't imagine never working—I had my first job at age twelve. But maybe you and I can help each other and have more time for our families."

Dawn wiped away more tears. "I think this would work nicely. Would that make us partners then?"

What Richard was about to tell her would change the rest of his life. It frightened him, but it was necessary.

"I was a sales rep for this brokerage when I met your mother. I'd like to stay involved. But I think this merged brokerage—this cross-country brokerage—should be run by one person who has a few more years left than I do."

Dawn's jaw dropped. "You mean…you're giving me Robinson Realty?"

"You'll buy me out—at a very good price. But maybe I can stay involved as a sales trainer and…" He chuckled at the next idea. It was too perfect. "As a specialist in moving seniors."

Dawn swallowed her tears through her laughter. "Why don't I fly over again to talk to you more about this in person? I just have to arrange chauffeuring the kids with Dean's parents— they can help out once in a while. They hate disciplining the kids, so this time I'll make sure to leave them large boxes of Smarties as bribery."

Richard laughed. Grandma Sutton lived on.

Dawn turned serious. "I can't say yes yet, but I want to."

They exchanged goodbyes, and Richard relaxed into his chair, pushing his own tears back. He couldn't recall the last time he'd experienced happiness and sadness at the same time. Happiness at the prospect of being able to help one of his children, but sadness because it meant the beginning of the end of owning a business.

CHAPTER 25

Much to Claire's dismay, Richard had again woken up before she did. He had left a note saying he needed to drop into the brokerage but promised to be at the tea shop well before it opened. She'd been hoping to enjoy a nice breakfast with him, followed by a walk to the tea shop.

Figures work comes first, she thought.

But she'd soon found a text from Todd that lifted her mood: *We'll stay home today. Thank you.* She informed Richard by text, adding a little happy face to her message.

It was the first of December. The month for Christmas had begun. Claire arrived an hour before opening to give herself enough time to inspect everything and set up. The place looked clean. One of Pauline's first major changes had been to contract cleaning out to a company Michael had recommended. Claire had been cleaning the place herself all these years.

"No wonder I was getting tired," she said aloud. "There's no way I'd want to do that now."

She inspected the jars of tea and noticed that many were

empty. She'd taught Pauline that people were more apt to buy if the shelves were filled with product. She checked the supply in the back room, dismayed. Most of the product lay on the shelves, but some of it was too high up for her to reach without climbing onto something, and some of the bags might even be too heavy for her to lift down.

"Would be nice to have a tall, strong, handsome man here to help me." She let out a sigh of frustration and began with the bags she could comfortably lift by herself.

About twenty minutes in, someone knocked on the front door. A squeal of happiness came out of Claire's mouth when she peeked to see who it was.

It was Richard, holding a huge wrapped bouquet of flowers already in a vase. Claire grabbed her cane, approached the front door, and let him in.

He was pretending it was the sixties again. Claire's skin tingled all over. As soon as she locked the door and lifted the bouquet out of his arms, Richard pulled her into his.

Then he produced out of his coat pocket the Monkees' Christmas CD Pauline had bought for her mother.

"I thought you needed a little pick-me-up before we got really busy today. And sorry about disappearing so early."

"Is everything okay? I fell asleep before you got home last night."

A big smile on his face, he kissed her fully on the lips. "We'll talk later, I promise. But now, let's make this the best day Pauline and Todd see in revenue this season."

After all the sadness she'd told him about last night, he had found a way to make her happy. On days like these, she wondered how she'd ever live without him.

"I'd suggest using the back room," Richard said, his voice low, "but I don't think we have enough time."

Claire's cheeks warmed at many memories of stolen

evenings in the back room. She drew a finger down Richard's neck. "We did promise a certain daughter that we could run this place by ourselves. If we start acting like teenagers, I think she'll ground us."

Richard kissed her finger. "But we have time for one kiss." He set the flowers and CD on a table, and before he could even bring his arms around Claire, she had her hands wrapped around his head and lower back. When she pulled away, she laughed.

"You should've told me you'd planned a romantic morning," she said. "I wouldn't have put on lipstick."

Richard disappeared into the washroom to remove the lipstick stains while Claire carried everything to the back, where she also applied fresh lipstick.

As Claire unwrapped the bouquet—a dozen roses—she remembered Todd's choice of tea for her. What she loved about tea was the many meanings one simple drink could embody for each individual. Black tea with rose petals always had a romantic feel for Claire, and Jan practically treated it like an aphrodisiac. But for Todd, it was about finding hope again.

Claire kept the roses in the back room so their scent wouldn't interfere with anyone sniffing any teas and popped the CD in the shop's player.

But no sooner was Claire singing to one of the songs than she gasped when she opened the fridge to restock the food display case. The fridge was full of food all right, but individually wrapped items from a grocery store. With the bar code and price on.

Richard entered the back room, his face clean. "Shouldn't you close the fridge door? You hate wasting energy."

Claire pulled out a sandwich and closed the fridge. "I think Pauline forgot to order food for today."

"What?" Richard studied the sandwich. "Are they all like that?"

"Seem to be. But why? Didn't our supplier come?"

Claire picked up the shop's landline phone and dialled into voicemail.

"You have seventeen unheard messages. To listen to your messages, press 'one.'"

Claire's jaw dropped. She hung up and faced Richard. "I have no idea. But I can either listen to seventeen messages —"

"Seventeen?"

"Seventeen. Or we can start rewrapping sandwiches."

Richard agreed that they had to use what was there. He began pulling everything out while Claire wiped down the counter with a bleach solution to ensure sanitation. She then found a hair tie under the counter and pulled her hair back. After Richard finished his back-and-forth delivery run, they washed their hands, pulled on latex gloves, and fervently rewrapped all thirty sandwiches.

They finished ten minutes before opening. Claire compared what they had with what was listed on the menu. "I'll need to write up something special for a few of these and add them into the POS system." She clapped a hand on her forehead. "I haven't done that in almost a year."

Richard admitted he was helpless there: buying a house didn't happen via credit or debit card. "But wait, none of that was dessert."

Claire gave him an exasperated look. She continued with the POS system while he double-checked the fridge and reported that they had exactly four brownies and five pumpkin squares.

"See what you can get from the surrounding bakeries," Claire says. "But start with Tracy and Ben. The more discreet we can be about this, the better."

Claire worked the counter alone for the first hour as

Richard popped in and out the back door with desserts. Some customers complained that Richard wasn't around—they were hoping to say hi. Claire did her best to make him sound like the hero he was without throwing Pauline under the bus, but it was difficult. How could Pauline and Todd have forgotten to order food for today?

That must have been why Pauline had come home so late last night: she had been trying to stock up before anyone realized the error. But then why not stay to finish the coverup?

But that wasn't all she noticed. People asked about the tea sale and party, and Claire couldn't find any postcards to hand out. Nothing produced this week? The event was in two weeks!

During the afternoon, Claire and Richard had fun working together filling tea orders, serving customers, selling giftware, sneaking in a kiss now and then. Richard even advised a few customers on home sales and possibly gained a new client.

As foot traffic died down an hour before close, Claire began to clean up. But the lack of preparation for the day worried her and she immediately looked for any sign of completed tasks for the tea sale and party.

Nothing. Not even any invoices with the local papers for ads. Claire checked what she could on the computer—she now regretted her lack of knowledge—and Richard soon stepped in and helped.

Still nothing. No announcements on social media or special orders confirmed via email.

Richard inspected the stock more closely. Full bags had been pulled to the front, hiding many near-empty ones. Claire hadn't noticed that this morning. Pauline had used their height difference to hide what she didn't want Claire to see.

Richard told Claire more of what he'd noticed while she'd been visiting Dawn, like the empty napkin holders and Pauline not entering his sandwich into the system.

"Why didn't you tell me while I was away?"

"I wanted you to have a good time and figured this could wait until you got back."

Talk about feeling out of sync with each other. Had they both said something to the other, some problems could've been solved, or at least reduced.

She needed to get Pauline out of whatever bind she'd found herself in, but she could only work with what she knew. "I'll listen to the voicemail, you check the books. I don't know how to use that software too well."

Claire listened to the seventeen messages while Richard opened the accounting program. All the messages were from this week. Three were from their usual food supplier asking for order confirmations. Claire reported back to Richard.

"It gets worse," Richard said. "They haven't reconciled their books in six months."

Staying on top of the books helped Claire know immediately when things were going poorly.

Upon further investigation, the bank account balance appeared healthy, but the company credit card was almost maxed out. Several payment due dates had been missed. Taken together, that meant Claire couldn't tell if they had enough in the bank.

Richard, who'd also been flipping through and opening a stack of mail he'd found in a filing cabinet drawer, lifted out a notice from the credit card company.

"The interest rate's been raised because of late payments, and here's a stack of unpaid invoices from the past two months."

Within an hour, Claire's worst fears had been confirmed: Pauline and Todd couldn't manage the store on their own, the store with Claire's name on it. That meant she had to step in immediately to fix things before Claire's Tea Shop became a newspaper article with the title, "Who Remembers This Place?"

CHAPTER 26

Richard rubbed his eyes after reviewing the numbers for the tenth time.

"We can't tell Pauline we've figured this all out. It'll humiliate her. I'm certain she's always carried the shop's banner with pride."

Claire picked up his hand-written math notes. "But we can help her get back on her feet. All of us."

Richard rubbed his eyes again. "It's Christmas, Claire. No one's going to have the time." Claire had called in friends to help numerous times over the years. But this wasn't the time to do that. They had to sort this out on their own.

Claire set the notes down and studied a report he'd pulled up on the screen. She let out a deep sigh. "How did I let this happen?"

Richard touched her hand. "You didn't. You gave up responsibility for the shop."

"So long as my name is on that sign, and so long as I'm alive, I have some responsibility for this place."

The back door open, and both startled.

Todd stepped in, a friendly smile on his face. "Pauline and I were worried that you hadn't arrived home yet..." But once he caught what Richard and Claire were reading on the computer, his smile disappeared.

Not too much rattled Richard, but how could a family not ask for help when the ship was slowly sinking?

Claire's mood changed instantly, too. "Like Pauline last night?"

Richard turned around to look at her. What did she mean?

"I knew something was up last night," she explained, "because Pauline came home a full hour and a half after the store closed. I assumed she was just avoiding me because I've been nagging about her health. But it's because she'd forgotten to order food for today, isn't it, Todd?"

So much for not telling Todd and Pauline anything. But at least Richard and Claire didn't have to figure out a good time to talk to them about this.

Claire glowered at Todd. "When were you going to tell me that Pauline wasn't going to hold the tea sale and party for the first time in fifty-one years? Or that neither of you has any idea about the shop's financial shape?"

Todd stared at the ground like a little kid who'd just gotten caught with a mouthful of chocolate. "Eventually."

Richard stepped in before Claire exploded. This shop was truly her lifeblood. To see it not cared for the way she'd expected also hurt him. "It should've been sooner, Todd, because it wasn't until an hour before closing that we figured out the tea party situation, and that led Claire to log into the bookkeeping system."

Claire crossed her arms. "Do you see those plans on the wall that say 'December fifteenth'? That's the date we gave out to easily one hundred people today."

Todd surprised Richard by how he could keep his composure. Only one deep breath showed that he had reacted strongly inside to Claire's words.

"What's going on?" Claire demanded. "The tea shop is low on stock, emails are going unanswered, I just listened to seventeen phone messages—several from creditors, a few from restaurants asking about orders this week—the books haven't been reconciled in six months. You and Pauline are worried about me running this place when it should be the other way around."

Silence filled the back room. Claire had said what she needed to. Now came the part anyone who knew her well dreaded: the wait. Claire simply waited until the person responded, and if they attempted to veer off topic, she gladly reeled them back in.

Todd ran a hand through his hair. "I'll lose the love of my life if I say anything."

"You'll lose your livelihood if this place shuts down because it's being managed poorly. And then try staying in love when neither of you has a job." Claire's eyes burned with anger. "I understand that what she's going through is extremely difficult, but Todd, if you're going to belong to this family, you have to act like it. That means going behind Pauline's back to get help when things are this bad. We love you, and we will do anything to help you—both of you—stay together and run this shop. *But you have to tell us.*"

Claire fell silent again.

Few people in Richard's life could make silence grow louder. His wife was one of them. Those who experienced it became unnerved. Maybe it was the sight of such a small woman commanding so much power. Maybe it was just someone calling them out on behaviours at times when they didn't expect to be called out. Richard's wife had certainly turned many people off over the years with her outspoken personality, but it had also kept the family together.

Todd swallowed, leaned against the wall, and stuck his hands into his pockets. The conflict Richard sensed inside him —listen to Pauline or her mother—was real.

Richard asked the question any Robinson asked when times got tough: "Can I make us all a tea?"

A weak smile on his face, Todd took a deep breath and nodded.

Ten minutes later, they were seated in the lounge area, each with a cup of their favourite tea in hand.

"I've seen depression in performing artists before," Todd said, "obviously including myself. I've seen how hard the transition is to a non-performing career. That's something else I also experienced." He outlined the handle on his teacup. "Pauline helped me through that. She even helped me reconcile with my family. But to see all that affect her now…so harshly…and to feel so helpless in bringing her back to the light? Then she kept saying, 'Don't tell anyone. Don't tell anyone. I'll get through this. I just don't want the attention.' I thought the best way to help her was to honour that request." He took a sip. "But to see what I thought was an indomitable spirit crushed through mental illness…" Todd used the tip of his finger to wipe away tears that were starting to form.

Richard passed him a serviette from the table. "Only without her costumes to hide behind, she hasn't gotten out of it."

"And without a new season to get her excited about again," Claire added.

Richard had felt guilty the night before about not helping his daughters as much as he believed he should, and he had begun taking steps to assuage that guilt. But he needed to do more.

"Claire and I can support you financially for a little until you get back on your feet." After all, that's why he'd had worked so hard all these years, wasn't it? To ensure his family's needs were taken care of?

"Thank you but that's not necessary. We'll—"

"Be fine?" Claire finished for him, her eyes cold as ice. "As of right now, Todd, I'm volunteering three days a week—in addition to our Saturday hours—from three until closing, until Christmas."

"But—"

"You both need the help. You can either work on cleaning things up, or—my preference—head home early and rest and let me get the shop in order. I also recommend asking Sedrick to help clean up the books."

"She's not going to like this."

Richard spoke up. "When someone needs help this badly, Todd, you have to step in. Your job is three-fold. One: help Pauline rest as much as possible. Two: ensure she's following through on physiotherapy. And three: tell her healthcare team that she's in a deep depression and needs psychiatric help."

"I suggested medication to her last night, and she almost bit my head off. She said she 'wasn't that far gone.' Her words."

"Then as someone with a wife who's just as stubborn—" Claire shot Richard a look— "and who I love very much, you have to start asking for help to get past that. It's clear she's not going to come out of this on her own. Talk to Tracy, talk to her surgeon, her physiotherapist, and find her a sports psychologist while you wait for the actual psychiatric referral. Pauline is not the only one who's ever refused medication when it's absolutely necessary."

Todd raised his teacup to his mouth. "I don't know..." He took a long sip.

Claire spoke up. "Both of you have a high level of empathy. Use that to reach her."

"To sum things up," Richard said, "you look after your partner, and you call me at the brokerage anytime you need help with her. Because—and I say this with all the love in the world—when Claire's ready to take care of things, it's best to stay out of the way."

~

BACK AT THE apartment and fully exhausted, Claire collapsed onto the couch. "I know I said I'd volunteer four days a week in total, but I think I should've said six. It's going to take a lot of effort to get the shop out of this mess." The list of tasks had already formed in her mind and continued to grow.

"You'll make it. I know you," Richard said. "But I have some good news on another front: I proposed merging brokerages with Dawn today."

What? Did that mean retirement? It must!

Claire tried to keep calm. Richard had said he'd proposed, not that Dawn had accepted. "How did that go over?"

Richard unwrapped sandwiches they'd purchased from the tea shop and placed them on plates while he explained what had transpired last night at the brokerage. "I wanted to celebrate a little with you this morning but without pulling your focus from the day's plans." He carried the plates to the table.

That meant Richard was pretty certain the merger would happen! *Retirement!* Claire jumped up and wrapped her arms tightly around Richard. "We'll have so much fun together! When is your official retirement date? I know merging two businesses takes time, but you need a firm date to be your goal. How about April thirtieth? Are four months enough? Then we can travel to Asia together!"

Richard pulled back from their embrace. Silence followed. Claire had had enough silence today to last the rest of the year.

Her heart sank as they sat down. "You're not retiring."

Richard leaned forward in his chair. "After everything Pauline's just been through from taking on your shop? Dawn can't go through her family issues and take over the brokerage at the same time. Plus, I love my work."

Claire stared at her plate. "I'm trying to be understanding. Seeing what Pauline's going through because she's no longer in a career she absolutely loves is not something I wish for you." She traced around her plate. "But after enjoying myself so much in Vancouver, I want to see more." She looked up. "I'm flying to Asia next spring, Richard. For at least four weeks. And I want you to join me."

Claire's dream was to see the world with her husband. He could take off a month from a business he'd owned for over thirty years. If he couldn't, then something was wrong with their marriage.

CHAPTER 27

Claire turned around the "Closed" sign.

"Wow," Austin said. "People really don't understand what it means to keep their nose out of your business, do they?"

All day people had asked where Pauline was. Thanks to Claire and Richard's advice, she'd agreed to take the day off since she'd begun it with a physio appointment.

"The downside to being well known in the community is that some people feel your business is their business," Claire said. "Great for marketing, not for privacy. You're sure you can spare a couple extra hours today? I don't want to interfere with your study schedule."

Austin confirmed that he was fine to stay later today and help out. "Mom didn't even suspect that Pauline was this bad. She's feeling guilty for not having been there more."

"She hid it well. I'm just glad we stepped in when we did."

It was six o'clock and therefore already dark outside. Richard said he had to work late today too, and that he'd pick up Claire at eight so she wouldn't have to walk home in the dark.

Claire asked Austin to help her move all the inventory—dozens of bags—to the counter and a few tables opposite it. She could take the half-empty wholesale bags one at a time, but Austin could carry several full bags at once.

"Deadlines are fast approaching to order for Christmas stock," she explained, "and unfortunately, Pauline and Todd stopped updating the stock in the system over the summer, so I can't reorder easily."

As more and more mostly empty bags came out, Claire couldn't believe she hadn't paid closer attention to her shop. *This is no time for self-pity*, she admonished herself. *I've gotten this place out of a bind before. I can do it again.*

About fifteen minutes into their new project, Austin came out holding a medical-grey cane.

"I found this on the top shelf at the back. Is it yours?"

So, Pauline was supposed to have been using a cane, and instead she had hidden it where no one could reach it. "Let's leave it here for now. With any luck, the physiotherapist may have spoken to her today about her not using this. She probably doesn't need it around the apartment since she can sit whenever she wants, but it might come in useful here."

Austin stared at it. "I do kind of get it, though. When your body changes, sometimes you don't want the reminder. Or other people asking. The looks I get from others at birthday parties when they offer me pop and I say no. 'Oh? Why?' I mean, I know I do a lot of advocacy for epilepsy now, but it's not like I want to talk about it *all* the time, you know?"

Jan had spoken to Claire often about how difficult Austin had found his epilepsy diagnosis. It didn't require a cane, but he had had to make some changes in his life, like not drinking caffeine.

"I can appreciate that."

Once all the wholesale bags were laid out in the front, Claire set Austin to work on counting everything, with instructions to note if the bag appeared full, half-full, a quarter-full, or full of dust.

A clipboard and pencil in his hands, Austin pointed his feet along the floor while he made notes. Always the dancer.

Claire carried leftover food from the display case back to the fridge. About a half hour later, Sedrick knocked on the front door, briefcase in hand.

"Hi, Grandpa." Austin gave his snow-covered grandfather a hug and then helped him dust himself off.

Claire remembered all the hugs she'd gotten in Vancouver. It was a wonderful feeling.

Austin returned to his inventory, and Sedrick pointed Claire to the lounge where they could sit comfortably.

After inquiring after Pauline, Sedrick got down to business. "I'm afraid I don't have the best news for you about this shop right now."

"I need to know everything or I can't do anything."

He showed her the financial statements he'd been working on over the past several days. "I only have May to August reconciled so it's possible something might change before I finish."

"I understand. What's going on?"

Sedrick shook his head. "Not only has the tea shop missed several tax payment dates, but Pauline and Todd have been paying themselves from the cash drawer."

"What?"

Sedrick pointed to a few figures, including Owner Draws. "It totals to maybe enough for rent and food, but little else. It wouldn't surprise me if they've been taking home sandwiches for supper—the stock and revenue don't match up. Richard told me that Pauline hadn't recorded his sandwich she gave him, which backs up that suspicion. But when I match up the cash withdrawals from the bank, they're equal to the money missing from the cash."

"I can't imagine how long it's taken you to figure this all out."

"Anything for family, Claire. You know that."

Claire looked at the numbers. "But we're still in a revenue position, right?"

"I think so. But I can't confirm that until I've done up to October."

"When you're done, I'll handle November."

Sedrick offered to stay on board until January, but Claire didn't want to take any more advantage of his time than she already had. Richard had been right: it was Christmas and Sedrick had commitments to family and friends. Besides, keeping detailed track of everything would give her a better idea of what kind of plan to suggest to Pauline next year. If Claire could use her experience to help Pauline prioritize more effectively, then Pauline might find a better balance between administration—where she could sit—and serving.

At least the tea shop wasn't on the verge of bankruptcy. But if Claire and Richard hadn't stepped in when they had, Pauline —as the business owner—would have missed important government deadlines, which would have resulted in hefty fines. Not to mention the creditors asking for payment. And since Pauline didn't have a huge asset like a house to use as collateral for credit, she'd have a hard time borrowing more money.

This could have spelled disaster. *Eventually*, Claire thought dryly, recalling Todd's answer to her Saturday.

"This makes no sense," Claire said. "The money's there. Maybe not enough to pay both of them full salaries, but there's no need for all this mess."

Sedrick sighed and leaned back in the armchair. "Depression makes no sense. I've seen it often over the years before a business shuts down. In the old days, we called it—"

Claire knew the exact word. "Laziness."

Sedrick nodded. "But when I used to work for the regional small business centre, I saw instances where a business consultant was able to successfully intervene before it got too far, and then things would turn around, often for the better. As long as the business owner got the right kind of treatment for themselves."

That left Claire a lot more hopeful.

Austin approached cautiously with the inventory list, and Claire beckoned for him to join them. "I think it's important for you to see what happens in the adult world when depression hits and you don't ask for help."

Austin's eyes grew sad. "Working with Todd to keep these photos up was the best I could think of, but I know she hates them. Pauline stood behind me last year. She changed my life. I just really wish there was something more I could do that wouldn't hurt her so much."

"You're helping with the sale," Claire said. "That's already a big relief. And you're helping with the inventory."

He handed her the inventory list with all two hundred and seventeen teas. "You're low on quite a bit."

Claire reviewed the list with Sedrick and asked if he thought they'd have enough cash flow to fill up.

"Technically, yes," Sedrick said, "but only if you sell it at full price."

If there was one thing that kept Claire's Tea Shop customers coming back all these years, it was that Claire had achieved the right balance of consistency and change. This sale would run as expected. But some of the teas that sold poorly could probably wait until next year to be restocked. A little shortage would encourage customers to come back sooner.

"I'll prepare the order at home tonight. Austin, how are your plans coming for the sale?"

"Terrific. Anything to make Pauline feel better," he said. "She turned my life around."

Claire could wrap that kid up in a bear hug. Such a big heart.

"Let's start by throwing out the empty bags and filling up the jars."

Austin pulled his heels together so his feet turned out, and saluted. "Aye, aye, captain."

Claire shook her head and laughed. She was going to set things straight if it took every last ounce of strength. Besides, she'd have her and Richard's trip to Asia in the spring to recuperate.

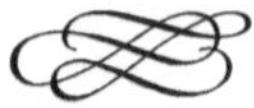

CHAPTER 28

Claire and Richard waited outside the door of Pauline and Todd's apartment.

"What's taking so long?" Claire asked.

"Maybe they're tidying up?"

"Pauline?"

When Todd opened the door and invited them in, Pauline's absence was the first thing Claire noticed. The second was that the bedroom door was closed.

"Is she okay?" Claire asked.

Todd nodded. "She's taking a nap."

Claire raised an eyebrow, and Todd gave an unconvincing smile.

Clearly, these kids had forgotten how to lie effectively to their parents.

"Maybe we should just go back to our apartment and leave them alone," Richard said. "It's getting late. She might be tired from her physio this morning."

Normally, Claire would agree. But given everything she had learned—and missed—she'd become very concerned about her oldest daughter's condition. She wasn't leaving until she saw that Pauline was doing all right.

She sat down on the couch, and Richard and Todd followed suit, both uneasy in their own ways.

"What did the physiotherapist say?" Claire asked.

Todd twiddled his thumbs in his lap. "I don't really know if she wants me to talk about that."

Claire was very empathetic, just like them, but her years of experience had taught her how to listen from a little distance. It seemed Todd and Pauline didn't have that ability, at least not with each other.

"This evening, Austin discovered the cane Pauline is supposed to be using. Whatever she's been trying to do isn't working. You can't look after her by yourself, Todd. We talked about that Saturday."

Richard lay a hand on her thigh. "Maybe just helping out at the shop is enough," he said. "I'm sure Pauline would like some peace and quiet as she sorts things out."

Claire removed his hand. "She was in good spirits Monday and Tuesday, and now she won't talk to me. I refuse to ignore what's going on in front of me. Todd, we're her parents. Every detail of her personal health isn't mine and Richard's business, but if we know the basics, we can help. I'm certain of it. And… we just need to know."

Todd glanced nervously toward the bedroom door.

"For starters," Claire continued, "I assume she's not taking a nap this close to bedtime."

Todd shook his head.

"Then let us help, Todd. Please. She's our daughter."

Todd took a deep breath, let it out, and nodded his agreement. "The physiotherapist said she's supposed to be using her cane, since walking still hurts." He raked his fingers through his hair, and his face turned red. "There was also something else, but it's, well, a bit awkward for me to talk about."

They were already discussing the difficulties of depression. What else could cause more discomfort than that?

She leaned forward. "I want you to feel comfortable enough in this family to talk to us about anything."

Todd stared at his lap. "The physiotherapist...mentioned, well, that, um, Pauline might be going through...what did she call it? Perimenopause. She said recent research says hormonal changes can affect mood." Todd let out a nervous laugh.

Ah. Women's hormones. Now Claire understood. But she could also imagine what Pauline's reaction to that had been.

Todd continued. "Pauline said, 'I'm not my hormones.' And, um, I'm not really sure what to do."

Even Richard looked away now. What was it with these men? Hormones were hormones. Not talking about women aging was one of the main reasons women often suffered in silence during this period of their lives.

Of course, for Richard and Claire's generation, talking about anything of this nature made many—men and women alike—very uncomfortable. A woman's sexual side—whether sex itself or her hormones—was viewed as inappropriate discussion. Yet how many commercials had Claire seen over the years for products and services that promised to reduce, eliminate, or even reverse men's receding hairlines? Not to mention the drugs that existed so aging men could still enjoy sex.

How were women supposed to age? By using wrinkle creams, hair colour, and makeup. Fine, some commercials for men's hair colour existed, but one look at a drug store aisle made the main target market for hair dye clear.

And women's hair also thinned during and after menopause, yet Claire didn't know of any reliable products that could treat that. All she had known back in the day, if she could find out anything at all, was that osteoporosis was a real danger and that she needed to take calcium pills. Her doctor—also a woman—had even recommended that she not take hormone replacement therapy, because it was only for the worst cases.

"We're done treating menopause as a disease," she had said. "It's just a normal part of a woman's life. We just have to grin and bear it."

So, Claire had suffered several years with hot flashes and horrible sleep, not to mention mood swings that she now understood had been part of menopause when she'd assumed it had been her inability to deal with life and business issues. But without the Internet then, and certainly without any desire to be seen borrowing or buying books on the topic, Claire had only her friends to talk to and her mother.

"Todd, can I talk to her? Please?"

He glanced in the direction of the bedroom door, seemed to think for a moment, and then nodded.

Claire gently knocked on the door. "Pauline?" When no one answered, she opened it a crack. Pauline rolled over on her bed so that only her back showed to Claire.

"My honey, we need to talk about your appointment this morning."

Pauline didn't respond. Claire closed the door behind her and approached her daughter. She heard a sniffle.

"Todd told us because I guilted him into it. Don't be angry at him, please."

A tiny, tiny nod of the head. Good. She was listening.

"No woman likes to feel like she's being reduced to a pile of hormones, but they can play havoc with us nonetheless. Did the physiotherapist say how perimenopause might be affecting you?"

Pauline nodded.

"Did she say depression might be part of it?"

Pauline nodded again.

Claire gently rubbed her daughter's back. After a few minutes, Pauline turned around, her eyes red. She spoke through sniffles. "She said that estrogen, progesterone, and even testosterone affect chemicals in the brain. And that…that I'm going through a lot of changes." She wiped her eyes. "She sees depression in…in a lot of athletes…and…former athletes. But with the change in my career…and my surgery…I can't seem to keep my head above water." Pauline covered her eyes as she cried.

So much change for such an open, giving person. How could Pauline be herself if she didn't feel like herself? "You know, when I was your age, I had depressive episodes, too. So did my mother. I'd hoped that maybe your dad's genes would be able to pass on something that would make it easier. But I see genetics aren't on our side here."

Pauline sobbed some more. "When am I going to feel better?"

Claire stroked her daughter's hair. "One step at a time. Come out and sit with us—we're all family and we love you very much. I'll make whatever tea you want to get your mind off things. But first thing tomorrow, call the family doctor to talk over perimenopause with her. And tell the receptionist it's urgent. I'm going to call you at ten tomorrow morning, and I expect to find out when your appointment is."

Pauline nodded.

"Now, freshen up and join us. You get your energy from being around others. Holing up in here by yourself won't make things any better."

Pauline sat up, her eyes still wet. "I didn't plan the sale because…because everyone wanted things to be the same as last year…and I would've done that, like I've kept everything else the same…but I can't make them happy."

Claire wrapped an arm around her daughter's big shoulders. "You're your own person. Be yourself. People will come to see *you*." She gave her a squeeze. "Todd loves you with his whole heart, and Dawn's coming Sunday, so the two of you can hang out a little."

"Dawn's coming? Because of me?"

"It's for…work. But I think it's good timing for you to hang out with each other."

"But Destiny's drawing…"

Claire gave her daughter another gentle squeeze. "I told Dawn what had happened—so she knew what to expect when she came—but we both agreed to tell Destiny that it accidentally blew away in the wind when you carried it to the shop. Dawn's bringing another one."

Pauline nodded and wiped her eyes. "I owe Dad an apology. And you. What I've done to the shop…" She cried anew. "I couldn't live up to everyone's expectations."

Claire faced her daughter square on. "You owe no one any such thing. You are going through so much right now, my honey, and we're here to support you every step of the way. I know relying on others isn't easy for you, but it gets easier with time. To start with, I'm going to run the shop full time until Christmas. You and Todd will only come in if you want to work the counter for a few hours to be around people."

Pauline wiped her face and nodded again.

Claire stood up and kissed the top of her daughter's head. She held back her own tears and smiled instead to show Pauline she was loved. The last thing Pauline needed was another person's sadness on her shoulders.

She'd shouldered far too much in her life.

CHAPTER 29

*R*ichard was already twenty minutes late for his joint shift with Claire. But a client needed to meet with him. He'd at least aimed to be at the shop an hour before it opened.

Now he was rushing.

Richard pushed the button for the crosswalk across the road from the tea shop and waited for it to change. He glanced at his watch. Twenty-two minutes late. He hated disappointing his wife. Now that she was working full time again, he wanted to help her however he could. For family.

As he peered across the street, he couldn't see anyone in the store other than Claire. What had happened to the line-ups from previous weekends?

The orange crosswalk lights flashed, and Richard hurried across the street. When he entered the shop, he was indeed greeted by an angry wife.

"You were supposed to help me open in case we had another emergency on our hands—which we don't, thank goodness. Todd has been helpful with looking after ordering from home.

But I still need you."

Claire was back in charge to help, which was great, but Richard was trying his best, too.

He whipped off his jacket—even though the store was empty—and hung it up in the back room. "I'm sorry. A client needed some information on a house, so we met early this morning. And I may need to leave early for a viewing."

"Figures."

Richard let out a sigh. "I'm doing my best, Claire. I can't let ten or twelve thousand dollars slip through my fingers."

"So because your business earns more than mine, you can't keep your commitments? We need to fulfill our promises to our customers."

Richard clenched his jaw. Obviously, he understood that. But a real estate agent worked seven days a week. Claire should understand that.

"Please don't do this," he said. "You know the tight spot I'm in right now."

"Don't do what?"

"Comparing whose situation is more important—usually yours."

Before Claire could reply, a customer walked in, and both turned on their professional personas.

"I'm glad you're open. I tried to get into the Christkindl market, but it was so packed, there was no way I was going to do my Christmas shopping there."

"We appreciate you stopping by," Claire said.

The customer purchased only a few packages of tea, but at least it was some business.

When he left, Claire pointed at Richard's head. "You don't have your Santa hat on."

Richard had left it off on purpose. He felt the complete opposite of jolly. Pauline had clinical depression and…women's issues… And what about Dawn? She hadn't felt comfortable coming to him for help either. Everyone talked to Santa. No one, it appeared, talked to Richard.

"Can't say as I'm in the mood for it."

Now somewhat calmed down after that customer visit, Claire took Richard's hand in both of hers. "I know it's hard to be the cheerleader when the cheerleader of the family is down. You could put it on, and we could take a few funny photos and send them to her. Like you and I did when you tried pickleball with Sedrick, and Jan and I went shopping."

If he didn't put on the hat, Claire would ask what was wrong. *You're only helping out for three more Saturdays*, he thought. *And if the client calls, then you simply have to leave.*

The only thing that was certain in his life right now was that selling homes provided for everyone. He enjoyed spending time with Claire and helping a family business, but real estate did bring in more money. Merging the two brokerages would allow him to work, still support his community, and give him more time with Claire.

She smiled when he joined her at the front again, this time with the Santa hat on. She gave him a peck on the cheek. "You always look so good in that."

On the other hand, if wearing that hat kept her smiling, he'd reconsider his opposition.

Claire pulled out her phone from under the counter. "Ready?"

They stuck their tongues out at the camera and gave each other funny kisses. For a moment, it felt like they were completely in tune with each other. But ever since Claire had returned to the shop, Richard felt like less of a couple. The feeling intensified with her full-time hours these past couple of days.

How did that happen? Their work schedules were back to

the way they used to be. Shouldn't that mean that their relationship should be back on track, too?

Claire sent a few of the phots to Pauline. Five minutes later, she received a short video of Todd turning on the spot, one hand on his hip, while Pauline appeared to be "stirring" him with a wooden spoon.

Mixing my hot toddy, she'd texted.

So, her mood had lifted. Even for a moment. Claire's suggestion about the photos had been right.

After another disappointing half hour of no foot traffic, Claire announced she'd make herself a tea and wondered if Richard wanted one.

Richard declined: he'd grabbed a coffee at the brokerage.

"I've been reading up more on Japan and even China," Claire said. "I really need to explore green teas. I only started stocking them because of their supposed health benefits and because customers wanted them. But I should be paying more attention to their quality and varieties like I do with black and oolong teas."

Asia again. Claire hadn't mentioned it since last Saturday, so Richard had assumed that she'd let the idea drop. When she got excited about something, Clare couldn't stop talking about it. Besides, with everything going on with the family, it wouldn't be right for the two of them to even consider a trip somewhere in the spring. They had no idea what condition their family would be in.

But maybe Richard was jumping to conclusions. Maybe she truly had just meant that she wanted to investigate green teas more.

It was best to ask.

"So you don't want to travel to Asia in the spring any more?"

Claire's eyes grew wide with excitement. "I most definitely

do! I dropped by Mayumi's Wednesday before coming in to get some advice on Japanese teas—she's given me her mother's phone number and email address, since Mayumi doesn't drink hot teas all that often—and she told me more about the cherry blossoms. Japan just explodes with them in the spring. It's so beautiful that there are festivals everywhere."

Cherry blossoms? Lots of people had cherry trees here. Wasn't that enough?

"With everything that's going on in our family, don't you think it's best to stay here?"

Claire adjusted a stack of dishes behind the counter. "Not at all. If our kids are doing so poorly that we can't leave for a month, then that means they need more help than you or I can provide. And if they're doing well, which I expect they will be, then we'll be fine to travel."

These ideas of Claire's were starting to go too far. Ignore her family to feed some new desire to travel?

"I have to disagree with you there. Quite strongly, in fact. A parent's place is by their children's side."

Claire stood up straight. "How do you expect us to look after everyone if we don't look after ourselves?"

"Going for a weekly walk, getting an extra massage… I think I'm going to join Sedrick at pickleball. Those things also let us look after ourselves without abandoning our family for a month. We're parents. We need to stick by our kids."

"Excuse me? Please remind me again which of us had the children at work when they were young? I have always stuck by my kids. You're the one who hides at work."

Richard backed down. What was he thinking? Of course, Claire had taken excellent care of both girls in their childhoods. Richard had learned that the best way to look after others was to ensure everyone had enough money to be fed and live in a functioning house. He happily spent time with his girls, but he was most useful at work. Something else he couldn't say without making it sound like his business was more important than hers. That conversation when he'd arrived hadn't gone well.

"I just want to make sure everyone's okay," he said.

"And I don't?"

"That's not what I said."

"You implied it, Richard."

"That's not it at all. I…I just don't want to travel that far away from anyone." He sighed. "If I could wave a magic wand, I'd move Dawn's family back here so she's closer."

Claire's eyes narrowed. "Since when did you start controlling everyone's dreams?"

Richard threw his Santa hat onto the counter. "Stop twisting my words, Claire." He marched into the back room, re-emerging with his jacket. "I'm not trying to control anyone's dreams. I'm just terrified something's going to happen to someone and I won't be there to help."

Richard was tired of defending himself against Claire's dreams. Why wasn't it enough to dream that your family would be healthy and well cared for? Or to dream that he'd grow old enough to watch his grandchildren achieve their dreams?

THE AFTERNOON only saw a handful of customers, and Claire was certain the Christmas market at city hall had something to do with it. That market habitually attracted tens of thousands of people in one weekend. At the very least, it gave her time to solidify plans for next week's tea sale and party and come up with a new tea blend. Pauline's notes had said, "Tea of Joy," but Claire wanted something more elaborate. Anyone could take a package of black tea and drop a cinnamon stick in it. But it was all she could come up with fifty-one years ago.

How could Richard not see what he was doing? Yes, it would be nice to have Dawn and her family here, but they lived in Vancouver. Claire and Richard could easily take the time to visit them more often. It was their job as parents to support their children's dreams—that Pauline hadn't found a new one bothered Claire. *That* was what made her feel like a failure: she hadn't helped Pauline see a new way in life.

Claire shook her head at Richard and referred to her to-do lists in the black binder. The remaining tea stock would arrive Monday. Thankfully Pauline had scheduled social media from home. Postcards, which Ben had quickly designed, were being handed out every day. Austin said his plans were falling into place, too.

But a pleasant surprise walked through the door an hour before close: Pauline, leaning a little on Todd.

Claire hurried around the counter to give their daughter a hug. "It's so good to see you out!" Claire said.

Pauline, still a slight limp in her gait, walked with Todd over to a chair, where she sat down. "I wanted to get out for a little, and I thought I'd update you on what the doctor told me yesterday and how things are going." Pauline looked around. "Where's Dad?"

"He had to go into work." Pauline didn't need to know that her parents were arguing. She had enough worries on her mind.

"Oh. But we've been advertising…"

"I know. And he's been here both other Saturdays. But today's really quiet, anyway." Claire clapped her hands together. "So? How'd it go yesterday? I didn't want to interrupt your evening, in case…" Claire let the rest go unsaid. *In case I mess things up again* were her actual thoughts.

"You wouldn't have," Pauline said. "The doctor was

convinced that I'm deep in perimenopause. She prescribed me hormones—a low dose to start—and asked me to report back to her if anything felt uncomfortable after a week. I have to admit, I'm already feeling a little lighter. Still down, but…" She smiled at Todd. "Better." Pauline looked around. "We thought we'd drop by to tell you before we head out to dinner and a movie tonight. For which I'll need my cane."

Smiling, Claire retrieved Pauline's walking aid from the back room.

"And I wanted to ask you something, Mom."

Claire sat down. "Anything, my honey."

Pauline swallowed. "I told the doctor everything. She's going to try and find a psychiatrist for me, even if we have to drive to Toronto. But she wants me in therapy as soon as possible and to also take time off where I can. At the same time, she also said I need to find ways to continue doing what I love. So…"

Pauline showed her mother a photo on her phone, asked her a few questions, and Claire happily agreed.

CHAPTER 30

Richard paced nervously back and forth while they awaited Dawn's arrival.

"What is with you?" Claire asked. "The plane landed fifteen minutes ago."

"Maybe something's happened…what if it missed the runway…?"

Claire stared at him. "Missed the runway? Richard, we would've heard about that by now. She's fine. It takes time to disembark. You know that."

But Richard wouldn't be able to settle until he saw his daughter safe and sound.

Claire leaned into him and whispered, "You're making people nervous."

Richard glanced around, and several people turned their heads away from him quickly, as though hoping he didn't see they'd been watching.

He stood still. Then he started pressing his fingers together. *Where was she?*

While he was thinking about one daughter, he might as well

think about the other. Claire said Pauline had seemed happy today at the shop, but what if side effects from her …medication…affected her and she wasn't telling them about it? Richard had no idea about those medications. He tried looking up what Pauline might be on, but he couldn't figure out which of the several options was hers.

The side effects looked appalling: increased chances for heart attack, stroke, blood clots… How did women live with these dangers in the back of their mind? How did she sleep knowing all that?

Would she wake up in the morning?

Then he remembered that age was a risk factor, and since Pauline was starting this therapy at her age and not in her sixties, her risks for some of those problems decreased.

But there were always exceptions, weren't there?

He checked his phone. Maybe she'd texted that she needed help and he hadn't responded—

"Richard," Claire said. "You're sweating." She touched his forehead. "Are you okay?"

He wiped his forehead with the back of his glove and nodded. "I'm fine."

Fortunately, Dawn exited the doors at that moment. Richard's heart rate slowed down. She was safe. He might have worried less if it hadn't been a midnight landing.

After tight hugs, Dawn asked, "How is she?"

They headed toward the exit. "A little better," Claire said. "She's taking a week off."

Dawn placed a hand on her chest and let out a breath. "Thank goodness. Then maybe we need to change our plans a little. What if Dad and I postponed talking about the brokerage, and I just helped Pauline and Todd as much as I can? Things can wait, can't they, Dad?"

Richard's heart sped back up. "We have a lot to discuss," he said. "And I think your mother said it'd be good for Pauline to work a little, be around people. She could go into the tea shop for a couple of hours."

Claire pushed open the door and held it for the other two. The night sky was crystal clear, and the air crisp and cold.

"I'm also fine if she takes the full week off. Dawn's here for a few days. I think Pauline would find it refreshing to have her sister to herself for a little," Claire said.

"I'd love to spend time with her. Almost every time I'm in town, it's with the whole brood, and with Pauline's last job...I feel like I've seen her more since she moved back to town than I have in the past ten years."

Luggage wheels bumping along on pavement took up the space where the conversation had been. Richard needed to know how things for his brokerage were going to move forward. He needed to know *now*. Everything else had changed so much these past few weeks, one reassurance would be welcome. Knowing the future was one of the reasons he liked real estate. Yes, the market took a dive from time to time, but people would always need a place to live.

"I'm sure you'll want a few breaks yourself," he said to his younger daughter. "We don't have to spend full days sorting things out, and with the brokerage so close to our apartments, it'll be easy for you to step away for an hour or two."

Claire glared at him. "You always find a way to work."

Once everyone was in the car, the conversation continued.

"Todd's been dealing with Pauline's depression for months," Claire said. "Are you really so married to your work that you can't let it go for a few days? A few days, Richard?"

"I just think Dawn needs to make the right decision for her business. That's all. She's made the effort to come here to take an initial look."

Dawn leaned forward from the back seat. "Everyone's tired. Why don't we just go to the apartment and get some sleep?"

Richard agreed as he carefully drove out of the airport parking lot. But a few minutes into the drive, when Richard looked in the rear-view mirror to check for oncoming traffic, he saw tears in Dawn's eyes.

"Dawn? What's wrong?"

Claire looked in the rear-view mirror, too.

Dawn wiped her tears. "I tried talking to Pauline a few times this week and she wouldn't say more than a few words. Usually, she'd talk my ear off." She took in a deep breath and let it out. "I'm just scared I won't be able to help her."

Claire turned around and reached for their daughter's hand. "She's taking medication for perimenopause. She's not out of the woods yet—she's also undergone major life changes—but I know she's looking forward to seeing you. And don't forget, we're going to the Christkindl market for a couple of hours this afternoon. She loves that."

Richard agreed. And now that he'd been driving for at least ten minutes, his own fears had calmed. Where had they come from? Of course, Pauline would sleep well tonight.

Was he the one losing his mind instead?

KITCHENER CITY HALL LOOKED MAGICAL, all decked out in Christmas decorations for the Christkindl market. The area outside was filled with little wooden cabins of vendors selling everything from toques and mitts to food. The inside would be even more Christmassy.

"Apple fritters!" Pauline yelled, drawing attention from those around her. But instead of feeling embarrassed, like Claire would have, she engaged with them. "They're amazing, aren't they?" Some nodded, one man held up his box with a grin, and others smiled.

Claire couldn't tell if Pauline's new medication was responsible for this excitement, or if it was an upward mood swing. Only time would tell. But for the moment, Pauline was back to her old self. Claire remembered the time, on a family conference call, when they had heard Pauline getting an entire subway station in Toronto to cheer for the Peregrines during the playoffs.

She truly had no fear around people, which had made seeing her checked out in her bed, ignoring every person around her, so hard to watch.

"Why don't Todd, Dawn, and I wait in line for the fritters, and you two walk around and see what else you'd like to eat or drink?" Pauline offered.

"Are you okay?" Richard asked. "Shouldn't you maybe sit down to rest? You don't want to overexert yourself."

Pauline eyed her father the very same way she had as a teenager, which gave Claire a good laugh. "Dad, we're good."

But Richard looked quite hurt at Claire's reaction.

A squeal startled Claire. She turned to where several teen girls were pointing at Todd. Her hand on her heart to calm herself, she asked him, "Why do I feel like you're more famous after retirement?"

Todd smiled as he acknowledged the girls. "I'm starting to get the same impression." To Dawn and Pauline he said, "I'll meet you in line."

Did Claire see a moment of hurt on Pauline's face? Based on what she'd asked Claire at the shop before heading out for a date night, Claire guessed yes. Often in the past, such attention would've been for her.

Hopefully, we can make her dream come true. In a safe way, she thought.

Plans were set to meet up again in a half hour.

Claire glanced around at the cabins outside but shivered. "I need items for the prize gift baskets for Saturday. Let's see what's inside. I'm already frozen to the bone."

"Sure," Richard said.

They headed first indoors, to the city hall rotunda. Tables and displays seemed to fill every nook and cranny in the spacious area, with vendors selling arts, crafts, baked goods, German entertainment, and...

"A trip! Richard, we could win a free trip to Germany!" Claire rushed over to the table and entered their names into the draw.

When she rejoined him, he said, "Please don't run off like that. I can't get to you fast enough."

"Excuse me?"

"There are tons of people in here. What if someone bumps into you and knocks your cane out from under you?"

"Then I'll fall and someone will help me, and we'll look after things at that point. You don't have me on a leash, Richard."

"That's not what I mean."

"But that's what I'm hearing."

They headed for the elevator.

"There's nothing wrong with caring for others," he said.

"Until you start to muffle their voice."

Did Richard just roll his eyes at her? Claire didn't want to ask in the crowd: the conversation was already getting too personal to have in public.

They took the elevator to the second floor where more Christmas greeted them. Claire found a few bath-and-beauty items at one vendor, some lovely Christmas ornaments at another, and wooden toy cars and trucks she thought would go great in a kids' prize basket along with Nutcracker Prince Tea.

Next to the wooden-toy stand was a European baker. Claire asked to have a few items explained to her before she made a decision.

"I've never had poppy seed strudel or walnut strudel," she said. "They look delicious. Should we get them?"

Richard nodded, although he didn't seem enthused. "How about these sugar cookies, too? Something familiar?"

Familiar? Or boring?

Claire didn't want to be rude in front of the vendor, so she took those, too, and paid for everything.

"Any gifts for the family?" Richard asked.

"We're already done with Dawn's family. I don't know about Pauline and Todd yet, to be honest. I'm more focused on the shop right now. We're advertising big gift baskets as prizes, and I'd like there to be more in there besides tea and tea wares."

They returned to the main floor where Claire stopped by some artisanal jewellers. She picked up a pair of Christmas earrings for herself, and then selected several more pieces of jewellery for the gift baskets.

As they left the rotunda for the cold outdoors again, she asked, "Are you all right? You're not saying much."

Richard shrugged. "I guess I was hoping to spend time as a family together today. Instead, we split up, and you're working."

Claire stopped in the middle of the crowd. "I wanted unique, ideally handmade items to add to the gift baskets. If I have a reason to support local vendors, I'll use it."

"Fine. Just please stop complaining about my work schedule."

"Excuse me? Your work schedule? I'm helping out at the tea shop while Pauline gets better. It's temporary. You're still working full time with no plans to retire. Don't start comparing our situations as though they were equal."

Richard pressed his lips together and continued walking toward the doors.

Since when were their situations the same? Claire couldn't figure out her husband, and after fifty years, that scared her.

CHAPTER 31

The next morning, Jaya's father, Wayne, smoked a cigarette outside Richard's childhood home while he, his wife, Richard, and Dawn waited for Jaya, her husband and son.

Richard's grandfather and uncle had smoked. He could see them sitting on the porch, his grandfather leaning back in his chair, the cigarette always held between his fingers, and his uncle casually leaning forward so he could easily tap the ashes into the tray.

"What's it like knowing you're selling homes to three generations of one family?" Wayne asked.

Richard and Wayne knew each other well as far as client-realtor relationships went. Wayne's father had been one of Richard's first clients, back before Richard and Claire had met. He'd passed away sometime ago. Wayne had two older sisters, who had also signed on with Richard at various times over the past thirty-some-odd years. When Richard could help multiple members of a family find the right home for their stage in life multiple times, a deep sense of satisfaction fuelled him through all the rejections a realtor encountered.

Richard smiled at Dawn. "Unbelievable. It's something I hope Dawn experiences."

Dawn beamed back at him. "So do I."

"Father and daughter. So wonderful. I wish even one of my kids had followed in my footsteps. Instead, one's in computer sciences, and this one is a journalist."

Wayne was a tool-and-dye maker.

"How long has this house been on the market?" he asked.

Richard checked his notes. "Forty-three days." He should've known that off the top of his head. "Old homes can take some time to sell because of all the upkeep needed. But this one had its roof replaced five years ago, and the windows..." He checked again. "Twelve years ago. So they're relatively modern by today's standards."

He should've known those details, too. Richard absorbed the details of any house he showed within mere minutes. It was simply a matter of remembering if a house had the common benefits and problems of its generation and noting the exceptions where it didn't.

Jaya arrived a minute later with Alain, her husband, and her son, whose name Richard didn't know.

Once inside, Richard apologized for the smell of smoke. "It's hard to get out of walls, unfortunately."

Jaya took an extra whiff. "No, that's my father you're smelling."

Wayne's wife, Madhura, walked away from her husband, toward a wall, also took a whiff, and nodded in agreement. "This house smells clean, unlike ours." She shot her husband a look of disdain.

It was happening again. Richard believed he'd prepared

himself mentally for this visit. His cheeks heated up. "My apologies. Didn't mean to insult you, Wayne."

Wayne clapped Richard on the back. "I'd quit if I could, but when you've been smoking since you were thirteen…" He shrugged.

Jaya and Alain were almost certain that they wanted to purchase the house. They just wanted to walk through it once more with her parents and son to make sure.

This house shouldn't be haunting me like this, he thought.

"Mom, Dad, can you see us all opening Christmas gifts here and celebrating Diwali in the backyard?" Jaya asked.

"It's a lovely house," Dawn said. "Charming, lots of personality, but kept up really well."

Jaya nodded. "Those were my impressions on my first visit. Alain, come see the kitchen."

They stepped into the small kitchen, with its modernized, white quartz countertops and stainless steel appliances.

Richard heard two kinds of sweeping: the short, slow strokes of a five-year-old whose mother had taught him the chore as soon as he could hold a broom, and the swift, long strokes of a woman — his grandmother — in her fifties. He associated comfort and friendliness with the sweeping, not the feeling most kids had to chores. Richard couldn't pinpoint the reason for the impression, though.

"What do you think, Richard?" Alain asked.

Not again. Why couldn't these memories just leave him be?

"I'm sorry, I didn't hear the question. Momentarily distracted." He caught a look of concern from Dawn.

Wayne studied Richard for a moment but didn't say anything.

"I asked if the neighbours would be accepting of Diwali celebrations," Wayne said. "The properties in the old neighbourhoods are so close together."

Jaya waved her father's concern away. "Like I said, Dad, they never complain during Canada Day or Victoria Day. What's one more day? Besides, this little guy…" She patted her son's head. "Still goes to bed early."

"It's not like everyone stops backyard fireworks at nine at night on other holidays, anyway," Alain said.

Except for Doris, Richard thought. He didn't know where in the neighbourhood she lived, but she'd certainly complain about any noise at any time of day.

Jaya walked to the front bay window in the living room, and her son followed. "Can you imagine a big Christmas tree standing right here, with all the lights and ornaments?" Her eyes seemed aglow at the images her mind was conjuring up.

"It would be beautiful," Dawn agreed. She grazed her hand across the old, wooden mantel, which now had a gas fireplace installed below. "And Christmas stockings here."

Richard tried to smile when he spoke. "Just make sure to leave room for the craft projects from school that they expect you to hang on your tree. Trust me, I speak from experience."

Dawn shot him a playful look. "You said you loved those."

"And we did! They just took up a lot of room." He tried to make the memory of their family tree larger in his mind so it would crowd out the memories from his childhood. He pictured their artificial tree in the living room of his and Claire's first family home. In kindergarten, the girls had made ornaments out of an outline of their handprint, pasted onto a white doily and then a Christmas-coloured paper plate. In grade one, popsicle sticks formed a frame that each child glued a photo onto. In grade two—

"I think we'll get our first one from junior kindergarten this year!"

Jaya startled Richard, her eyes full of excitement as she

gazed down on her son. "It's a big window, isn't it?" she asked. He nodded vigorously.

That window doesn't bring back your parents, just so you know, Richard thought. "Shall we go upstairs?" The memories of the Robinson family Christmas tree had vanished.

The young boy bolted up the staircase in excitement.

Wayne surveyed the main floor one more time before heading up. "Don't you think you'll want a washroom on the main floor of your home?"

Alain shook his head. "I'll be designing a new edition in a couple of years, anyway. We can add a powder room then."

The boy's family followed him upstairs, but Dawn held her father back.

"What's wrong? You look lost in thought, and not in a good way."

If Richard said anything about what was going through his mind, he'd begin to cry. *And with my age, they'll think I've gone senile.*

"I'm fine, it's okay. Just thinking of the many things I have to do this afternoon."

Dawn nodded. "I can relate."

The tour continued, but the longer they stayed, the more Richard needed to check his notes and deal with concerned looks from Dawn. No matter how much he tried to bury these wayward stories that kept surfacing, they kept dancing around in his mind, ghosts of Christmases past returning to taunt him. What was the point of reliving so much sadness this late in life?

"Which room's mine?" the boy asked.

Mine, Richard almost replied, the word fortunately getting stuck in his throat. The boy's exuberance contrasted starkly to whatever young emotions the second floor had reawakened in Richard.

When Richard showed the large room again, grief struck

him. It hadn't bothered him last time, so why now? Could the smell of one cigarette open such a large box of unwelcome recollections? Richard was twelve by the time that room had become empty. His grandfather had died of a stroke, and his grandmother after a hip fracture caused too much blood loss while she was home alone and everyone was gone for the day.

A hip fracture. How could I forget that?

He had gotten his first job—paper boy for the local daily—soon after this to support himself as much as possible. His uncle wanted to ensure someone was home for Richard every evening, so he quit his second job. Richard's income from selling papers went to clothing for himself and occasional treats.

"Richard?" Wayne asked.

Damnit.

"You all right, man?"

Everyone save for Wayne and Dawn had already moved back downstairs.

Richard nodded. "I'm so sorry. Too much going on right now. It's not an excuse, just a reason." He refused to dump any of this on clients, no matter how long he'd known them for.

He met everyone on the main floor, where Jaya was still staring out the front window, her son's head tucked into her hip. "I love it."

"Why don't you think about it some more?" Wayne said. "These century homes require a lot of work. Let's at least have lunch over it?"

Richard nodded. "A smart decision. The agent hasn't told me about any offers on the table currently—it's a hard sell because of its age."

He led the family back out to the front, and after they drove off, Dawn spoke. "What was going on in there? Are you okay? Do we need to get you to a doctor?"

Richard shook his head. "I'm fine, Dawn. I promise."

"You spaced out, Dad, multiple times. Does Mom know about this?"

"Trust me. I'm fine." Big boys didn't cry about past hurts.

Richard reached again for the passenger door for Dawn, but Dawn took hold of the handle. "I'm driving. Something's wrong with you, and I'm concerned."

In the car, Richard kept his face turned away from Dawn. Christmas was becoming increasingly less appealing. At least once that sale agreement was signed, he'd never have to see that house again, and those feelings of abandonment and loss could be buried deep in his mind, where they belonged.

CLAIRE HAD SPENT the afternoon trying to lift Todd's spirits at the shop while Dawn hung out with Pauline. Dawn had told them both that something was up with Richard—that he'd "spaced out" several times while showing a home. What was he not telling her?

Richard burst into their apartment, startling Claire at the stove.

"We sold three homes today! I'm going to be able to reach my charity goals!"

Claire smiled. Maybe Dawn had overreacted? After all, when was the last time she'd watched Richard sell a home? He'd been busy for several weeks now because of staff fluctuations. Maybe his mind had just wandered? "That's wonderful!"

Richard almost threw the hanger with his coat on it into the closet.

Or was he finally going through his midlife crisis? He did seem a little over the top.

"I created a bonus program for agents to encourage them to find more homes, and it worked! I've still got it. You should've seen the faces of the staff when I told them how much I felt comfortable donating this year: one hundred and twenty thousand dollars!" He hugged and kissed Claire. "It feels so good to give back like that. And now that two new agents have begun, I can leave by five or so almost every day again. Only a few clients refused to switch, so once I'm finished with them, I'll be back to regular hours. At least until Dawn and I start working through the merger."

In other words, he might have reduced hours for a week or two, maybe three. Then it was back to crazy schedules. Claire turned off the stove and lifted the lid on the boiling potatoes. "Well, that's good news indeed. Todd worked a few hours this afternoon, so we reviewed the plans for Saturday." The oven beeped and Claire pulled a meatloaf out. She pushed a smile onto her face. Trying to force Pauline to talk to her hadn't worked. It certainly wouldn't work with Richard either. "I made your favourite. Dawn's going to hang out with her sister and Todd. I thought we'd celebrate progress with our girls, but it looks like we have more to celebrate!"

Richard squeezed her and gave her a tight kiss. "One hundred and twenty thousand dollars! I could just burst. But listen—I only have an hour and a half. Sedrick's picking me up for pickleball."

The news took Claire aback. "I was hoping we could spend some time together. Maybe talk about something else besides work? I know it's too cold for a walk this evening, but even just cuddling in front of the TV, after everything we've been through, would be lovely."

Richard seemed to barely listen. "I had some good talks with Dawn today. Things are looking good to solve our problems. We're going to talk some more. Since physical activity is good for the brain, I thought engaging in a little sport would clear my mind for our discussions tomorrow."

Claire forced herself to gently place the cutlery on the table. "Work again. Where do I fit in all this?"

Richard stared at her like the answer was as plain as day. "What do you mean? We're back to normal, don't you see? You could keep working at the tea shop—I'm sure Pauline and Todd will appreciate the help—and I'll stay involved with my company. It'll be like it always was."

Claire threw her arms up in the air. "*I don't want it like it always was!* I want something different! Yes, I love my shop and will do anything to help, but I'm not committing myself to returning to full-time work. I've said it before: I only have one life to live. So do you. When are you going to join me on the last part of our journey?"

Richard slopped food on his plate. "I can't do this with you anymore, Claire. It's like you decide what's important and when, and I'm supposed to follow along. I'm excited for what I accomplished for my business in just the past few days, and for how many other people I can help. You keep talking about these 'last years' as though we're going to die soon. I'm going to stick around for my kids as long as possible." He headed to the den with his plate. "I have paperwork to review."

So much for talking to him about what happened at the showing today. Of course Claire was going to step in to save the business she'd founded. But how did Richard not comprehend after all these years that Claire Sutton/Claire Harris/Claire Robinson would continually change?

How could he not understand who he'd married?

Claire leaned against the counter and wept.

CHAPTER 32

Claire reviewed the checklist for the tea shop's sale and party on Saturday. Everything was in order. Food would be delivered Friday, fresh tea stock had arrived, and she hadn't needed to order more of the tea wares. Unfortunately, people hadn't taken as well as they'd hoped to the celebrating-fifty-years-of-marriage concept.

"Can't say I am excited about it either," she said dryly to herself. She and Richard had said barely a word to each other since their blowup two days before. She couldn't remember when they'd last fought this much.

But she needed to move on with her life.

She was just about ready to open the tea shop for the day when Todd approached the front door. *My marriage is fine, my marriage is fine,* she told herself. She didn't want Todd to pick up on anything.

She turned the sign around to "Open," unlocked the door, and pulled it open for him, letting in a blast of cold December air.

Todd stamped the snow off his boots. "I hope you don't mind if I help you a little this morning?"

Claire smiled. "Not at all. Are Pauline and Dawn having their last morning together to themselves?"

Todd laughed. "Maybe? I offered them tea at breakfast. Dawn had said yes, Pauline no, after which Dawn launched into something about Pauline always drinking tea in the morning and that she's just being difficult. That led to some argument they'd had thirty years ago about ice cream that they had never settled."

Claire laughed as she shook her head. She had no siblings to argue with over long-not-forgotten problems, but she and Jan had regularly exchanged stories over the years about their children and their squabbles.

"Oh, dear. Yes, I remember that one. It's certainly funny to recount today, but back then, it had to do with Pauline's very strong personality sometimes leaving Dawn feeling like she didn't count."

Claire paused. Was that how she was treating Richard? Like he didn't count? But with him claiming Monday that he'd be back to fifty hours a week once the merger began, she couldn't handle his need to work any more. At some point in time, he had to admit they were aging and maybe didn't have much time left. Didn't it make sense to spend that time together? Why all this talk about sticking around for family? Of course Claire wanted that, too, but Richard appeared to be obsessing over it.

Todd nodded. "That's how I felt in my family for so many years. I know my dad and brothers have changed, but some hurts you can't erase."

"That's true."

She began reviewing their task list and plan for Saturday.

What if this hurt Claire was feeling would always remain

with her? That every time she looked at Richard, she would remember his preference for his job over their relationship?

Work over her.

He could slice it and dice any way he wanted to, but ultimately, Richard Robinson was married to his business, not Claire.

CLAIRE FOLLOWED Elfie the Elf and Todd into the back room, where Austin and another boy and two girls from dance class were waiting, all dressed in beautiful ballet costumes in white, burgundy, gold, and dark green.

It was Claire's Nutcracker Sale & Party. Her updated version of her very first Christmas-themed tea, appropriately called Teas of Joy, included a blend of black teas, Christmas spices, cranberries, and caramel. She'd also put her daughters' teas on sale: Dawn's Delight and Belmont Blizzard. Although the latter didn't carry Pauline's name, it encapsulated her personality: the spark of tart cranberry, the calming refreshment of peppermint, the punch of flavour from dried ginger, and the uplifting feel of black tea.

Austin and his classmates had about thirty minutes of dances that they would do every hour, alternating with Pauline's Elfie the Elf character, with a break for everyone over lunch.

Todd had taken what he'd choreographed for the students' *Nutcracker* production and made a few adjustments to accommodate the relatively small space and allowing them to perform toward the window to the street, too.

"You did amazing!" Claire hugged her daughter in costume, and Elfie hugged back.

When Pauline had shown Claire the image of the costume and shared her ideas for how to play the character safely, Claire had agreed immediately. Pauline had needed to pull some strings in the industry to get this enormous elf costume shipped in time for the party and didn't want to do so if it would cause issues. But local costume businesses had already had all their Christmas costumes booked. To compensate for the cane, Pauline had carefully wrapped it in the recognized colours of a candy cane.

Pauline removed the elf gloves, then reached under the mask for a moment. Claire heard something click, and Pauline lifted the mask off her head, the biggest grin on her sweaty face that Claire had seen in ages.

Todd asked if she needed an ice pack, and Pauline shook her head. "But water and some paper towel would be great."

Todd retrieved the items, and Pauline wiped her face down and took a big gulp of water. "It feels so good to sweat like a sauna again." She laughed.

Austin held up his Nutcracker mask beside Elfie's. His mask covered just the eyes and nose and attached to his face with an elastic. It was mostly white but with some exaggerated colours for cheeks and around the eyes. The nose protruded a little, and a wavy moustache had been painted underneath.

"I still can't believe I have Todd Parsons's Nutcracker mask." He beamed, and his friends eyed him with a little envy.

"And I can't believe I'm inhaling disinfectant in my mask." Pauline chuckled as everyone else wrinkled their nose or turned down their mouth in disgust. She shrugged. "You have to sacrifice something to do what you love."

After making sure Pauline was okay, Todd corralled the ballet students, and they ran out to the front on the balls of their feet as though running onto a stage. They looked so beautiful. Claire would certainly catch one of their performances later.

"Speaking of costumes." Pauline opened her shoulder bag

and pulled out a folded piece of paper. "Check out what Destiny and I have been working on." She handed Claire the paper.

Claire unfolded it and gasped. "A mascot for the tea shop?"

Pauline nodded enthusiastically. "A purple cat—gender non-specific—with a happy smile. Its name is Paws. Destiny came up with that. I guess you said they needed a pause and made them tea?"

Claire smiled at the memory.

"Unlike Perry, where I had to look through the eyes, I can look through the mouth of this one, so my field of vision will be better. We'll also keep the feet close in size to mine just to be sure." She took the folded printout from Claire's hands and pinned it next to a photo of herself as Perry.

Her daughter was coming back to her. Claire understood Pauline would still have a bit of a journey, but this was the first step, and a big step at that.

Richard came into the back room, an empty jar in hand. "I don't know why you're allowing her to do this," he said to Claire, pointing at the elf costume. "She could really hurt herself."

Pauline tipped her head to the side. "Dad, I've been acting as a mascot for over three decades. Todd's ensuring the kids don't sit on the side of my new hip, the chair I'm in is the right height for sitting safely, and I've been really good with my physio, including no longer running. I have my bad days…" She looked to Claire. "But you have no idea how much fun that was out there. One mom said to me that she'll be bringing her son this afternoon. He uses crutches to get around, and mascots almost always look fully healthy. Another kid wanted his mother back for Christmas—she'd passed away earlier this year." She pressed her hands to her heart. "I didn't realize how much I'd been missing those conversations."

Richard filled the jar, almost throwing the tea into it.

"Careful," Claire said. "That one's expensive. If you break the leaves, I can't sell it."

"You're more concerned about your tea than your daughter," he grumbled.

Even Pauline looked hurt now. "I know I'm going through some rough times, but Dad, come on, give me a break."

Richard popped the metal lid back on. "Which is what will happen if you trip or if a kid runs into you."

"Actually," Pauline said, "they see the cane, and most under-stand immediately to be careful. Todd just explains that Elfie has had an operation and that his leg is sore, so it's important to wait until he sits down before giving him a hug. I've been out there twice so far, a half hour each time as promised, and no issues."

"Yet."

Richard walked back out.

"What's gotten into Dad? I thought he'd be happy for me. Anything to do with his spacing out at that home viewing?"

"I don't know what's with him," Claire said. "He won't talk to me about it."

WHY HAD he suggested and committed to helping Claire every Saturday until Christmas? He was exhausted beyond belief—fifty-hour work weeks at the brokerage plus five hours on Saturdays at Claire's Tea Shop. He could really have used the day off today. His schedule wasn't letting up as anticipated.

Of course he had attended every annual tea sale and party, even when he was no longer needed to play Santa. Claire's Tea Shop had always been about Claire, and he had always respected that.

But that was what was eating at him now. How often had

she helped him with his brokerage over the years? He could probably count the occurrences on his two hands. How often had Richard helped Claire with her business? He'd lost count years ago.

His dedication to his business had resulted in him donating more money this Christmas than ever. Although he'd started in commercial real estate when he and Claire had begun dating, he found residential more fulfilling. Only two of his reps looked after commercial these days.

To keep hearing time and again how happy clients were with having found the perfect home for their family gave Richard an immense sense of pride.

But Richard also felt pride in being there for his family whenever they needed him. He absolutely would not fly anywhere—except Vancouver. Dawn would be extra busy in the coming months, and Richard would take on whatever work he could to give her time for her family.

Parents needed to spend time with their kids, because that time could never come back.

And Pauline wasn't going to be able to live inside those costumes she loved so much. Even though her new medication appeared to be helping, she'd had several depressive episodes this week, according to Claire. After the exhilaration of today had worn off, she'd probably be crumpled in bed, depressed again.

It was not acceptable to leave the family for six weeks in the spring to fulfill some silly bucket-list dream.

Richard's dedication to his family meant keeping his promise to help out at the store until Christmas. But then that would be it. He'd give Pauline and Todd all the moral support and business advice they wanted, and he'd happily lend them money, but he wouldn't spend another hour working there. He had a brokerage to prepare for sale.

Richard sighed. Pauline had lucked out in that this first medication appeared to be helping her—she probably wouldn't have to switch, so long as side effects didn't become too much of an issue.

But didn't working in a foam snowsuit raise her body temperature significantly? Could that lead to a stroke, one of the side effects of those medications?

A customer approached the counter.

"Just one minute, please," he said. "I'll be right back."

PAULINE PLACED Elfie's head over a small fan. "I'd spray the inside with diluted mouthwash, but it's not my costume." With Todd's help, she slipped the costume off so Elfie could air out a bit. Pauline always wore tight-fitting fitness clothes underneath to help with the sweat and to protect the costume.

Claire wrinkled her nose. "Isn't there somewhere else we can hang that?"

Pauline laughed. "Sorry, Mom. Not unless you want to frighten kids with a decapitated elf on a hanger."

Point taken.

Richard marched into the back. "You can't go back out there in that."

Pauline crossed her arms. "I absolutely can, Dad, and I will."

"What about your medication? Your increased risk of stroke? You're putting your body through a lot of stress."

"I'm familiar with the side effects. The doctor said this would be okay, so long as I don't pull the same two- or three-hour stints I used to. That's why I'm making the effort to undress during my breaks."

"I don't think that's enough."

Claire stood next to Pauline, her arms crossed, too. Why would Richard put down his daughter like that? Couldn't he see how happy she was?

"It's what the doctor allowed," Claire repeated.

To her surprise, Richard grabbed her by the arm and pulled her outside, into the falling snow.

Claire yanked her arm back. "Don't you *ever* do that to me again."

Richard didn't appear to notice. "We need to present a unified front with our girls. Pauline's putting herself in danger. We shouldn't be allowing her to do any of this."

Claire blinked as she still rubbed her arm. "Allowed? Have you not noticed that our daughters are adults? There's nothing to *allow*. We *accept* and *love*. Then we ensure we're there in case they fall."

"Does ensuring you're there for them mean you won't go to Asia?"

Claire shook her head. "I don't know what's gotten into you, but I thought we shared everything with each other. I'm sorry about not saying more about David, if that's what's bothering you. I kept it to myself with the best of intentions." Claire shivered. She needed to get inside. "But if you *ever* handle me like that again, I will move out."

"All these years, you're comparing me to him, aren't you? Your level of measurement for a man is an abuser, not someone who loves you and would give you the world if you asked for it."

Claire's mouth froze. He was accusing her of measuring him against David Harris? Claire had never felt more insulted in her life.

"I may be who I am in part because of what I'd experienced back then. But I have always been outspoken—Jan helped me realize it started with my father returning home. So no,

Richard, I am not measuring you against him. I just know what it's like to be held on a short leash, and I won't stand for it. I guess I'll be flying to Asia *on my own*."

She stormed back inside, not caring if Richard followed or left.

CHAPTER 33

*R*ichard stared at his hands. "What have I done?"

The snow fell around him, landing on his shirt and his shoes, as though trying to cover him in its silent whiteness.

"What have I done?"

The words kept repeating themselves, bolting his feet to the asphalt.

Why?!? his mind screamed at his memories. *Why did you show me all those sad times from my childhood? Why?!?*

He had to make this right. He knew Claire's history. He *knew* it! He'd felt her pain from it, wiped away her tears when she'd shared all the cruel details with him.

He'd tried to bury his memories, and yet they wouldn't stay quiet. What use were they to him except to apparently torment him like this?

The back door opened, and Pauline stuck her head out. "Dad? You okay?"

Still staring at his hands, he shook his head.

"Mom's trying to serve people, but she's mad. *Really* mad. What's going on?"

Richard couldn't talk to his daughter about this. He was the father. He was the one who was supposed to have all the answers. He was the one everyone was supposed to be able to rely on. All those memories reminded him of that. *His* parents weren't there for him. He wasn't going to make…

He gasped as the full memory returned.

"I always thought my parents had made a mistake…" His voice was low.

Pauline stepped out into the cold with him. "You're starting to look like a snowman. Here." She dusted him off. "What mistake, Dad?"

"Of leaving me."

"What? Dad, no. Why would you think that?"

Richard didn't know. As an adult, he understood why his parents had died. But as a child hoping for their return, he now realized that he'd believed they'd forgotten him. They weren't dead. They'd just gone off somewhere and would come back once they remembered they had a son. His father had always been imaginary to him—his family showed him the few baby and family photos they had, but the rest was fantasy. Richard had envisioned his father to be tall, strong enough to lift him up over his shoulders, so jovial that he'd let Richard have all the sweets in the world at the fair. In Richard's buried memories, his father had just flown away and forgotten to return.

And since he didn't know what asthma was, he'd assumed his mother had been taken to the hospital and had forgotten to come home. He knew she had difficulties breathing, but he didn't know it was chronic. "Chronic" simply wasn't in the vocabulary of a preschooler.

We moved to a new home, didn't we? When Dad died. The memory felt like a snow squall: whirring all around in his head but almost impossible to see. *And we moved close to the factories,* he thought. *The air must have been horrible for someone with asthma.*

He never saw his father's body—that was understandable—but his family had decided he was too young to attend the visitation and open casket for his mother.

He never had closure.

You closed a door, a window, a deal…you also needed to close some parts of your life.

Pauline gently took Richard's hand. "Come inside. It's cold out here."

Richard allowed himself to be led back into the shop like a little child.

RICHARD LAY in their bed on his own. Claire had moved into the den, not saying a word.

He was certain now that she'd travel to Asia by herself. If she won that trip to Germany for two, she'd take Jan.

Given what had happened at the tea shop this afternoon, he couldn't blame her. But he'd still worry for her safety the entire time she was gone.

He hadn't meant to grab her like that. He'd truly believed that what he had to say was urgent and not for Pauline's ears. But any attempt at apologizing, even tonight, had been met with silence.

But he understood.

He loved Claire with all his heart. It was going to take more than roses to win her back.

If she wanted to be won back at all.

He could hear his mother in his mind now. Just fragments of a full conversation. But he could hear her voice.

Always keep a clean house, she'd told him. *You want people to feel at home in your house as much as in theirs.*

He remembered now, too, why she'd cleaned so often: volunteers came regularly, either from the church group, or any other group—Richard didn't know most of them—to sew for the war effort. Groups of ladies chattering away, their hands busy, patted him on the head as he walked through the room.

Their sadness. He remembered now. Lots of men didn't come back from the war, like the man Richard had never known.

He swallowed. "It's just a panic attack, Rich," he told himself. "Just a panic attack. That house is now sold. You don't have to see it again. Your wife will come back to you. Just keep the house clean."

RICHARD HAD GRABBED HER.

Grabbed her.

He was not the husband she'd married. What had possessed him to act like that? In fact, why had he suddenly become so controlling?

"Don't travel, don't perform, don't move…what does he really expect of us?"

Claire stared at the ceiling in the den. Richard had admitted once he shouldn't have declared at the wedding that he wouldn't change a thing. And now? He didn't want anything to change, and yet he had changed so much these past few weeks. She wanted to help, but after being grabbed like that, she didn't know when she'd next see that side of him.

David Harris she could predict: after work, before a social evening, whenever Claire had ostensibly not performed her domestic duties to his standards, and certainly whenever Claire had raised her voice.

Richard had never touched her roughly in all their years of marriage. The rational side that knew Richard so deeply and intimately told Claire something was wrong and he needed help.

The more powerful side—the fearful side—told her to keep away in case he snapped again.

RICHARD HAD a splitting headache and came out of the drug store with a fresh bottle of painkillers for himself. He and Claire had been arguing since they'd woken up, and anytime he moved toward her, she moved away.

He'd frightened her yesterday. Truly frightened her.

The falling snow left a light dusting on the sidewalk, covering the treacherous wisps of ice that could knock even the most skilled skater onto his back.

Richard walked carefully.

Belmont Village was quiet on Sundays—only establishments that served food would open today. He remembered when he was a new agent, helping rent out the units in the original plaza. He knew all the store owners by name from the moment they moved in. Now, some stores came and went quickly, but Richard usually met the owners as soon as he could. He needed to anchor himself to something, and no matter where in Kitchener or Waterloo he lived, he always came back to this shopping district.

It was home.

As Richard approached the tea shop, he could see that Todd was still teaching Austin inside. Of course. It was Sunday morning.

Such dedication. After a full day of performances yesterday, Austin was back practising the following morning.

Richard remained dedicated to his wife of fifty years, but she looked at him now as though he was David Harris.

Why was it that the more Richard tried to focus on his career, the more harm he caused? Why couldn't he pursue his dreams without hurting those he loved?

CHAPTER 34

Richard was poring over reports at six on Monday night at the brokerage when Sedrick walked in.

"I thought I'd find you here," he said.

"I'm not in the mood. Dawn has me on some tasks for our merger."

"That can wait. Your marriage can't."

Richard had tried for two days to apologize to Claire, to explain what had happened without dumping his past on her. But she wouldn't listen and instead kept on about dreams and such.

Now he was angry. What good were fifty years of marriage if they didn't include an opportunity for forgiveness?

"Hey!" Richard said as his report disappeared from under his hands.

Sedrick held it over the shredder.

"I can print out a new one," Richard said.

Sedrick paged through it. "You're already halfway done. You'd have to start all over again."

Richard tossed his pencil onto his desk and leaned back. "Fine."

Sedrick set the report out of Richard's reach and sat down. "What's really going on? Why did you grab her? I'm not leaving until you tell me the whole truth."

Richard ran his hand over his head. "I just want this all to go away."

"It won't until you're open with someone, Rich."

Richard had made the biggest mistake of his life when he'd grabbed Claire's arm like that. Of all the emotions humans felt, regret was the horrible one. You couldn't travel back in time to fix things.

Richard took in a deep breath and let it out. He didn't know how much time had passed while he told Sedrick everything — his feelings and emotions, his memories, his attempts at pushing it all away. Sedrick sat still and listened, only interrupting to ensure he understood what Richard was saying.

By the time Richard was finished, he had no more space for anger. "I've really messed up. Aside from a massive argument Sunday morning about…I don't even know what it was about… we haven't talked to each other."

Sedrick shook his head. "Richard, I'm so sorry."

"You said I'm brilliant at what I do, but sometimes I'm a dolt when it comes to Claire. We'd been fighting so much lately, and then my childhood home… I couldn't take it anymore. But I don't know why I didn't stop when I did."

"Trauma, Rich. Tracy had it with Austin. You never dealt with the trauma of your childhood."

Richard shrugged. "That all happened over seventy years ago. I don't get why…" He stopped himself. "Yes, I do. A part of me blamed my parents for not coming for me." He scratched at a mark on the desk. "I never had closure with either of their deaths. I didn't think that was necessary." He buried his face in his hands for a moment, and then looked up at Sedrick again. "I don't know what to do next. She won't talk to me."

Sedrick held up his phone. "Let me look after that. In the meantime, you and I are getting a drink. You need it."

CLAIRE STOOD in the back room of the tea shop, ready to lock up. It felt good to be there, almost like a second home. She'd lived in several places while she'd run Claire's Tea Shop, but Claire's Tea Shop had always remained in the same unit.

"In a way, it hasn't changed," she said out loud.

She pulled out the chair from the desk, ready to sit down and count the cash. Instead, in her mind's eye, she saw Richard sitting there, inspecting the books. She remembered how concerned he'd been for their daughter. That night, he'd contacted Dawn to discuss merging their brokerages.

Those weren't the actions of someone hateful.

Her memories began racing back in time, replaying all the times they'd made love in the back room.

But a marriage was more than sex. It was love, support, understanding, and compromise.

And Claire and Richard clearly couldn't find any compromise anymore. She wanted to travel; he wanted to stay put. She wanted to enjoy the retired life; he wanted to keep working.

Claire pulled out a cash sheet and began with the nickels when a knock on the back door surprised her.

Momentarily nervous—shopkeepers could get robbed precisely at this time—she held her cane in one hand and opened the door.

And let out a sigh of relief as Jan...and Brenda...and Cecilia marched in.

"I knew you'd be here late," Jan said, "so I rallied the troops. We need to talk."

"I don't really have time right now…"

Brenda marched past Claire and out to the front. "We'll be ten minutes, and then we'll help you."

Cecilia nodded as she, too, marched past Claire.

Jan indicated with her head. "Let's go. And don't worry about tea." She locked the back door, clearly an experienced shopkeeper herself.

The women sat in the lounge area.

Claire shrugged. "All right. What's this about?"

Jan started. "We're hoping you can forgive Richard."

Claire's back immediately went up. "He grabbed me, Jan. How can I forgive that?"

Brenda leaned forward. "No man should treat you like that. But please listen to what we've learned."

Cecilia touched Claire's hand. "You don't want to end your life with a list of regrets."

What did Claire have to lose? She'd already moved to the den to sleep. The next step would be to move out if needed, though she didn't know where she'd go.

She nodded, indicating she wanted to hear more. Her eyes opened wide as Jan told her about Richard having to sell the childhood home where he'd been raised by his uncle and grand-parents, about the memories that had begun to surface, and about his difficulties at pushing everything away.

His childhood home? The one he'd moved into after his mother had passed away? Claire couldn't think a straight thought. She'd asked him a few times what was wrong, and he'd said, "Nothing."

This was why they were called the Silent Generation, at least in her mind. Don't complain, pull up your bootstraps, and get to it.

"He's been trying to handle all that by himself? Without talking to me? After I told him everything about my first husband?"

The women nodded.

Cecilia spoke. "Don't be angry with him."

"He grabbed me."

Brenda took a deep breath. "I don't know what it is about me or my life, but I gave up looking for the right man ages ago. But you have a love for the ages, Claire."

Cecilia nodded. "You know how the men of our generation are: they hold absolutely everything inside."

"Look at Austin's generation, even Todd's," Jan said. "More men are willing to share what they're feeling, understanding that the world isn't counting on them to keep it spinning—it'll spin on its own just fine. Sedrick's learned a thing or two from Austin, but he still keeps some things to himself."

Cecilia teared up. "My husband didn't tell me about his cancer diagnosis until it was too late. I didn't have time to prepare for anything."

Claire gasped. "I had no idea."

"He worried others would think him weak for 'catching' cancer, and nothing I could do or say would change his mind." Cecilia's face darkened. "Promising not to tell anyone was the stupidest thing he ever asked me to do. How was I supposed to relieve my own sadness and pain without betraying my husband?"

Claire studied each of her friends: Brenda, consummately single; Jan, still happily married; and Cecilia, recently widowed. They each had a different perspective on life.

And love.

Jan spoke up. "If you don't find a way to move past this, then David will destroy the fifty years you and Richard have built. Richard's actions were not acceptable—we're with you on that—but they came from a different place than David's. We're absolutely certain he'll never do that again."

Claire covered her eyes. "He was right." She began to sob. "I have been comparing him to David all these years. I have to go to Richard, tell him that I'm willing to talk…and to listen."

Jan smiled. "We'll walk you back to your apartment."

Claire embraced all her friends tightly. "I don't know how I'd ever get through life without all of you."

"YOU DO WHAT?" Brenda asked.

"Drink it."

Claire had made them all her "punishment tea," as Jan now called it.

"I'm a coffee drinker," Brenda said, "and even I know you shouldn't drink over-steeped tea."

"This is the last time," Claire said. "I promise. On the count of three?"

They all nodded, holding their cups close to their lips.

"One, two, three!"

Everyone took one sip.

And everyone spat the tea into the sink, standing back up, laughing uncontrollably.

"Oh my god!" Jan said. "After all the years of such amazing tea from you, you make me drink this?" She was laughing so hard, she was crying.

Claire couldn't tell if she herself was laughing or crying. This was the last time she'd think about David. Jan had called Sedrick, and the men were out for a drink. The ladies opted to keep Claire company until Richard returned.

"I'm sorry, Claire, but I can't," Cecilia said as she dried her tears of laughter. She poured the tea down the drain.

"An excellent idea!" Brenda exclaimed and followed suit.

So did Jan.

And finally, Claire.

Jan grabbed the box of tea out of Claire's hands. "We're getting rid of this, too." She began ripping the bags open and dumping the contents into the garbage. "David doesn't even deserve to be composted."

Claire doubled over in laughter again.

"Claire?"

None of the women had heard the apartment door open. Claire saw Richard standing there through her tears of joy. She sniffed…

"Vanilla?" After she dried her eyes, she saw Richard holding several vanilla beans in his hand.

He shrugged. "It was the one piece missing from your bouquet at our anniversary."

The women each patted her shoulder or squeezed her hand as they passed her, slipped into their outerwear, and disappeared.

Both stood in silence, staring at each other, breathing, hearts beating.

Richard took a step toward her, and Claire did the same.

"I am so, so, so sorry," Richard said.

Now that Claire was standing closer, she could see tears welling in his eyes, too. But tears of regret, not of joy.

"Jan told me what you told Sedrick." A little anger rose in Claire, but she kept her voice even. "I wish you'd come to me."

Richard nodded. "We were so occupied with the girls, and then…to be honest…you kept talking about travel, and all I could think about was how far away you'd be from me. Your dreams are what attracted me to you in the first place."

"And your kindness pulled me in before I knew what was happening."

Richard took another step closer. "I'm sorry for..." He wiped his eyes. "I'm sorry for touching you as I did."

Claire's tears began anew. "And I'm sorry for pushing my dreams on to you. I'm sure we can find a compromise." She took a step closer.

Richard held out the "bouquet" of vanilla pods. Claire accepted them as though they were a dozen roses. She inhaled and then laughed. "These are rather strong."

Richard laughed with her. "I realized that after I opened the first container. I had to wait until Sedrick parked so I could open a window in the blustery cold to pull each one out of its packaging."

She pulled Richard into an embrace, and they cried out everything they had been through.

Claire understood in her heart that she would have to accept Richard's dreams. He'd shown her that kind of respect for over fifty years. It was time she paid it back.

CHAPTER 35

Claire turned around the sign so it said "Closed," and then ensured that the extra sign that explained the shop's Christmas hours was well-affixed to the door.

As part of her Christmas gift to herself, she was going to attempt to forget about the shop for a week for the first time in her life.

Okay. Maybe she'd drop by once to check on things.

Or twice.

"Or I can ask Todd to come and have a look so I can take a full vacation," she said aloud.

"I like that idea."

Claire jumped and turned around. Richard had snuck in the back door and was now standing just at the entrance to the back room, a wrapped bouquet in hand.

"But I assume he's not coming tonight?" Richard eyed Claire up and down. "I had plans for Christmas Eve."

Shivers ran all over Claire's body. "I told him not to worry about a thing, that I'd lock up everything securely. I'm even taking the float home in case anyone breaks in and is looking for cash."

She used her cane to walk around the counter to Richard. "I was just going to check everything one more time, turn of the lights…and then I'll be free."

Richard eyed her body again, and sparks danced through her as they always had with him.

"I thought I'd see if you needed some help." He stroked the top of her dress. "I wanted to check a few things myself." Then he stepped back and presented her with the bouquet.

Claire opened it to see a beautiful mixture of white and red roses against a backdrop of spruce, some cinnamon sticks inserted here and there for accent, and all tied together in a wide red-and-gold bow.

"Oh, Richard, they're so beautiful. We should put them in a vase."

Richard kissed her neck, then her throat, and then her breastbone. "I'll find a vase. You finish locking up. You have two minutes, or I'll be undressing you with the lights still on."

Claire giggled and rushed as best she could—but carefully, so as not to invite another accident.

The lights off in the front, and all doors securely locked, Claire met the love of her life in the back room.

Claire placed her hands on Richard's chest. "I've been waiting for this moment for well over a month now," she said, her voice low.

Richard lifted one hand and kissed it. "We have had lots of fun back here, haven't we?"

She unbuttoned his shirt while he reached around to her dress and slowly, longingly, enticingly pulled down the zipper.

One thing had never changed with Richard in all these years of dating and marriage: his ability to make her feel like the most desired woman in the world.

~

"Ow," Claire said as she and Richard, laden with gifts, hobbled together down the hallway to Pauline and Todd's apartment for Christmas Day celebrations.

Richard rolled his shoulder. "There's a reason we use the bed now, isn't there? That chair was not comfortable."

"Modern-day office chairs. Great for sitting, not for sex."

Richard kissed her on the cheek. "As much as I'm looking forward to Christmas celebrations today, I'd honestly rather go back to bed. With you, I mean."

His eyes, which had always reminded Claire of lapsang souchong tea, teased her with their hint of excitement and longing. Shivers ran down Claire's spine.

"Unfortunately, Pauline and Todd only have one bedroom, and I have rules about that," Claire said, a coy smile on her face.

"Our place is just a few doors down. I think we can make it if an emergency arises and I need to unzip that dress."

Claire giggled. "Stop it. You're making me blush. Everyone's going to know what we were talking about the moment we walk in."

They reached the apartment door. Richard transferred the gifts he was carrying to one arm, knocked, and then placed his hand behind Claire's back, where he let his fingers trail a short distance down.

He was evil.

But a child's voice snapped them both out of it. "I'll get it!"

Was that Destiny?

The door flung open, and Destiny was indeed standing in front of Claire and Richard.

"Surprise, Grandma and Grandpa!" she yelled.

Claire's heart filled with joy. "What? Where…?"

Pauline came up behind her niece. "It was hard, I won't lie."

A mischievous smile lit up her face as she passed some of the gifts to Destiny to carry inside. She whispered to her parents, "I came to the store to see if I could help with closing up for the holidays. You were…busy."

Claire's eyes opened wide. "What? You saw us?"

"And I can't unsee it." Pauline gave her parents a big hug. "But it let me know that you'd be occupied this morning, too, so we could sneak Dawn's family in. I'm glad the two of you have reconciled."

Richard shook his head. "I think last night was the last night of our escapades back there." He rubbed his shoulder.

Pauline raised an eyebrow. "I happen to know a good physiotherapist."

Richard burst out laughing as he patted his daughter on the back.

Claire and Richard entered the apartment, which now seemed crammed with the entire family there.

Including Dean.

Claire opened her arms to the big man. "I'm so glad you could make it. But I'm afraid we don't have any gifts for the kids—I gave them their gifts at your place last month."

Dean hugged Claire back tightly. "And they know that. The point of visiting was to celebrate Christmas as a family and see Richard open his gift in person. I'm sorry for not being around while you visited. Work was just ridiculous. I have to fly back ahead of the family so I'm ready to go on the twenty-seventh."

Ahead of the family? "How long are the others staying?"

Pauline wrapped her arms around them. "A whole week!" She grinned at Todd, who smiled back at her. "But Mom, do you and Dad have room for Dawn? The kids want to sleep over without their mother."

The room broke out into laughter. Claire and Richard looked at each other and nodded. Destiny jumped for joy, and

Danielle and Dave smiled, still apparently attempting to look like the cool, calm, collected teenagers they most definitely were not.

The apartment phone rang, and Todd picked up. He let someone in.

"Food's already coming," he said. "Adults on the couch, kids at the table."

"Where do I sit?" Danielle asked.

"Table," Dean answered automatically. "'Kids' is a generational term."

Danielle sulked.

After a joyful meal with merriment and laughter, it was time to exchange gifts.

"Mom goes first!" Pauline yelled, and the room fell silent.

Claire glanced at everyone. "What's going on?"

Richard pulled a gift from under the tree: a gift bag with "Merry Christmas" in bright red letters, and red and green tissue paper stuffed in the top.

Claire's heart beat in her chest as she lifted the tissue paper out to find several envelopes. She opened the first one and unfolded the piece of paper inside. Her hand flew to her chest.

"Japanese language class?"

Richard nodded. "For two."

Claire did a double take. "You're going to learn with me?" She quickly opened the next one and unfolded that paper. "Tours of Japan?"

"I knew you wanted to go there. I wasn't sure where else you wanted to travel. But from the middle of April to the end of May, I'll be incommunicado from Robinson Realty."

That didn't sit right with Claire. She'd promised herself to support Richard's dreams. "I'd love to travel with you, my Keemun, but what about your dreams? Your life?"

Richard put his arms around Claire. "I'll be very busy—

except when we take our lessons—preparing the brokerage for the merger. But Dawn has offered to take over for the six weeks we're gone, and to only interrupt me if it's critical. We thought it'd be a way to see if our ideas work. If they don't, then we'll iron things out when I get back."

Claire kissed him passionately.

"I guess it's my turn now?" She looked around the room, and everyone nodded.

She pointed to a large gift bag, and Dean passed it to Richard. She'd put just as much effort into wrapping this one as their anniversary gift, including decorating it with cinnamon sticks tied together with red and green ribbons.

Richard set the bag on the couch so he could more easily open it. When he finally removed the tissue paper, he couldn't stop laughing.

"What?" Pauline asked, trying to peer over his shoulder.

Richard started coughing, he was laughing so hard.

"Dad?" Dawn asked. "You okay?"

Richard held up his new athletic clothing, including a T-shirt that said, "Fit as a fiddle and ready to smoke you," new running shoes, and a pickleball paddle.

Everyone laughed almost as hard as he had.

"Sedrick said you needed to look more intimidating on the court," Claire said. "That's supposed to be an excellent paddle."

Richard hugged her tight. "I will scare the beejeebies out of my opponents to win your heart anew every week, my love." He kissed her again.

Claire marvelled at how she and Richard embraced change but kept some things the same. That balance had kept her married for fifty years to the most amazing man in the world.

EPILOGUE

 ichard stood in his office, a pair of scissors in his hands.

A very big pair of scissors.

He took a deep breath. "I guess this is it."

Claire stroked his arm. Dawn smiled as her eyes welled up. Pauline jumped up and down in excitement. Richard and Claire had learned over the past eight months that Pauline would always have jumping beans in her, especially since she'd given up jogging for good back in the winter.

Dean laughed as he wrapped his arm around Dawn. "I have no idea how you grew up around your sister."

Dawn dabbed at her eyes and glanced warmly at her sister. "I'm sure I drove her nuts, too."

Pauline nodded. "'Turn the music down! Stop jumping around the house! I'm on the phone with my friend!' *For three hours.*" Then she hugged her sister. "I claim that I trained you for management."

Richard had just turned eighty the week before and couldn't believe his luck in creating such a wonderful family with his intelligent, sexy wife: two successful daughters, three wonderful grandkids, and two upstanding sons-in-law.

Claire snapped her fingers several times in succession. "Let's go go go! I know we're all nervous, but your father and I have a weeklong trip to New York City and we still need to pack."

Richard gave Claire a kiss. "That's two trips in one year for us. I can hardly believe it."

"And when you get back, Dad," Dawn said, "your new office will be ready and waiting." She slid her hands along what had been Richard's large oak desk. "Nice to know I'll have this beautiful one waiting for me whenever I fly in."

"Be kind to my desk," Richard said. "It still has a lot of years left in it."

Terry knocked on the door. "Mr. Robinson, we're ready."

"That's a nice way to tell your soon-to-be-former boss that everyone's waiting."

Terry blushed and adjusted his glasses.

Dawn added, "And if you ever call me Ms. Glover, you'll be relegated to hard-drive cleanup."

Terry laughed as he nodded. "Understood…Dawn."

Richard held the large, gold-plated scissors in his hand and walked out to where a small crowd awaited this final moment in the opening ceremony. His family followed behind as the staff and several members of the Belmont Village community—including Jan, Sedrick, Tracy and Ben—clapped. Dawn stayed up front beside him while the others moved off to the side. Pauline held out her phone to take pictures.

Richard addressed the crowd. "Sorry to keep you waiting. I needed a few moments to collect myself." He smiled at Dawn. "Passing on Robinson Realty to my daughter was something I didn't think possible twenty or more years ago, when she fell in love with that man over there, Dean Glover, and moved to Vancouver." Dawn and Dean smiled at each other. "I know she'll run the brokerage well." Richard swallowed as he tried to blink back tears. His voice shook gently. "Of course, I won't be gone. You'll see me every week training new agents and advising on how to help older people like me transition from their family homes." Richard went on to thank the many people in his life who'd helped him become the man he was today, from his parents to his uncle and grandparents, and even to Brenda, "for putting up with me since day one." At that, his former long-time assistant raised her glass of wine to him, and he nodded in return.

"But the one person who's been here throughout almost all of it has been my wife. If it wasn't for her, my life wouldn't have ever changed. Through Claire, I learned compassion, had the most stupendous daughters a man can have, and created such a stable life that I could be here for all of you." He smiled over at her, his tears now spilling down his cheeks. "Thank you."

Claire blew him a kiss, and her smile gave him the strength to finish his short speech. This ceremony was the final, official action to publicly transfer the brokerage to Dawn. He wiped his face quickly with a tissue from his pocket, grateful that Sedrick had insisted he carry a few.

Richard and Dawn moved behind a large red ribbon that had been tied between two posts. He invited his younger daughter to hold the scissors with him.

"Welcome, everyone, to Fits Like a Glove Realty."

Father and daughter cut the bow as everyone cheered and cameras flashed. Richard was soon engulfed in a huge embrace with Claire, while Dawn was wrapped in a congratulatory hug from Pauline.

"I can't believe this has finally happened," Claire said. "We've found our balance: a little work to keep us engaged with life, and lots of playtime to enjoy our families and each other. I'm glad you showed me that it's possible to do both."

Richard kissed her again. "Actually, I have you to thank for showing me that, with the way you stepped in at the tea shop and have now found a schedule that really works for you."

"So…maybe nothing will change?" Claire said with a wink, remembering his words at the anniversary party.

"Oh, lots will. But it'll all be for good."

Both smiled and kissed one more time.

For the next couple of hours, the new and old owners milled about, engaging and celebrating with their guests.

By the end of the evening, Richard and Claire were exhausted.

"Do you want me to close up?" Dawn asked.

Richard shook his head. "That's okay. I know you want to get back to the kids at Ben and Tracy's house."

Austin had happily stayed home to hang out with what he now called his "almost-cousins."

That's how close the families were, and Richard loved it.

"I just hope they've gotten along," Dawn said.

Richard patted her on the shoulder. "You've raised them well. I'm sure they haven't torn down the house."

Claire and Richard's daughters and sons-in-law said their goodbyes, and Richard sat in his chair one last time.

"This is really it," he said. "Legally and publicly, Robinson Realty is no more. After thirty-three years."

Claire locked the door to his office and gently swayed her hips as she approached him. "Last time in this office, eh?"

Richard's skin tingled. "Last time."

Claire walked around him, one hand trailing along his chin, and then headed for the windows, closing the blinds with the sexiest glance in his direction he'd seen in a while.

"Then I think we need to commemorate this wondrous occasion. And do something we've never done before."

Richard swallowed.

Claire returned to him, sat on his lap, and mussed up his hair a little. She gave the lightest kiss on his cheek, and he shivered. Her delicate hands lifted his tie as she leaned in for another kiss but stopped just short of touching his skin.

Richard took in a deep breath, trying to restrain himself.

Claire outlined his ear with her finger, then gingerly undid his tie. "This is in my way," she said. She took her time pulling the tie out from under his collar, and Richard's skin burned in anticipation as she tossed his tie aside.

He couldn't handle it anymore. He pulled her in with one hand and pressed his lips to hers tight while his other reached for the zipper of her dress. Claire reciprocated with undoing his buttons while their mouths explored.

Claire sat up, panting. "My Keemun," she breathed.

Richard, his breath just as frantic, said, "My Darjeeling."

He was still fully in love at eighty, with change happening all around him.

Life couldn't get any better than this.

SETTING THE RECORD STRAIGHT

Love on Belmont mixes real locations and situations with fictional ones. Here are some of the facts.

WORLD WAR II AND CANADA

I love reading and writing romance: if a person can write a book that describes how at least some of life's pain can be healed through love, then I believe love can heal much. Maybe not all —I'm also a realist—but much.

That's how the themes of this book came about: war transfers its pain to subsequent generations. It breaks up families. Alters fate. Creates wounds that leave lifelong—and generational—scars. But all kinds of love—familial, romantic, platonic —help us through.

However, I also like to introduce my readers to topics they may not have thought of before. As well known as World War II may be, many of its stories are not. Most Canadians, I believe, when they hear about World War II, think about the European theatre of war. If they think about the Asian theatre, the attack on the US via Pearl Harbor jumps to mind faster than any Canadian involvement.

So that's why Claire and Richard's fathers fight on different sides of the world.

Canadian soldiers did liberate a transit camp in Holland: Westerbork in April 1945. The website for the Canadian War Museum says this is the camp where Anne Frank and her family were taken in 1944. Unfortunately, Canadian troops didn't arrive there soon enough to free them. Visit www.warmu seum.ca/liberation/ for more information.

Canadians also fought in Hong Kong, at the time a British colony, and did surrender on Christmas Day 1941. Search with the keyphrase "Battle of Hong Kong" at warmuseum.ca for more information. (Please keep in mind that archival content, such as newspaper clippings, will use the reporting language of war, including how enemies were portrayed at the time. Some of the content may be offensive to some readers.)

I do need to explain where I took poetic licence. The Battle of Hong Kong was fought, so far as I can tell, by the Winnipeg Grenadiers and the Royal Rifles of Canada. Men joined mainly from Manitoba and Quebec, respectively. Richard's father lived in Ontario. Although I've found a few graves from Ontario in the Sai Wan cemetery via the Commonwealth War Graves Commission's website (cwgc.org), they were few and far between. I overlooked this detail, though, because covering a little-known battle was more important to me.

PERIMENOPAUSE AND MENOPAUSE

Because of my age, I've begun paying attention to my hormonal health so I'm ready with information once I need to discuss treatments—if any—with my doctor. As much as I hate to admit it, the effects of hormones sometimes do creep up on us when we really don't want to deal with them. Just look at dopamine: it can keep you staring at your phone or leave you unmotivated in bed all morning. We love dopamine but, my goodness, when dopamine's low—which can happen, for example, when you have ADHD—life can be extremely difficult to navigate.

The same happens with our sex hormones. I won't put any specific medical information here because science changes almost daily but if you're at the age of perimenopause, there are many evidence-based resources out there for you, and treatments are available—hormonal and not. Also, if in any way you feel uncomfortable talking about a woman's sex hormones, know that you're not alone and that your doctor is a helpful source for further guidance.

VANCOUVER

Definitely the highlight of writing this book was travelling to Vancouver for four days in September 2023. It was my first time, and I loved every minute of it. We've had direct flights to Vancouver out of Waterloo Region Airport for several years now but still I was surprised with how easy it was to travel from such a small airport. I'll definitely do it again sometime.

And yes, Vancouver's flashing green lights are different from almost all of Canada (the Yukon being the other exception). You can find out more with a quick search online.

BELMONT VILLAGE

Belmont Village is real and is a wonderful, quaint shopping and eating strip on Belmont Avenue in Kitchener, Ontario, Canada. You can learn more about it at TheBelmontVillage.ca.

Although the stores and businesses I use in *Love on Belmont* are fictional, if there's overlap with a real store, I speak with the owner(s) first to ensure they're comfortable with me moving forward with my idea. Claire's Tea Shop is partially inspired by All Things Tea, owned and run by George Broughton. Their website is AllThingsTea.ca. They can ship their delicious teas anywhere within Canada where Canada Post can ship. At time of printing, American customers are welcome to place orders to the US by calling the store at (519) 574-4774.

Some stores, like Tracy and Ben's The Belmont Village Chocolate House, are completely fictional.

If you ever find yourself in Kitchener, Ontario, Canada, drop by Belmont Village for a bite to eat, a package of tea, a lovely gift, or just to see where Claire, her family, and her friends could be hanging out…

ENJOY ALL THE LOVE ON BELMONT BOOKS

Join all your friends from *Love on Belmont*, where love and tea create a magical blend 🤍.

THE LOVE ON BELMONT PREQUEL SHORT STORIES

1. Claire's Tea Shop
2. Trick or Tea
3. Oh, Christmas Tea

THE LOVE ON BELMONT NOVELS

1. Tea Shop for Two
2. Oh, What the Fudge
3. Teas of Joy

Visit LoveOnBelmont.com to buy your next book!

STAY IN TOUCH

Did you enjoy the book? You can stay in touch with Lori by visiting LoveOnBelmont.com and signing up for Lori's newsletter. She writes each one herself, so it's her words to you. You'll receive updates on *Love on Belmont* and other books, be the first to hear about specials, and get deleted scenes. Plus, if you haven't read the short story prequels to *Tea Shop for Two*, you can download them for free by subscribing.

ACKNOWLEDGEMENTS

A book is never written alone. I'd like to thank the following people for their help:

- My business group, run by Lois Raats, for encouraging me through this novel and hooking me up with a real estate agent in Vancouver for my research.
- Isadora Maria Kuipers of Dream Party Productions in British Columbia for renting me an Elmo costume so I could get some kind of idea what Pauline's previous career felt like, at least physically.
- Ariel Hudnall from ZG Stories, my marketing consultant, for her feedback on the initial idea for this story and tourist tips for my trip to Vancouver. (ZG Stories operates out of the city.)
- My mentor, ali macgee, for her feedback on early drafts of this book and for acting as a sounding board when I got stuck and needed someone to hear my thoughts out loud and reflect them back to me.
- Susan Fish, my editor, for her feedback and substantive line edits to the manuscript.
- Phoebe Wolfe, who helped proofread the manuscript. Any remaining errors are mine.
- Michelle Fairbanks of Fresh Design for the lovely cover and for her patience in working with me.

- My family for their continued support: Mom, Dad, and Kristin; Corey, Khristopher, and Jonnathan.

And most importantly, thank you to my readers for joining me on this journey.

ABOUT LORI

Lori's first memory of the Belmont neighbourhood is of her falling out of her bed at her grandparents' home when she was perhaps three. Opa, her grandfather, sadly passed away in his mid-60s, but that didn't stop Oma, her grandmother, from creating many, many happy memories in her home for her family.

Across the tracks and up a set of cement stairs was Belmont Village, a quaint shopping strip. Oma always bought her lottery tickets there and often took Lori and her sister to the convenience store to buy them a sugary treat.

But at the time, Lori had no idea Belmont and Belmont Village would be the source of the most wonderful romance in her life: her future husband.

When she met her future in-laws about 20 years later, they learned they had already met: Lori's in-laws had run that small convenience store until the mid-eighties. Moreover, their paths had crossed often with those of Lori's mom's family before Lori was even a thought.

Happy memories, shared fates, love…

And shopping.

How could Belmont Village *not* be the perfect place to set a sweet romance series about different couples in different stages of a relationship?

Lori lives in Waterloo, Ontario, with her husband and two sons and visits Belmont Village whenever she can.

facebook.com/loriwolfheffner

x.com/LoriWolfHeffner

instagram.com/loriwolfheffner

goodreads.com/lori_wolf-heffner

bookbub.com/author/lori-wolf-heffner

pinterest.com/loriwolfheffner

amazon.com/author/loriwolfheffner